SLOW
RECOIL

SLOW
RECOIL

C. B. Forrest

RendezVous
Crime

Text © 2010 C.B. Forrest

Cover design by Emma Dolan
Author photo by Stephanie Smith

Le Conseil des Arts | The Canada Council
du Canada | for the Arts

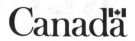

We acknowledge the support of the Canada Council for the Arts
for our publishing program. We acknowledge the financial support of the
Government of Canada through the Canada Book Fund for our publishing activities.

RendezVous Crime
an imprint of Napoleon & Company
Toronto, Ontario, Canada
www.napoleonandcompany.com

Printed in Canada

14 13 12 11 10   5 4 3 2 1

Library and Archives Canada Cataloguing in Publication

Forrest, C. B
        Slow recoil / C.B. Forrest.

ISBN 978-1-926607-06-1

        I. Title.

PS8611.O77S56 2010   C813'.6   C2010-904967-5

For Abby

Who never ceases to amaze me.

JULY, 1995

<u>A farm field outside Kravica, Bosnia-Herzegovina</u>

The men—although to say "men" is inaccurate, for many of them are just boys—stand in rows, stripped to the waist. Their flesh is stark white except on their faces and arms where the sun has touched. They are terrified of the unknown—or worse, the expected—their chests working like bellows as they try to sort out what comes next, how this works. As though the logistics matter. The bus ride offered time to think, too much time, and it seemed it was true after all, how your life really did flash before your eyes. Or at least these bits and pieces. Moments of happiness, tears, first sex and first cigarettes, the simple pleasure of a smile induced at a moment when needed most, a bottle raised in celebration. Sons, daughters, wives. Fathers, mothers, holidays, and smells of cooking, of home. All of the small gestures we take for granted across a lifetime.

Even as they are coming off the bus, they hear the gunshots. The crack that breaks across the skyline. Pungent cordite hanging in the air. The stink of death is unmistakable, sweet sickness wafting in the light summer breeze. For they all know what death smells like after these years of war, neighbour to neighbour, street to street, house to house. *My god, the things we have done to one another...*

This one thinks briefly of trying to make a run for it—perhaps there is something nobler in being shot while attempting to flee. But there is no time. Their captors are efficient, mechanical, managing this as though it were a line in a factory. Drill here, move the thing down the line. Drill. Next. Drill. Next...

The shots report, and the men jump, expectant. Tense. Blindfolded. They wait. Hear the jagged breathing of the man in front and behind, the whimpering of these big men you schooled with and lived with and drank with, and the shots make you jump, and there is no dignity to be salvaged in this place, not here, not now.

Hear the bodies folding to the ground like dropped bags of chicken seed.

You're crying, too, and you don't want to give them this final piece of your possession.

To face this chin up, shoulders back, is all you want to do. But it is hard, the hardest thing you have ever done in a life that has never been what you would call easy—though right now you would trade the worst day of your past for one more tomorrow.

Even to will your legs to move ahead takes energy, focus.

Crack!

And it will be your turn now to anticipate the slow recoil of the final shot.

I should be dead by now, but there is work to do.
- Czeslaw Milosz

PROLOGUE

He was sitting on a bench at Queen's Quay watching the late-summer tourists stroll along the Toronto harbourfront with their cameras and their holiday smiles, just sitting there with a soft-serve ice cream cone melting down the side of his hand, when he heard the screams for help. A girl's voice, shrill. He sat bolt upright, turning his head to decipher the location of the distress. A flash of movement, a commotion within a gaggle of people gathered on the dock beside one of those tourist charter boats that charged a fortune for a two-hour putter around the harbour. McKelvey dropped the cone, closing the distance in a dozen fast strides.

He came to the dock area just short of the Amsterdam foot bridge. Couples sat reading magazines on the decks of moored sailboats or were busy tidying ropes to set sail for a sunset cruise out past the quaintness of Toronto Island. Some of them stopped what they were doing and looked around, unaware of what exactly was taking place. McKelvey spotted a woman in her early thirties pointing frantically at the green-blue water.

"My daughter fell in!" she screamed. "I can't swim! *Please!*"

McKelvey saw it then, the flail of arms, tangled dark hair like a mess of seaweed out there in the water a few metres off the bow of a yacht painted blue and white. He beat a young man who was taking too long to kick off his sneakers and jumped feet first into the space between the boats. The water was colder

4

than he would have guessed. When he broke the surface, he saw the girl had slipped under, likely having panicked and swallowed a mouthful. He took three or four strong strokes and reached beneath the water with both hands, raking the darkness. His own breath was coming short now. He took a long haul and let himself drop beneath the water line. He opened his eyes to the murk, the silt too thick to see more than a foot in front of his face. It stung his eyes like vinegar. The world shimmered above in the dull silver of muted daylight. His fingers made contact with a patch of hair, and he pulled the girl to himself, using his legs to propel them this last distance to the surface. He came up, vacuumed air into his lungs like life itself and coughed a little. He pulled them towards the dock with a one-armed breast stroke, his other arm locked in a V around her head to keep it above the water.

The girl was limp in his grasp. She was light, maybe forty-five pounds, and McKelvey guessed about six or seven years old. A mop of thick black hair that for an instant, just a flicker, reminded him of his own boy's head of hair. The young man who had taken off his shoes was already in the water, halfway down a wrought iron ladder. He accepted the girl as McKelvey held her up, the frantic mother already there, right there. He pulled himself up the ladder just as the girl turned her head to expel a mouthful of Lake Ontario, then immediately started crying in a loud, shivering wail, teeth chattering, the mother threatening to crush the girl with her hugs. He heard the girl let out a belly-empty belch and knew that she'd be all right.

When it was done, he crouched on the hot pavement at the end of the dock to catch his breath, drenched clothes chilling his skin despite the strong sun. He could smell the stink of the lake on him, motor oil and algae, poison and piss. People were gathering in a large crowd now, tourists and passersby drawn by the current of human tragedy and excitement. The EMS workers came through with a folding stretcher and black medical kit that looked more like a large fishing tackle box. A middle-aged man from one of the sailboats came over and handed McKelvey a bath towel. He dried his hair and cleaned out his ears and wrapped the towel around his shoulders.

"That was a quick response," the boater said, looking over at the mother and the daughter. He was dressed in pressed khaki shorts and navy golf shirt, the tanned face of a Bay Street trader who had retired at fifty to a life of sailing and country club golf. "Let me guess, you were a lifeguard when you were younger."

"Something like that," McKelvey said.

It was the six hundred and twenty-third day of his official retirement. And thirteen hours. Not that he was counting; not exactly. But still, he missed it. Getting wrapped up in the details of the work, the drive. That was it mostly, the sense of purpose the work had provided in his otherwise meandering life. Once again his mind's eye conjured an image of himself dressed in a blue smock, pushing shopping carts toward idiotic shoppers at the crack of dawn, a sickening smile plastered on his face. Have a nice day, asshole!

The *Sun* the following day carried on page 5 McKelvey's reluctant picture and a brief article with the headline: *Shootout Copper Pulls Girl from Harbour*. A young reporter intent on bringing McKelvey's history into the story asked how it felt to save the life of a child, considering his own son's life had been taken by the hand of another almost four years ago. It was a good question. But McKelvey didn't have an answer. He could have told the fresh-faced scribe there were no scales at work in this conundrum. We trust in the laws of karma because we need to believe that what goes around does indeed come back around.

In McKelvey's experience, it was a line of thinking that had delivered disappointment more often than not. Not that he was keeping score; not really. Sometimes it came easy, sometimes it came hard. Life was just what it was; no exchanges, no refunds. Down here, your good luck charms hold no sway…

*   *   *

"You're my hero," Detective Mary-Ann Hattie said when she called the next morning. "You just can't stay out of the papers, can you? Are the paparazzi camped outside?"

A little more than a year earlier she had presented him with the laminated front page of the *Sun* featuring news of the shooting at McKelvey's house. *Shootout in the Beaches.* The tabloid had jumped at the opportunity to conjure images of the Wild West, gunslingers settling old scores. It made for good copy. At least in this instance it wasn't too far from the truth. McKelvey and Duguay in that darkened hallway, pistols drawn. The smell of gunpowder, the ringing in his ears.

> *Reputed Quebec-based biker Pierre Duguay was shot and seriously wounded yesterday morning as he allegedly broke into the home of a recently retired Toronto police detective. Sources indicate Detective-Constable Charles McKelvey was conducting his own unauthorized investigation into the unsolved murder of his son, Gavin McKelvey, who was killed almost three years ago over alleged involvement with the now-defunct Toronto chapter of the Blades biker gang. Unconfirmed reports suggest McKelvey had fingered Duguay for the killing even after the courts dismissed charges against the*

Montreal native due to the suicide of star witness and fellow biker, Marcel Leroux.

The province's Special Investigation Unit has opened an inquiry along with the force's own Professional Standards Unit.

"They're going to make a movie out of you one day, Charlie," she said. "You know, like *The French Connection*. I wonder, who do you think should play you?"

He shrugged, standing there in his boxers in the kitchen of his small apartment condo, early morning light catching the dust in the air. Hearing her voice made him want to see her, for her to come and stay the night. It had been a week or so. He remembered what it felt like to be with her, how they seemed to lock together. But this was the bargain they had struck, and he had to stick to the conditions. "I love you to death, Charlie," she had said finally, after trying for nearly a year to negotiate a space in the man's life, within his stubbornness and his dual afflictions of guilt and grief, "but I can't live with you… "

"I don't know," he said now, "how about Steve McQueen."

"Cool guy," Hattie said, "but last time I checked, he was still dead."

"I know," he said. "Perfect."

The truth was, the only thing McKelvey was thinking when he dove into the water of the harbour was the same thing he was thinking when he raised his pistol in that dark hallway to fire at Pierre Duguay: *I am fully prepared to accept the consequences of my actions.* It was about getting lost in the intent, within those seconds during which time slowed, wherein everything was brought into a sharper focus—life, in all its ragged promise… and yes, in that single instant, Charlie McKelvey had a purpose.

8

In McKelvey's evaluation, if modern history were a book, things were whittled down to the last few chapters. There was little left for the human race to turn against except itself, and a quick scan of the headlines proved that's precisely where they had come to as a collective multitude; like a bunch of half-drunk tourists, too ignorant to ask for directions or consult a map, they were lost and stumbling in the hills beyond the safety of the resort complex. The morning the twin towers fell to dust in New York City, McKelvey sat and drank beer in his boxer shorts, watching the anchors on CNN grapple with the enormity of the moment, the sheer unspeakableness of it, and he knew something had shifted within the entire mechanism of the western world. This was the coda of the modern times, the epilogue of all the great wars fought without final resolution; the simple and unalterable fact remained that mankind was incapable of leaving the scab alone.

It was this vein of morose talk that finally caused Hattie to shake her head and step aside for a breath of fresh air. Cops grew cynical as a matter of course, and given his personal history of loss, she did not expect smiles and giggles from McKelvey twenty-four seven. But it was his inability or refusal to meet somewhere in the middle that finally pushed her to lease an apartment, to regain some of her independence after their year-long experiment in co-habitation. McKelvey had sold his matrimonial home with its memories of his son and his wife and the shooting of Duguay, and he'd taken a nice little apartment condo on the top floor of a converted warehouse in Olde Town on the edge of the so-called "Distillery District" between The Esplanade and Front Street. He settled into the new neighborhood with its little pubs and cozy restaurants, the bustle of the St. Lawrence Market just up the street—those busy stalls with their hanging meats and bags of cheeses, varieties of fish he'd never heard of, these slippery reds

9

and yellows on beds of ice. It was about the old bricks, the way Front Street split at King Street in a "V" that defined the whole bottom of the city with that vista of the Flatiron Building set against the golden, shining bank towers, the CN Tower a spire among the clouds beyond. The unique mix of old and new made him sometimes feel he was on the set of a movie featuring a borough in some other city like Boston or Chicago.

There was a pub called Garrity's right next door to his place, and it was all a man could ask for with its good bartenders and dark wood. Hattie kept her frayed toothbrush and a drawer full of clothes at his place, jeans and sweaters hanging in the closet. They were together, she supposed, no more or no less than any other modern couple. She loved him, and she knew that as much as Charlie McKelvey was capable of it, he loved her right back. She looked into his eyes, those blue eyes, and she saw something that was beautiful and broken all at the same time.

ONE

Thursday evening before Labour Day weekend, the school teacher left a message on McKelvey's answering machine—something about a missing friend. Had McKelvey known this message would ultimately propel him towards a foreign brand of darkness, something beyond the experience of his thirty years on the force—had he known what this one call would bring into his life—well, he certainly would not have checked his messages that night or any night thereafter. He could live without a phone, it was true. In the very least, he would have been more careful in what he wished for; retirement was a killer, to be sure, but it wasn't deadly in any literal sense.

As it was, his friend the school teacher, Tim Fielding, left the message while McKelvey sat in Garrity's drinking a pint of Steam Whistle pilsner, scanning the classifieds for a used vehicle. McKelvey's beloved Mazda pickup, the little red machine, had shuffled to its earthly end. That fateful day, his trusted mechanic had put a hand on McKelvey's shoulder—understanding something of the man's loyal if illogical commitment to the vehicle—and he had simply shaken his head. Like a surgeon standing before an anxious family huddled in a waiting room, the mechanic relayed the long odds at play, the parts and the labour required. There had been a good run in there, oh yes, a few

11

years where McKelvey did little more than perform oil changes, spent a few hundred here and there on brake pads, a muffler. Despite the spread of malignant rust along the wheel wells, and the clouds of pungent dark smoke that belched from its rear-end upon ignition, McKelvey had never really prepared himself for this eventuality. Now it seemed as though the machine's entire organ system was shutting down in succession: transmission, timing belt, radiator, water pump…

McKelvey's rested his elbows on the dark wood of the bar, grooves worn deep. He circled a few promising listings. There was a Honda Civic alleged to have been driven solely by an "elderly female", as though that explained everything or anything. Another promoted the mind-boggling economical merits of a Suzuki. He said the word aloud—"Suzuki"—and asked the bartender, a former minor league hockey enforcer named Huff Keegan, about the specific model mentioned in the advertisement. The young man was a trunk of solid muscle, thick-chested like a farmer's son, and his face, at just thirty, looked as though it had been put through a grinder both frontwards and backwards. There were incalculable scars, grey and white flecks peppered across his eyebrows and the bridge of his crooked nose. He shook his big head and laughed.

"Does it come with a can opener?" Huff said.

"Is that the model with the lawn mower engine?"

"Good on gas. Great for parking downtown," the bartender said as he filled a patron's mug with amber Stella Artois. "Probably have to bring your groceries home one bag at a time, though."

"I suppose I could always get a roof rack," McKelvey said.

"And maybe a trailer," Huff added.

"Jesus, I hate this," McKelvey said. He took his pen, scratched out the circled ads, folded the paper under his arm, and got up from his bar stool. "Maybe I'll just get a goddamned bicycle and a pair of those Spandex shorts."

He paid up his tab, said goodnight to Huff, and stepped into the night. One block over, streetcars shooked along their tracks, moving across then up the city through old Cabbagetown, where the earliest and poorest immigrants had carved a life, then on past the gay village at Church and Wellesley. It was a beautiful evening of late summer. The air was dry and still. It was the sort of evening that reminded McKelvey there was hay being cut somewhere beyond the suffocating concrete and chrome of this city, large round bales left standing in fields like something constructed and abandoned by an earlier civilization.

This was the long weekend that brought with it the end of summer, if not officially, then at least psychologically. It was the Jerry Lewis telethon during which the hundred-year-old comedian removed parts of his tuxedo in hourly increments, mopping the sweat from his face with a balled-up hankie. It was the harried mothers with their bratty kids at the office supply store, baskets piled high with binders and pencil cases, ruled paper wrapped in plastic. McKelvey remembered how his own boy could never fall asleep on that final Monday night before the start of another school year.

"I've got a tummy ache," Gavin would say.

Or it was a headache. Or German measles. The sudden affliction of polio.

It was an area in which McKelvey felt a kinship with the child, for he had also detested that final sleep before entering the battlefield of another school year. Wondering which burned-out teacher you'd get stuck with, rating their defects on a scale—I'll trade halitosis for dandruff, body odour for the stench of half-digested vodka. He would stare at the shadows on the ceiling, willing some natural disaster of biblical proportions. But his hometown in the north knew no floods or tempests. The deep freeze of winter was broken up by a couple of months of moderate summer. The closest they came in Ste. Bernadette to an act of God were the infinite blankets of blackflies that hatched in early May like the spawn of hell itself. McKelvey had swallowed them by the dozen while riding his bike, choking on them, digging them from his ears and the corners of his eyes.

The sidewalk in front of his condo apartment off Front Street East was undulating with human traffic now, couples and groups of young people on their way to eat wings and sushi, or simply to sit and look good on the patio bars. All of these young people, McKelvey thought, with their bodies at the apex of health and strength, carefree as though life would always be just like this, filled with free time and spending money. He figured there was no sense in telling them the truth about what lay ahead. They would find out, just as he had, by navigating through one shitstorm at a time. Every year that he lived, he grew fonder of his late father and the example the man had tried to impart. That is to say, he let the man off the hook for all the things he had or hadn't done as a father. The way things had worked out between McKelvey and his own son, well, it put a man's view of himself in a clearer context. There was no end to the second-guessing, playing with the pain and regret like a tongue poking a canker.

The sidewalk gave off a warmth still, as though it were the collective embers of all those golden days of July and August, when the tourists shuffled along on their way to a Blue Jays game or to visit the Hockey Hall of Fame. McKelvey lit a cigarette and enjoyed the rush of dope to his head, the effect of which always seemed compounded after a couple of pints of beer, as though the cigarettes knew his defenses were already weakened, so they

14

took the opportunity to carry him across the threshold. He coughed a little and cleared his throat. It was the third and final allotted ration in what was his latest scheme to maneuver within this habit, for breaking it all together seemed utterly futile. Old dogs and all of that business. He had become, in his advanced years, a proponent of compromise.

He walked the three or four paces to the door of his condo building. An attractive woman in her early forties walked by in a group of mixed company, and she caught McKelvey's eye. A nice red dress that fit her well, fit her very well, a white sweater tied across her shoulders to guard against the evening chill. They gave each other this shy little smile, kids flirting in a schoolyard, and McKelvey shrugged as she walked on past, shifting her eyes to the sidewalk when she could no longer hold his gaze. He pinched the glow from the half-finished cigarette, dropping the ash to the sidewalk, twisted the end and put the remainder of the smoke in his shirt pocket. There was a measure of consolation in knowing he would start the next day up half a cigarette in the debit column. It was all just games that grownups played, this mental masturbation. One had to be grateful for the small mercies won or awarded in a day.

McKelvey climbed the stairs. Each unit had its own landing and a small velvet-topped bench against the wall in case someone was waiting for you and for some strange reason you didn't want them in your house. It was a new building and they were collectively the first tenants. There was the old Italian, Giuseppe, on the main floor, a former member of the resistance in Italy during the Second World War, the *Resistenza*. McKelvey had tried to tell the old man to stop using a stone to prop open the inner door of the building, saying it defeated the purpose of a so-called secure entrance. The old man shrugged and said he could never remember to bring his keys with him when he limped up to the St. Lawrence Market to buy his coils of sausage. On the second floor was a young gay couple, Chad and Russell, both of whom appeared to be lawyers or perhaps financial traders, always dressed in these expensive suits and ties. On the third floor, just below McKelvey, there was a divorced woman in her late thirties or early forties who made Hattie a little jealous because she was cute with her short hair, and she sometimes smiled at McKelvey. It had been an adjustment to leave The Beach, the old neighbourhood off Queen East and Gerrard with its converted cottages and the boardwalks, the first home he had made for his wife and his son; he accepted the fact it was a geographical cure of sorts, the shaking of ghosts. It had been an adjustment, but he was getting used to it. The people in his building were as good a collection of wayfarers as he could imagine.

Now McKelvey stood in front of his door for a moment to catch his breath, embarrassingly dizzy from the short climb. Stars and pins of light across his vision. He sat on the little red bench, the first time he'd used it in almost a year. It struck him that he had forgotten to eat lunch. A slip, perhaps, a sort of backsliding to old ways. It began with forgetting to eat. Then it was the laundry, or lack of it, wearing the same pants three days in a row, the stubble on his face coming in thick and silver. That living with Hattie had kept his life on track by offering a division of workable quotients seemed glaringly obvious in moments such as these. Living with someone gave reference to each part of the day. They became your gyroscope. There was the time you got up, the time you ate breakfast, the time you went to bed, the time you swept the hardwood, cleaned the toilets. Left to his own devices and vices, McKelvey had only himself to worry about. And therein lay the problem, at least according to Hattie.

She said, "You'll jump in the harbour to save a stranger, but you won't take the time to fucking feed yourself. God, Charlie, what am I going to do with you?"

He unlocked the deadbolt and stepped inside, the smell of the six strips of bacon he'd fried that morning still heavy in the air. The light was flashing on his answering machine across the darkened room. He drew toward the beacon like a ship guided to a distant shoreline.

The first message was from Jessie Rainbird, the mother of his granddaughter and the last person to love his son. A runaway from Manitoulin Island, the girl had seen more than her fair share of life and all of its darkness on the streets of the nation's largest city. She had grappled with the curse of addiction, and the myriad lessons it brought. He knew there were times when the pressure of straight life and the memories of Gavin came back to her, a haunting refrain. He knew also that she stumbled sometimes but always managed to pick herself back up. He was proud of her and had come to love her in a way he had never thought possible—they had a history, this girl and McKelvey, and he knew without doubt he would always come through for her.

Jessie's year-long hairdressing course was wrapping up now, and she was planning to head back to her Aunt Peggy's place on Manitoulin Island to take a break and contemplate her next steps. She said in the message that she wanted to bring Emily over for a visit before the two of them took the Sunday morning Greyhound up Highway 69. Before signing off, she admonished McKelvey for the Coca-Cola he had served the curly-haired Emily the last time she had left the child in his overnight care while she went out with some classmates.

"And no Krispy Kreme donuts, either," she said. "She's turning three, Charlie."

17

He smiled as he made a mental note to buy groceries in advance of Saturday to supplement the jar of mayo and the heel of dark orange cheddar cheese in his fridge. The smile faded as the next message came on. It was Tim Fielding, the young widower he'd met at the men's grief group up at St. Michael's Hospital. There solely to satisfy his wife's desire to see him progress within the realm of healing from grief and trauma, McKelvey had somehow ended up befriending the young man. And it was through tagging along while Tim got a tattoo in memory of his wife that McKelvey had made the strange discovery of Jessie Rainbird. That Polaroid photo of Gavin and Jessie tucked within the pages of a portfolio at the tattoo shop, the fated young couple there to get matching tattoos. The young girl pregnant. Lovers from the street. Everything had unfolded out of that moment of sheer serendipity. And it was for this reason he felt his relationship with the young man was meant to be.

"Charlie, it's Tim. Tim Fielding. I'm sorry I haven't called in a while. Listen. I need your help with something. Please give me a call. The number's the same. I really need your help, Charlie... someone's gone missing."

It was the sound of Tim's voice that did it. There was something there, a desperation. He replayed the message. *Someone's gone missing.* Surely to god the man knew enough to call the police. As a retired detective with the Metro Hold-up Squad, formerly of the Fraud Squad and a lifetime in patrol cars across four divisions, McKelvey certainly had connections and numbers to call, names to drop—the fraternity of the police lasted for a lifetime, after all. But he wasn't on active duty. And the connections he did have were growing fewer and farther between as new-generation careerists on the force tried to distance themselves from his maverick investigation of Pierre Duguay and all the fallout that had come from it—the files opened by Professional Standards and the Special Investigations Unit. For McKelvey had been correct in his hunch that the lead investigator on his son's case was off the mark. That Detective-Sergeant Raj Balani had turned out to be truly dirty—that he was on the payroll of the bikers and directly implicated in Gavin's murder because the boy had recognized the man hanging with the biker Marcel Leroux—well, it was a black eye for the force once the story hit the press. A crime writer with the *Toronto Sun* apparently had a book in the works. He'd called a few times, but McKelvey had yet to return the call. There was nothing to say; what was done was done.

He flicked the desk light by the window overlooking the alley and the brick face of an old warehouse preserved in its original character. In this neighbourhood you could turn a corner and walk straight into 1923, half expecting to see old-world mobsters with tommy guns, scuttling barrels of illegal whiskey on the flatbed trucks. He thumbed through his small black address book, most of the entries long ago scratched out. Mutual couple friends, well-meaning folks who had simply drifted away from him and Caroline in the dark days and months that followed the murder of their boy. It was the sort of extraordinary event that made people look a little too closely at themselves, into the fragile nature of this strange arrangement.

He glanced at his wristwatch and saw that Tim had left the message just over an hour ago. He dialed the number and chewed at the skin on the side of his thumb. If smoking was his worst habit, then this was his oldest. He'd been doing it as long as he could remember, to kill time or boredom or anxiousness. As a boy he'd sat on the floor and looked up as his father did the same thing, sitting at the kitchen table with a stubby bottle of Labatt 50, there in body but somewhere else entirely.

"Charlie?" Tim said as the lines connected.

The creepiness of call display never ceased to amaze McKelvey. "I got your message," he said. "I was down at Garrity's."

"I don't know what to do here, Charlie. This woman, this student of mine. Not a day student but a night school student…"

"Slow down, Tim," McKelvey said, using his cop's measured, authoritarian voice.

"Donia. Donia Kruzik. She's taking English as a second language courses at the high school on Wednesday nights. I've been teaching night courses since last September. It gets me out, I make a little extra money. And…and anyway, I'm sure you know how the story goes."

"How do you know she's missing? Maybe she just went away for a while."

"She didn't show up for class last night. I called a half dozen times. Then this afternoon I stopped by her apartment and—"

"Whoa, hold up," McKelvey said. "Back up a minute here. Did you say you left a half dozen messages? You stopped by her place? You do that for all your students, Tim?"

He heard Tim's long exhalation. He pictured the younger man removing those glasses with the round lenses that made him look just a little like John Lennon, rubbing his eyes with thumb and forefinger.

"It's more complicated than that," Tim said.

McKelvey said, "I figured as much. It always is."

"I didn't sleep last night," Tim said and there was defeat in his voice. "I need to get some rest. I can't even think or see straight. Will you meet me for a coffee tomorrow morning, Charlie? I need someone to talk to. Someone I can trust."

"I'll be over first thing," McKelvey said.

He opens the medicine chest above the toilet and stands there a full minute, perhaps two, this game he plays on odd or even days. *The dance* is how he thinks of it. Or jerking his own chain, more like it. At last McKelvey sighs, pushes aside the roll-on deodorant, the striped can of Barbasol shave cream, and his fingers find the little plastic bottle—always pushed to the back, as though this will somehow delay the inevitable. Spills the remaining tablets into his palm, counts them, measuring them across days or weeks not unlike the way his own father used to stand in front of the refrigerator on a Saturday night, lips moving in thought as he worked through the mental calculations: bottles of beer against hours remaining until the start of work on Monday. He funnels all but two of the tabs back into the bottle and swallows them back with a snap of his head. The white powder residue tastes of bitter chemicals. He stoops over the sink and scoops up a palm of tap water.

Looking at his face in the mirror, he is unable to meet his own eyes for just an instant. He knows how slippery a slope this is, for his life's work revolved around wading through the mess caused by this very thing: the getting of it, the keeping of it, the trading and selling of it, the killing and hurting for it. The motive for the majority of crimes, at least in McKelvey's experience, could be boiled down to one of three things: drugs, greed or passion. And when those three elements combined to a single force, watch out. It was madness. Every man for himself. Working the Hold-up Squad, McKelvey had come face to face with the desperate things a man would do in order to maintain the flow of his dope. It was always simply a variation on a story as old as time itself.

In his case, the doctor—the same doctor he'd been seeing

without any sense of regularity for the past sixteen years—had prescribed the Oxycodone tablets to help treat the recurring pain that was the residue of the gunshot wound. A crease of sliced flesh along the top of the inside of his right thigh. The .45 slug from Pierre Duguay's pistol had by some miracle missed his femoral artery—not to mention his balls. The scarred flesh was grey and shiny as plastic, and it ached now and then with a strange and unnameable pain, as though it were a radio signal emitting from the inside out. Some days it gave his walk a limp. Other days he forgot about it completely until he was stepping from his boxers and into the shower, when he looked down and saw it and his mind registered that yes, he had dueled in the hallway of his home; he had drawn and won.

In those moments of utter clarity that came at three o'clock in the morning—when the city was quiet, his apartment was still and he had only himself to betray—McKelvey was incapable of providing a satisfactory justification for the ongoing prescription. Everything hurt, and Christ it felt good to get a little numb, that was all. Numb the way a dentist made your gums before delivering a filling. It seemed as though the things in life which should have been getting easier, the hitching of the belt and the squaring of the shoulders, were in fact becoming more of a struggle. There was a cumulative weight to his movements. His energy was on the wane.

He moves now to the small living room and sits back in the loveseat Hattie forced him to buy at some ridiculous high-end import place on Queen Street West that had these African masks all over the walls. He had assumed his work was done with the selection of the loveseat, but oh how wrong he had been, for there had followed a litany of questions: selection of fabric covering, selection of throw cushions, selection of accompanying ottoman, and on and on. McKelvey had at one point asked the wafer-thin sales clerk if he was in on this gag with Hattie, like where were the hidden cameras. The thing had cost about as much as his first car, a point that was lost on Hattie in her mission to propel the vessel known as SS *Charlie McKelvey* towards the twenty-first century.

There is nothing on TV, so he settles for the late news with Lloyd Robertson. The medicine mixes with the two large beers he drank at Garrity's, and the flow of ease comes across him as though he is being lowered into a bathtub from an overhead hoist. Warm. And good. Top of the skull, across the shoulders, down through the spine, until finally there is no pain, just the opposite in fact, the absence of pain, a vacancy where once there had been full tenancy. All the old, haunted places were filled with sunshine…

TWO

McKelvey sparked his first cigarette of the day on the sidewalk in front of his building. A morning of blue skies, a hint in the air of the autumn to come. This city was at its best, he had always believed, in those in-between seasons of spring and fall. The winter was as grey and as dirty as the slush kicked up from buses and cars, and the dead of summer brought with it a muggy, suffocating heat that made the city stink of garbage and the lake. The owner of a flower shop across the street was busy hosing off the sidewalk, and McKelvey wondered briefly if the Dart & Feather pub located next door had anything to do with it. He smiled as he conjured an image of staggering young men sloping sideways down the other side of last call, holding one another for support as that ninth pint of ale began to percolate with the deep-fried fish and chips.

He tugged on the smoke then suddenly held the mustard gas in his lungs as a lithe jogger rolled around the corner, catching him by surprise, a woman dressed in expensive exercise shorts and tank top that left no part of her a mystery. She had a life-affirming spring to her stride that made her golden ponytail bounce. You weren't allowed to smoke anywhere any more, McKelvey thought, because people believed that by taking a few extra measures they could stretch their life to infinity. What is this prize we seek, he wondered. To outlive all contemporaries, to while away those last long empty days withered in a nursing home with a shawl wrapped around bony shoulders, some jaded and underpaid support worker celebrating like it was your birthday every time you took a shit—*"Good for you, Mister McKelvey, that's a good boy now!"* When the moment came, that very instant that he was no longer of any use to himself or others, he'd much prefer to cross the yellow warning line and stumble onto the electrified tracks of the subway. There was no question. Find the ice floe and hop on board.

He exhaled the captive smoke once the perky jogger had taken her perfect rear end to the next block. A twinge of guilt reminded him there was a full gym in the basement of his condo, a dark corner he had yet to grace. It was one of the perks of paying exorbitant condo fees. There were stretches of weeks, though, wherein he returned to the regimen of pushups and sit-ups, enjoying the surge of energy and strength that came back to his body like a remembered sense, touch or smell. All in all, and considering the places he'd been and the things he'd twisted and torn in his career as a division street cop, he figured he wasn't in bad shape. At least not for his age, and that was the slide ruler against which he found himself increasingly judged. Retired, pensioned off, not yet sixty but more salt than pepper in those curls. He was suddenly eligible for a broad new variety of discounts as though he were a member in a secret club—young pimple-faced clerks smacking bubble gum, asking him, *"You want the seniors' discount?"* Of course he did.

He had every intention of taking the subway north on the Yonge line, getting off at the urban hip crossroads of Eglinton Avenue and Yonge Street, and catching a streetcar or cab the rest of the way east to Fielding's new place. He missed his little truck, hadn't felt his freedom restricted in such a manner since he first arrived in the city as a young man with a duffel bag and the forty bucks his father had given him in lieu of advice. In those days he'd hoofed it everywhere he went, and in that way he got to know every side street and corner of the growing metropolis. The geographical knowledge had come in handy once he'd found himself behind the wheel of a patrol car seeking out the opportunity to make a good collar, to sweep the streets.

Public transit made the most economical and environmental sense, to be sure, but the last time he'd taken the subway, he'd come close to assaulting a teenager. This eyeliner-wearing ignoramus sat there with a pound of steel pierced into his head, listening to headphones that may as well have been loudspeakers, this drone of cyclical drums and repetitive bass lines bleeding out like a screwdriver in your ear. McKelvey gritted his teeth, felt his blood pressure thrum, a spider's web of heat across the back of his neck that was a sort of advance warning system. But he rode out that wave of electricity, urging his thick knuckles to reach out and provide a lesson in civil decorum.

The so-called "Megacity" was stumbling in its infancy. A little over three years earlier, the provincial government had amalgamated the six municipalities that comprised Metropolitan Toronto—the original city, East York, North York, York, Etobicoke, Scarborough, everything and everybody—into a monolithic City of Toronto. It was a trend that was popping up all over the country, from Halifax to Ottawa, this notion that somehow things would be easier, more efficient, with one level of municipal government. In McKelvey's mind the whole thing was a big goddamned boondoggle, a colossal waste of taxpayers' dollars, and rather than more efficient, everything seemed more obscure, doubled and tripled up. People asking if garbage day would stay the same. Would the fees for public swimming increase? And anyway, the people weren't in favour of it, hadn't been from the get-go.

A municipal referendum found the vast majority of citizens overwhelmingly opposed to the concept of amalgamation, worried their borough would lose its uniqueness, get swallowed up by the Megacity—the precise reason why they lived "here" and not "there". Which is of course what had happened, near as McKelvey could gather. It didn't help matters that the Megacity's first mayor was a clown who sold bargain sofas and washing machines through these horrible television ads in which he gave you the thumbs up and a conspiratorial wink like he was your long-lost buddy from grade school.

Now McKelvey hailed a cab easing its way along Front Street. The driver seemed glad for the fare, yanking his wheel to the curb. He was a young man, perhaps thirty-five, and like the vast majority of cab drivers in this and every other North American city, he was dark-skinned and from some faraway place. He spoke with a thick accent, Middle Eastern. McKelvey was never quite able to read, let alone pronounce the names of the drivers posted on their taxi license in that plastic card tacked to the back seat.

"Please," the driver said. "Where to?"

"DVP to Eglinton East," McKelvey said as he slid in the back. There was a lingering scent of alcohol and sweat back there, the residue of late night fares.

Tim Fielding had moved to a building overlooking Wilmot Creek Park. The young man was on his third residence in the two years McKelvey had known him. These geographical adjustments seemed to cure a man of memory and melancholy, at least for a time. And that was worth something. McKelvey saw no shame in a man taking comfort where comfort could be found; he was in no position to judge. He had himself contemplated many times making an exit from this city with its memories of his wife and son, of the bad ending for all of them. It was a thought, at least for him, that had never moved beyond conception. He loved and hated this place, worshipped and despised it. It was what it was; it was his city.

"Just starting or have you been on all night?" McKelvey said to pass the time.

"Since midnight," the driver said. He eyed McKelvey in the back, and McKelvey thought of those towers coming down like soft ash to the ground, how it had changed everything, and what it must have meant for a man with dark skin and a name like—he squinted at the taxi license photo folded over the back seat—a name like Hassan. McKelvey wasn't naturally sympathetic to the plight of immigrants, for he believed every man had to make his own way, but this new world had opened his eyes to the obstacles faced by a very specific group. The media called it "racial profiling", but the police, well, they just called it the law of averages.

"How's business?" McKelvey said.

The driver looked in the mirror. His eyes were bloodshot, weary. "Bad, very bad. Airport travel is down forty per cent. Tourists are not coming, you see. Affects us very bad. This is my cousin's car. I rent from him. I pay the gas and his fee and have barely enough left to pay for my apartment. In my country I am an engineer, but not here. Here I drive a taxi, deliver pizzas."

McKelvey shook his head and looked out the window. He let the conversation die. There was nothing he could do to change anything. Things were what they were. Traffic was lighter than usual on the Friday morning of the long weekend. People calling in sick or booking an extra day of vacation to stretch that last bit of summer. McKelvey knew the highways would build through the afternoon as families scattered northward up Highway 400 to cottage country, west on the Queen Elizabeth Way to Niagara Falls, or east on the 401 to places like Ottawa and Montreal. You wouldn't want to be on the Gardiner Expressway or the Don Valley Parkway at four o'clock this afternoon. The sign said the Greater Toronto Area was home to five million souls, but it felt like double that when the commuters flowed into the downtown each weekday morning from the sprawling suburbs.

As the cab passed beneath the Bloor Street Viaduct, McKelvey was reminded of the great leaps taken from that high arch. Over the years, this connecting span had served as the exit point for many an overwhelmed soul. He had responded to a jumper call there in his patrol days, this thirty-year-old salesman who had argued with his unfaithful girlfriend and decided to teach her a lesson by taking a nosedive from the rail. McKelvey saw in his mind's eye the man's limbs twisted at awkward angles, the internal structure completely re-organized, dark blood sprayed like graffiti across the rocks onto which he had landed. You noticed the smallest details, and they got burned into your memory. How the man's blue necktie was folded back across his shoulder, eyes grey and dead and milky, flies already buzzing at the nostrils. McKelvey wondered now how this had affected the unfaithful girlfriend, what sort of weight she had carried through the days of her life, where she was now, and what she was doing—and how often she stopped to think of that day the way McKelvey did.

The deep and rugged ravine of the Don River had until 1919 served as a natural obstacle to movement and growth. Construction of the Prince Edward Viaduct—or the Bloor Street Viaduct as it came to be known—linked two major thoroughfares: Bloor Street on the west side of the ravine, Danforth Avenue on the east. The span had played a crucial role in Toronto's history as a young city in terms of bringing together boroughs previously divided. McKelvey wondered now if the designer, Edmund Burke, would accept as part of that progress the fact his

29

viaduct had eventually become North America's second most-used suicide bridge after the Golden Gate in San Francisco. It was, McKelvey figured, the give and take of modern life.

The driver exited the DVP onto Eglinton Avenue East and slowed as he searched for the address McKelvey had provided.

"Right up there," McKelvey said, and the cab pulled up to the front of a fourteen-storey building. The fare was twenty three dollars and change. McKelvey gave the driver a twenty and a ten and told him to keep the change.

"Thank you, sir," the driver said. Then, as McKelvey walked toward the entranceway, he called out. "Please, if you need a driver, sir, give me a call. I give you my card…"

The man had scrawled his name and cellphone number across a taxi receipt in the shape of a business card. The entrepreneurial spirit impressed McKelvey, and he stuck the card in his shirt pocket, giving the top of the car a tap before he walked away.

The elevator in Fielding's building was mirrored floor to ceiling. If the designer had been after some element of class or chic, he'd missed the mark. The effect was disorienting, slightly creepy. The glass was smudged with hand prints and the smeared smacked lips of toddlers. McKelvey punched the button for the ninth floor then stood back and checked his reflection in the yellowish light. He was dressed in jeans with a white dress shirt and navy sports jacket, still unable to leave the house without looking something like a plainclothes cop. Which is what he was, in his heart of hearts, and what he always would be. It was his skin, it was his DNA—the alpha and the omega of Charlie McKelvey. Which was somewhat ironic, considering he had stumbled by chance into the job as a fresh-faced kid off the bus from the isolated northern mining town of Ste. Bernadette. It was a steady paycheck at first, and he'd never expected it to become a lifetime, to define everything about

30

who he was and what he believed. One day you simply woke up and The Police was your marrow.

He buttoned and unbuttoned the jacket, turned to the side, sucked in his modest paunch. Those draft beers at Garrity's, the always-at-hand bar peanuts. He thought he didn't look as bad as he felt. He was holding his weight steady at one ninety, better than the two fifteen he'd carried around his last few years on the Hold-up Squad, eating fast food and guzzling too much coffee. The soft lighting in the elevator was flattering too, and his curly hair seemed to have more pepper than salt. But as the floor chimed and the doors whooshed open, he saw that it was all an illusion: every mile was etched there, and he had been both city and highway driven.

*   *   *

Tim Fielding was the sort of man who could not easily conceal the internal workings of his life, something McKelvey had learned from their time together in the men's grief group up at St. Michael's Hospital. The young widower wore his guts on his sleeve, the type of man who would never hold up under police questioning. That morning, when he opened the door, McKelvey thought Fielding looked as though he hadn't slept in a week. His usually clear eyes were red and glassy, and his face had taken on a new paunchiness.

"Thanks for coming, Charlie," he said. "You must think I'm crazy."

"To be honest," McKelvey said, "you're the most rational person I know."

Fielding went to the kitchen and poured two coffees from a drip machine. He handed a mug to McKelvey, and McKelvey

31

read the swirling blue letters that proclaimed "World's Best Teacher.'"

"You take sugar and cream, right?" the younger man said.

"Just cream," McKelvey said. "I'm supposed to go for skim, but what the hell. It's a holiday almost."

Fielding stood with the fridge door open, staring. After a moment he turned and held his palm up.

"Sorry," he said. "No cream. And the milk's expired."

McKelvey nodded, accustomed to his own lack of fresh groceries. He sat in the living room on the sofa and set his coffee on the table. It was one thing for his own fridge to carry little more than a block of crunchy orange cheese, but Fielding was better organized and took better care of himself than that. These were the variety of observations that allowed a cop to form his appraisal of a situation. Everything meant *something*. It was the part of his job had that always driven his wife crazy. On the way home from a house party, Caroline might say, "Charlie, for god's sake, those are our friends. Do you always have to watch people like that, like you're on duty?" And for the most part he was unaware he was even doing it. The insinuation seemed to be that he wanted to find the dark spot in every soul.

"Donia," Fielding said, coming around the kitchen island to join McKelvey, "she's a student in my night school course I was telling you about. She's Bosnian, a survivor from the war. Her family was destroyed. She came over less than a year ago to work in a factory as a seamstress, working these industrial sewing machines. She wanted to get ahead, but her English isn't strong enough. She's from a small village. Her people were simple people, farmers and tradesmen. She always said that: simple people, but good."

McKelvey took another mouthful of the black coffee. It was caustic, like Liquid-Plumr running down the back of his throat.

32

His doctor had warned against this sort of carelessness, for the peptic ulcer which had hemorrhaged and escalated his retirement meant a lifetime of vigilance against those four horsemen of the apocalypse: booze, cigarettes, stress and coffee. He had grown sick of the bitter and bland low-fat yogurt, of a life lived on the narrow margin of the health food aisle. A man could only eat so much plain rice and couscous before he snapped, walked into a steakhouse off the street and bought a twenty-two ounce prime rib with all the trimmings.

"You met her through the night school," he said, getting his facts down.

"I just…we hit it off. It sounds stupid, Charlie, I know. She's a beautiful woman, and there was something there. She's wounded, I suppose, and I'm obviously not a poster boy for the well-adjusted. We just seemed to fit." Fielding threaded the fingers of his hands as he might do in demonstrating a point to his students. "We went for coffee and then it was lunch and then it was dinner. And then, you know…"

"You slept with her," McKelvey said. Going easy here, for if he had been making inquiries on the job, he would have used guttural language in an attempt to draw some emotion, indignation— *yeah, that's what you did with her, isn't it, you dirty dog?*

Fielding nodded and said, "I hope you know me well enough to know there was nothing untoward about the situation."

Untoward, McKelvey thought. Was that a fancier way of describing the act of a teacher putting his prick in one of his students?

McKelvey said, "Go on."

"We're adults here, Charlie," Fielding continued. "She's not one of my Grade Six students with braces and a training bra."

McKelvey pushed the mug away a little so he wouldn't keep

reaching for it out of habit. He regarded his friend, saw the truth written across the man's face, and in fact had never suspected otherwise. Tim Fielding was one of those people walking the streets, bless his heart, who happened to lack the gene necessary for telling bold-faced lies.

McKelvey said, "So what happened?"

"She stopped answering her phone two days ago. She missed class on Wednesday night, and she hasn't missed a class in six weeks. Something's not right, Charlie. I'm no cop, but it just doesn't feel right."

"You have a key to her place."

"No, but she has a key to mine. We didn't spend the night together more than a few times, but when we did, she always stayed over here. She said her place was too small."

"Where does she live?"

"She was in a unit off Blevins Place in Regent Park when she first came over last year. She said she had heard enough gunfire during the war, so she found a little apartment she could afford at Roncesvalles and Dundas, near the tracks over there."

Fielding gave the address, and McKelvey pictured its approximate location. On the edge or even within the boundary of the so-called "Little Poland" neighbourhood. But first she had lived in Regent Park, having come to this country to escape war and instead having found the darkest the city could offer in terms of social housing gangs, handguns going off like firecrackers in Regent Park, *pop, pop, pop*—where the tough boys of 51 Division did all they could to prevent young black men from killing other young black men while witnesses stood by with their mouths sewn shut for fear of reprisal.

"Have you been to her place?" McKelvey said. "I mean her new place?"

"Just inside the lobby. I picked her up one time, about two weeks ago."

McKelvey nodded, already working through the language he would use to somehow tune his friend into the workings of the big bad world out there without destroying this new ray of light that had entered his life. As far as he knew, Fielding had been on something like four dates since his wife's death at the hands of a repeat drunk driver more than four years ago. The wrong woman, or the right woman, would see him as an easy mark.

"So she's gone for a few days," McKelvey said. "Maybe she's visiting a friend, a relative. You've been seeing each other what?"

Fielding shrugged and said, "Four weeks, I guess."

"A month. Jesus, Tim. Maybe she's screwed off for a few days and doesn't feel like she owes you an explanation. Has that entered your mind?"

Fielding removed his glasses and rubbed his eyes with the pads of his palms. He put the glasses back on. He sat back, exhaled a long sigh. "Something's not right, Charlie. I know it in my gut. It's not like her to just take off without a word. I mean, she missed a mid-term on Wednesday night. She could fail the course, and she's put a lot into it. She's trying to make a better life for herself. But there's been something there that I could never quite put my finger on. Like she was waiting for something to happen."

McKelvey saw that his soft approach had missed the mark. "How well do you really know this woman, Tim? That's all I'm saying. We can be friends with people or work with someone for fifteen, twenty years, then one day they do something that seems completely out of character. But is it really out of character? Or are we just shocked because we thought we knew every aspect, every angle to that person?"

35

Fielding sat there looking into his coffee and didn't answer.

"She could be in a hotel room in Montreal right now with her husband," McKelvey said and stopped his foul imagination from going further. "Or maybe she's with her other boyfriend playing the slots down in Vegas for a long weekend getaway. Or anything else you can think of. You said yourself that you never stayed over at her place."

"She's not married, and she doesn't have another boyfriend. I believe that much about her. Her husband was executed by rogue Serbs in the war. Listen, I know you're cynical, I know you think like a cop. That's why I called you, Charlie, because I'm not stupid enough to assume I can place a missing person's report on a thirty-two-year-old woman I met four weeks ago. They'll laugh in my face. I thought if I told you about us, about her just disappearing, you of all people would believe me."

McKelvey sat there and ran his hand across his face, the extra day of stubble coming in rough as iron shavings. The things a man would do, would say, while in the throes of love or lust never ceased to amaze him. It was in this regard that all men were indeed created equally—pauper or prince, it hardly mattered: we all fall the same. He remembered this particular collar from his first year on the Hold-up Squad. Guy's married and has four kids, starts screwing around with a girl at the office. The girl has expensive tastes, she likes the thrill of opening gifts, that ooh-aah moment. She wants to eat out at all the hot places, dance at all the cool clubs. The guy's kids need braces and hockey equipment. His credit card gets maxed, he takes out too many loans that he can't pay. When McKelvey finally had the poor bastard sitting there in the corner of the interview room—showing him a black and white single frame printout from the security video capturing him standing in front of the bank teller—McKelvey asked him what could possibly make a guy with no criminal record walk into a bank with a pellet gun on a Tuesday afternoon in May. The guy got this look on his face—a mixture of sadness and stoicism—and he said, "I had no choice, man. I couldn't afford to keep her, and I couldn't stand to lose her. Either way I was screwed. You know what I mean?"

Now McKelvey exhaled a long breath across the room, across the morning that had begun with such promise. The end of summer, the beginning of autumn. He had some grocery shopping to do before the girls came to visit him on Saturday. He had a good coffee to buy and get into his system—something that wouldn't act as an instant laxative—and later still he had a stool at Garrity's on which to sit and circle classified ads for used vehicles he would not purchase. Ragged and ridiculous, perhaps, but he had a life to live. But yes, at the end of it all there was no denying that he did in fact have the time to go through some motions here, to give Tim Fielding a sense that at least something was being done.

"Listen," McKelvey said, "I don't know what you're expecting from me. I'll go on over there and check out her place. Maybe ask a few of her neighbours or the super, or something like that. That's all I can do here, Tim. I'm not on the job any more. I'm not a private detective."

"I'd appreciate it," Fielding said, relief written on his face.

"If and when it comes to that, I can put you in touch with someone on the force who won't laugh in your face," McKelvey said, getting up and moving for the door. "But that's about all I can do here."

"I'll get my keys," Tim said.

McKelvey got to the door then turned. He said, "Thing is, I

should head over there myself, take a look around. I think it's better that way."

Fielding stopped and took it in. He nodded as though he understood this was a requirement of police business, how things worked. McKelvey didn't want to explain the fact that Fielding would be the first obvious suspect if anything *untoward* had happened to the woman, god forbid. Begin at the nucleus, work your way out. McKelvey saw the school teacher leaving his fingerprints all over the apartment…

"I can at least give you a lift over there."

McKelvey smiled, pulling the card from his shirt pocket. "I've got a driver."

He used Fielding's cordless phone to call Hassan. He asked the driver to meet him in front of the building. Then, against his better judgment, he shook his friend's hand and promised to report back within the hour. In the elevator he shook his head at himself, at this whole thing, and dug his fingers into his pants pocket, where he found a half tab of the painkillers—he had broken a few of them in half, and he carried them around from time to time like loose change. In case the pain got too bad, or whatever. Maybe it was boredom, or maybe it was simply because they were there, and he could. Too much to think about, and anyway, he didn't need to make any justifications here. He was far beyond the days of reporting to any sort of supervisor, real or imagined. He pressed the button for the ground floor, snapped his head back and swallowed the tab dry.

THREE

Hassan pulled his cousin's cranberry-red Crown Victoria up to the front entrance. McKelvey watched the big boat swing in on a wide arc, just like an unmarked cruiser from the old days, and his mind spun back: him at the wheel and a partner riding shotgun, easing the unit up to the curb to put the screws to a crew of the usual suspects the morning after the armed robbery of a Mac's Milk—where were you around eleven last night, Alexander? And what about you, Damon James? The inherent sense of authority and purpose that flowed through his being as he stepped from the car, sunglasses on, big gun slung in its holster. The Man, the 5-0, the Heat, the goddamned King of Kensington. It was the best and worst job in the world, and like the city itself, he wanted to be able to say that he could leave it all behind, just walk away, but it was a lie. He knew in his heart of hearts that a part of his identity had been forever altered: now that there was no squad room, no courtroom prep with an ambitious Assistant Crown looking to make a career case, no administration or backwards bureaucracy to buck and bitch about, no drinks with the boys after the late night shift, no stakeouts with bad coffee and cold pizza, no sense of pride at the making of a good collar, no shield, no more no more. Welcome to civilian life, Charlie. Ain't it grand?

McKelvey got in the back of the taxi with the nagging sense that a mild depression was settling in, this imperceptible autumn frost. He had no idea what he thought he was doing here, pulling some part from a *Spenser for Hire* episode. Maybe Hattie wasn't so far off the mark when she accused him of "reckless meandering in retirement". She said the point was to slip out of his uniform and into a whole new life, a new world—but he was stuck, a man without hobbies, a man without a plan, without a family. He saw the coffee mug again, "World's Best Teacher." The world needed all the Tim Fieldings it could get, the ones who, despite all evidence to the contrary, still believed the promise of the advertisement. McKelvey knew it was the string that held their friendship together—the chasm that fell between his own bleak view of humanity and the school teacher's unflagging investment in the future generations. He saw something there within the younger man that he either wanted or knew he ought to want. Right now, the half-pill was performing at half duty, confronting the impending depression with a small smile. Perhaps it was a smirk.

McKelvey gave the address, and Hassan said, "Thank you, sir, for calling back."

"My truck died a couple of weeks ago," McKelvey explained. "I'm having trouble finding a replacement. Who knows, maybe I'll become a regular until something turns up."

"Try Auto Trader online," Hassan suggested, like they were old friends now.

"Online, sure," McKelvey said. "I don't have a computer at home."

"They have it for free, sir, the internet. At the public library. That is where my children use it for their schooling. We can't afford a computer of our own. Not yet."

"I guess I'll need to apply for a library card first," McKelvey said.

The guy on the AM sports station was going on about the Blue Jays, how Clemens took the loss last night in a tough game against the Yankees. *The bastards*, McKelvey thought. He hated the New York Yankees not for winning all the time, but for winning the way they did. They were just a hateful team, overpaid braggarts and loudmouths—so perfect in their prancing starched pinstripes. Tonight Pete Walker would hit the mound for the Jays, and McKelvey had his money on the home team. Walker was the sort of guy who could keep his cool and get himself out of a tight spot. It was a characteristic that would have made the man a good cop.

Hassan pulled up to the curb outside the low-rise apartment. It was a working class neighbourhood, the fringe of so-called Little Poland. As the metropolis grew, these self-proclaimed neighbourhoods seemed to blossom from beneath the sidewalks as though the roots had been there all along, defining themselves by block and intersection. Little Italy, Greektown, Chinatown, Portugal Village, Koreatown, the Gay Village, there was something for everyone, for that was the essence of Toronto, the heart pumping blood through this massive body: a hundred different languages, a million different stories, the past preserved and the future a shared dream. This new city, it belonged to everybody, the last best frontier.

"Here," McKelvey said, getting out and handing the driver a twenty. "Wait here for me for ten minutes, will you?"

Hassan took the bill, folded it once and set it on the clipboard at his side. "I am at your service, sir."

McKelvey made his way up the walkway to the four steps that led to a set of double glass doors. Suddenly he was filled with a sense of foreboding, the cop's instinct that gave his stomach a quick flip. He thought he was probably going to walk in on the woman and another boyfriend, or maybe her and a whole crew of reprobates holed up in the love shack with the phone turned off and poor Tim Fielding sitting across town going crazy. The whole thing was a misunderstanding. Inside the foyer was a wall of mailboxes to the right, flyers and coupons for pizza and carpet cleaning scattered on the floor. To the left was a listing of tenants set in a glass case next to a keypad and speaker intercom. He ran his finger down the list until he came to D. Kruzik. He pressed the buzzer and waited. Nothing. He pressed it again, this time for a full minute. Nothing. He pulled at the main door, found it sloppily unlocked, and slipped inside.

The apartment was on the top floor of the eight-storey building. He rode one of two elevators, noting the drastic difference in design and upkeep compared to Fielding's newer building. This elevator was small and the carpet was stained and marked here and there with black cigarette burns. It smelled like the inside of a cab mixed with something else he couldn't quite put his finger on. As the doors opened, it came to him: boiled cabbage.

He found the unit—801—at the end of the hallway on the left. A narrow rectangular window on either end of the hall let in the only daylight, and it was a good thing, because the whole place had the feeling of 1960s Eastern European Cold War modesty. He knocked and waited. He put his ear to the door and listened. Nothing. A door opened up the hall, and a woman in her mid-fifties, dressed in a dark coat with a kerchief tied over her hair, glanced at him quickly. He fished his own house keys from his pants pocket and pretended to look for the right one. When the woman was inside the elevator, he knocked again, put his ear to the door, closed his eyes. Nothing. And then something. What, a sound of movement? The subtle resonance of a human presence on the other side? He reached out and turned the doorknob. It was unlocked. He took a step back and gave it a moment. He stepped in and listened again. Nothing. He turned the doorknob quietly in his left hand.

"Hello," he called.

He was startled to find the apartment empty save for a few papers scattered across the top of the kitchen counter, old direct mail flyers. Tiny and spare, a one-bedroom for eight-fifty a month. But it was empty. He left the door ajar as he stepped quietly into the hallway that opened on the right to a small kitchen and continued straight ahead into a living room. He surveyed the emptiness, and spotted a single magnet stuck to the fridge, an item of information stored for later testimony perhaps.

"Hello?" he said. "Donia? I'm a friend of Tim's…"

He listened. Nothing. And then it was there again, the sense of human energy. It wasn't a sound, not quite, it was some frequency coming through on the channel of the sixth sense. He had entered enough rooms and vacant buildings in his day to trust in the feeling, to believe in its root. In an earlier life he would have reached then, hand hovering above the holstered sidearm at his side. But he was unarmed now, standing there alone in a stranger's apartment. What a fool's errand. What the fuck had he been thinking…

He was turning back to the door when the rush came upon him, the kinetic surge of a body in motion. From a bathroom down the hall, four fast strides—McKelvey turned, pivoting at the knees just in time to catch something thick and hard across the side of his skull, heavy metal: explosions of pinwheels scorched across the blackness.

McKelvey twisted, falling sideways, reaching out, hands curled into fists, and he saw his mistake—goddamned rookie patrolman's mistake of turning his back before every single room,

43

every single closet had been checked and cleared—and the son of a bitch was right there, combat jacket and jeans, hair shaved close to the bone—and McKelvey caught another sledgehammer of a blow square in the centre of his face, an atomic detonation.

He was splayed on the floor, a beetle turned the wrong way.

The door slammed shut.

He squinted through the tongue-thick ether. Numbness spread across his face, a dull pulse knocking from behind his eyes. Then his hearing went garbled as though he were under water. He could taste blood down the back of his throat, iron and copper, and he knew, even before he sat up, that his nose was broken, his fucking nose was broken.

*　*　*

The taxi driver was pulled up to the curb listening to callers on talk radio share their opposing views on the so-called "War on Terror" when he noticed the big man in the green army jacket come bursting through the main doors. He ran across the street— mere feet in front of Hassan's car—and jumped in a silver Honda Accord (probably a '94 or '95, Hassan thought). The car peeled from the curb, gone. Hassan strained to make out the plate. APVB and three digits, maybe a nine in there. These were the details he provided to McKelvey once his passenger had also come stumbling from the building, a clutch of bloodied paper towel held to his face, a darkness crawling beneath and between his eyes.

"What happened, sir? Are you all right?" Hassan's wide eyes told McKelvey all he needed to know about his own condition.

"You see a guy come out of there the last few minutes, which way he went?" McKelvey said, his voice thick, nasal.

A lifetime on the force, and he'd never been punched in the face

44

with such velocity or precision. Kicked, spat upon, stabbed at, and yes, even shot at on two occasions—once at the deadly shootout intersection of Jane and Finch, the other time in the hallway of his own home as he and Duguay drew like gunfighters—but this, this was otherworldly. He had come as close to blacking out as his fragile male ego would allow. Held on there to the tassels of faint hope, pulled himself up through sheer stubborn determination, an ode to his Celtic ancestry. It was the fucking pill, that little half tablet that had dulled his edge. As bad as taking a drink on duty, for Christ's sake. Rather than being ashamed of himself, he was angry and embarrassed and wanted to get this asshole face to face in a fair fight, no sucker punches thrown from the dark.

Hassan relayed the facts as he had processed them, his cab driver's eyes always recording—which is what made drivers such a great source for the dicks of the various crews working in Hold-Up, Homicide, Sexual Assault. McKelvey put his head back on the headrest in the back seat and took a haul of air between clenched teeth. His face could come off if he pulled hard enough. He could pull it off and hand it to Hassan and walk away and find another face somewhere. He was cotton-headed, tongue-thick. He had the four numbers from the plate, the general description of the asshole wielding the sledgehammer in his right hand. He closed his eyes and centred himself, willing forth the last of the reservoir, the needle well past "E". His mind flashed to the image of the stark white refrigerator and that single square magnet stuck to the door.

"I'll be back in a minute," he said, opening the door, and stepping out on legs no longer connected to his hips. "I forgot something."

"Please sir, let me take you to the hospital," Hassan said.

"That's our next stop," McKelvey said.

FOUR

<u>Three days earlier…</u>

Kadro stands on the balcony of the cheap airport-strip motel smoking a Canadian cigarette. Du Maurier. The cigarette is smooth. Fine. Back in the war, he liked those mornings best when the sun had not yet burned away the fog completely, and he could stand alone with the gun slung over his shoulder and enjoy a cigarette all to himself. The fields seemed peaceful then and not at all associated with the gruesome acts of war. The bullets, the bombs. The effect of shrapnel on the human body. The sweet, sick stink of the dead, the sounds they made in their moment of dying. None of it seemed possible inside the stillness and clear sunshine of those fields. He would smoke his cigarette and watch the morning glow within itself, and it made a man feel grateful to stand with his legs wholly intact, heart still beating, still pushing blood. He understood in those moments what it meant to be entirely alive, because he was already dead—his generation expendable as a matter of birth and name and timing. The great lottery of life. His number was accounted for; it had been waiting for him just up ahead all the days of his life. The next field, the next town.

"Always daydreaming," that's what Krupps used to say. The weary squad leader with the perpetual smirk, the crooked grin. The dimpled cheeks of a farm boy contrasted against the dead eyes of a killer, their best shooter. Removed the head from an

46

enemy soldier at six hundred yards. At dusk. With a hard wind blowing at them. Krupps had collected on the bet from every man in the squad, including Kadro. It was supernatural.

But it was Krupps who was dead and not him. Dead going on seven years now. And only just yesterday. Life was funny that way, how time shifted, played tricks so that even now Kad could close his eyes and actually smell the cordite, the blue-grey smoke from their guns—and then the other smells that came on, the stomach-curdling stink of death, the foul funk of bodies left to bloat and swell in the hot summer sun, a smell that settled in your mouth like a taste, something that stayed on your tongue for days.

"This," Krupps said, handing him a pint of plum brandy, "is the only thing that gets rid of the stink. Drink it. And then smear some under your nose… "

Yes, life was funny. Kad's brother Tomas had studied at a school in Chicago, because he was the smarter of the two, always reading these thick books, preferring conversation and debates to sports or roughhousing. And it was Kad who'd stayed home with the rifle and the grenades, the bayonet that he could mount on his rifle when the fighting got that close, that dirty. Kad was not jealous of his brother. He was proud of Tomas and happy that he had been spared these years of war. To see the world come to an end, to stand each day in the midst of the apocalypse. To have killed men, to have witnessed the cause and effect of the bullets stored in the belt slung across his back. Kad had seen the brochures for his brother's school in Illinois. *Ill-in-noise*—how many times had he said that word as he tried to imagine this unknown world his smart brother had flown to with scholarship dollars. The fields that looked like a golf course, the thin white girls with blonde hair, always blonde. What perfect timing Tomas always had. He had graduated and earned his scholarship—his ticket out—in the very months before the war came to their villages, to their homeland. At first it was the whisperings of independence that reverberated around the world.

"I will come home to fight," Tomas had told his brother in their last phone call.

"Father will not allow it. You are the only hope we have… Stay where you are."

Everything happened so fast. But not really. No, this was two thousand years in the coming. It was always there, as Kadro's grandfather had said, this wound without stitches. When Bosnia voted for independence from Yugoslavia on February 29, 1992, the dominoes teetered. In the days following the vote, the Yugoslav Amy disbanded, looting the Bosnian reserve units of their weapons and ammunition, equipment and uniforms. There remained the fledgling and poorly trained Armija—the government army of the Republic of Bosnia-Herzegovina, or perhaps the 7th Muslim Brigade of the Armija for the truly devout. Neither option appealed to Kadro, for he was neither devout nor interested in guaranteed annihilation as part of an ill-trained and ill-equipped army fighting for a country so new, it had barely had time to ink a national emblem.

The storm clouds gathered and the fates conspired. Yugoslav Army soldiers fresh from the killing fields of Croatia paused to catch their breath in Bosnia, there along the Drina Valley at the Bosnian border with Serbia. A pileup of tanks, artillery, personnel carriers, soldiers smoking and stewing and drinking in the local pubs—drinking and talking and fermenting their hatred, this notion of revenge for the homeland.

The line of dominoes toppled and fell with the Siege of Sarajevo, the guns in the hills opening with salvos of artillery and incendiary tank shells. And so Kadro's new Republic of Bosnia-

Herzegovina—recognized as sovereign by the U.S. and most of Europe—was truly a nation born into war. The days were merciless. It was mayhem. Kad's father would meet a group of men at the tavern in their small village and return with updates, fragments of news. To his wife and daughter he would say only that the war would be over before it reached their town, and anyway, what did anybody want with a bunch of poor farmers this far from the city? They were but a dot on a map, of no strategic value. But to his son he spoke the truth. This village had fallen, such and such official had been hung from a telephone pole. He told Kadro of the reports from the front, what the men were doing in the villages to the women, the girls.

"I am too old to fight," his father had said, "but I will. To my last breath those bastards won't touch your mother or your sister. I will burn my own home to the ground before I give them the satisfaction. There is no choice now, my son, you must fight. Either with our small army or with one of the units forming up… "

And so it was that Kadro joined a handful of his classmates in a paramilitary unit that was rumoured to be funded by a wealthy landowner with business connections in Russia and the Balkans—this never-seen figure referred to simply as "The Colonel". They were a rag-tag jumble of farm kids and country kids who could shoot well but lacked any formal military training, no understanding of comportment. The commander of their unit, whom they referred to as "Captain", explained to them their predicament.

"This is not the fucking regulation army, boys. You are not protected by any international laws or conventions," the Captain told them, standing on the tailgate of a black half-ton truck. He was the only one among them dressed in full camouflage, new trousers bloused over new black boots, his grey and black beard neatly trimmed. "But that hardly matters now. This is not a conventional war. We have only one mandate, and that is the mandate as declared by the Colonel. We are to take back as many of our villages and to kill as many of the enemy as we can before we ourselves are terminated. Any questions?"

Kad looked out now across the parking lot of the fifty-dollar motel. The sun was rising, giving birth to his purpose in this life. The burden of his brothers and sisters squarely on his shoulders. The load was heavy, but he didn't mind. He had no family now, no past, no future. He was invisible; in fact, he had never been born. He turned and slipped inside the glass patio door and surveyed the room: the ugly artwork on the wall, the red shag carpeting worn from a million footsteps, the brown water stains painted like a map of Africa on the stucco ceiling, the cheap plastic cups wrapped in more plastic, the bed with its sloping mattress, the floral-print comforter.

This was Canada. The word made him think of the UN and the blue helmets and the white troop carriers shipped to a war that was none of their business, these fresh-faced boys sent halfway around the world to stand at roadblocks and witness murder. *Canada.* Smooth cigarettes that did not burn your throat, soft beer, soft women. The place where people apologized even when it was you who bumped into them. That was the word that came to mind: *soft.*

Out on Airport Road a car backfired, and Kad ducked low, hunching at the shoulders. The automatic reaction even after all these years. His mind worked to decipher the sound, incoming or outgoing, mortar or something worse, something larger—an American five-hundred pounder sent to level a street, a block.

"We have to move," Krupps says, kicking at Kad's boots, waking him.

"What about Ahmet? He's too fucked up to move. He needs blood," Kad said.

Standing in the motel room and the fields of war all at the same time. Standing and seeing Krupps, seeing everything as it was, as it always will be. Outside the traffic of Toronto ebbed and flowed.

"Leave him for the UN. Give them something to do for the morning, those bleeding heart blue helmets. Thirteen minutes, Kadro. Let's move."

He took a final long haul of his cigarette, tossed the butt to the ground. He exhaled the tobacco and looked out across those fields. The places he had played as a boy, the small wonders of a boy's imagination at work in those deep woods. The trees and hedgerows were forming now, coming to life, the fog burning away to reveal the true nature of the torn landscape.

There was a knock at the door.

Kadro opened his eyes and blinked. Here in the room. Here in Canada.

The man with the guns had finally come for him.

*   *   *

Now Kadro was at the wheel, and the man with the guns was in the passenger seat. Riding shotgun is what the Americans called it, from the days of the Wild West, the stagecoaches carrying payrolls across the bleak prairies. The driver had to keep his hands on the reins, so this required a second man with free hands and free eyes to shoot at Indians and bandits. Kadro had watched dozens of black and white westerns when he was a boy. John Wayne and Gary Cooper with their six-guns. Sitting around the TV at his uncle's place, five or six cousins sprawled on the floor, their fathers getting drunk on plum brandy and filling the old farmhouse with choking cigarette smoke. How he and his cousins had fashioned sticks and branches for guns, playing in the woods and the barns, shooting each other out of trees, trying to squint like the American cowboys. If only they had known what their life was to hold, of the killing that was to come for their generation.

The passenger was a Canadian, but he was a blood brother in this. He was fully vetted. His name, or at least his operational name, was Turner. He was to be Kadro's primary contact after landing at Pearson International Airport, to get him the tools he would need for the job. Turner looked like an accountant or a government auditor, slim with brown hair parted on the left, a nondescript face save for one feature: a patch on his left eye. Like a damned pirate, Kad thought when he opened the door to see the man standing there. For two days he had sat in the motel listening to the flights take off and land, listening to couples on either side make love in hourly appointments, nothing to do but pace and smoke Canadian cigarettes, watch idiots on game shows, and scratch those lottery tickets he found at the Shell station down the road. That first night he had ventured from the room in search of air and perhaps a bag of potato chips. Beneath a plastic display at the cash register he had discovered the opportunity to win one million Canadian dollars. Two dollars a chance. Why not?

"The vehicle is registered to a numbered company," Turner said. "Try not to get into any accidents. Don't speed. And whatever you do, don't drive drunk. That's generally frowned upon over here."

"I know how to drive," Kadro said. "Since I was ten. Tractors, trucks."

"This isn't a fucking tractor, and this isn't a cow lane in Bosnia," Turner said.

Kad stopped himself, as he was trained to do, trained to swallow instinct, smother emotion, follow orders. In any other situation he would have addressed the profane insult with a hard flat-palmed chop to Turner's throat, grabbed the back of his neck and driven his accountant's face into the dash of the car. The man would be sucking for air through a broken windpipe before he had time to wet his pants.

"Your ID is good enough to throw a beat cop off your scent," Turner continued, "maybe buy a little time, but don't screw around. Since nine-eleven, you can't go to the bathroom without a note from your teacher. Follow the plan. Don't deviate or you'll bring us all down. You have the cellphone, you have my number. After today, it's the only way you'll reach me. The number will be de-activated in seven days. By that time you should be on your way out or…well, it won't matter anyway."

Kadro found everything—the streets, the shops, the women on the sidewalk, the signs in the stores, the grass and the glass and the chrome and the sheer number of brand new vehicles on these city streets—it was more than he had imagined. This city was so *new*, so young, it looked as though it had been built a month ago, not at all like the cities of Sarajevo or Banja Luka, Visoko, Srebrenica, with their ghosts on every corner, their architecture from the earliest centuries. This place was a movie set, it was a shopping mall, it was a picture you saw in a magazine. The year he'd spent locked away on the farm waiting for the last trace of his identity to be erased, existing for this and only this, it had been the life of a monk. Five a.m. wake up, cold water wash and meal parade, exercise and studies—both the English language and overviews of maps and cultural explanations, the security rehearsals, sitting in a chair and reciting his new name and the details of his invented life until they became real. The handler had warned him of the dangers of over-elation, of too much excitement, of meandering in the great North American arcade. No drinking, no drugs, no sex, no chance to get in trouble. Get in, get out.

"Take the next exit," Turner said, "and merge to the right lane. Easy, easy."

Kad saw the sign for Highway 7. They were north of the downtown core now, the CN Tower reduced to a souvenir a few inches tall in the rear-view mirror. Turner gave him directions one at a time, feeding him only the necessary information, until finally they pulled up to a self-serve storage complex. It was a sprawl of low-rise warehouses with tin roofs and yellow garage doors separating each unit, the whole place circled with eight feet of chain link and topped with razor wire.

Kad said, "Like the prison camps."

"This is where Canadians store all the shit that won't fit in their houses," Turner said. "Pull right up to that little stand there and swipe this across the transponder."

It was hard to believe, Kad thought, how people could need more space for their belongings. The things they owned. So much. He had lived the past seven years out of a duffel bag, washing his clothes in sinks, eating only enough to stave off starvation. And this is why his body was as hard as stone while the people around him were soft and slow. Turner handed him a blank white card with the words "Secure-Store" on it, and Kad waved it until the machine beeped and the chain link gate slid open.

"Number sixty-two," Turner said.

Kad drove slowly up and down the rows until they found the unit. He put the car in park and killed the engine. The motor ticked as it cooled down. Turner dug in his coat pocket for a key then looked over at Kad quickly, perhaps one last check of this stranger he was about to arm. Kad stared back at him. He didn't like this Turner with his orders and his "this isn't a cow lane in Bosnia", as though he thought Kad was some dumb farm kid from the hills. He had been that at one time, yes, as a boy. But he did not remember that boy, could not place himself in those shoes.

Turner unlocked the door and lifted it just high enough to get a boot under it. He gave the door a good heft with his foot, and it rolled all the way up to reveal a storage unit twelve feet deep by eight feet wide. There was nothing inside the unit except for a large green trunk. Kad recognized the box as a military foot locker.

"Close the goddamned door," Turner said, standing there at the box. Kad turned and rolled the door down, enclosing them in darkness. Then a light came on, a glow of bright blue-white from an LED lantern. Turner's face was rendered pale and eerie in the light, and the eye patch suddenly gave him a new and sinister impression. Kad saw then the potential that existed within the man for violence; it was there, yes, he could see it now. And this was so true of life, how sometimes the things a man needed to see only became clear to him in the darkness. How a man like Turner navigated through life by appearing just as he presented himself: harmless, insignificant. It was a tactic, of course it was, because everything they did had a tactical purpose.

Turner knelt and unlocked the foot locker. He pushed the lid back and moved some things around. He came back up with a black attaché case. He flicked the latches and revealed a handgun, ammunition clips, a couple of other accessories, stainless steel death. Turner took hold of the sidearm, heavy and black. Checked the safety, racked the action to check for live rounds.

"SIG P225. Recoil action, 9 millimeter NATO cartridges in a nine-piece clip. Canadian Navy boarding parties use these beauties. Close security teams, you know—the cavalry. Cleaned and tested it myself," Turner said.

"I know guns," Kad said, and he took the piece.

He held it in his hand. Regarded it. Turned it over in the way that felt natural now, the way a guitar player held a new instrument—weighing it, getting to know its body and character. For weapons were a lot like humans: they could look alike, perhaps, but no two weapons were exactly the same in personality, in temperament. He had thrown aside expensive German hunting rifles with thousand-dollar scopes for a worn and beaten lever action 3-0-3 simply because of the feel and the response, the nature of the weapon. Simply because it felt right in his hands, an extension of his will. You for me, and me for you.

"Good," Kad said, sliding the action.

"Accessories," Turner said, and handed over a black silencer attachment about four inches long. "And your ammo. Thirty-six rounds. That's it, so don't waste it."

"The rest," Kad said. A directive.

"Hold your horses," Turner said. Then he turned back to the foot locker. He looked over his shoulder—because he had handed over a weapon with ammunition—then turned back to his rooting. He stood up and held what looked like a men's shaving bag. He unzipped the bag and held it open. Kad stepped closer and looked inside. Four syringes, four vials. Clear liquid.

"Be careful," Turner said. "You as much as prick the end of your little finger when one of those is loaded up, and you're fucked six ways to Sunday. I mean *gone.*"

"Do I look clumsy to you?" Kad said. His eyes were hard.

Turner looked at Kad from across the storage room. Dust filtered through the LED light. Turner blinked his one eye. So easy to offend, these types, he thought. Nothing to lose, for they owned nothing but their family name, their pride. They were machines to a great extent, and like all machines they could only be programmed to a point. There were limitations.

"Relax, sparky. I'm just saying, be careful," Turner said. "This shit is straight from the play book of the Mossad. Get it? I'm talking covert black ops. One CC, and the poor son of a bitch exhibits signs of a heart attack—not even detectable in a routine autopsy. Boom, dead. The trick is to get the needle somewhere it won't leave a bruise, signs of puncture. Under a toenail, back of the hairline, around the anus, that sort of thing. Use your imagination."

Kad put the pistol back in its case and zipped up the shaving bag. "The girl is ready?" he said.

"Oh she's ready, all right," Turner said.

"Take me there," Kad said, "now."

Turner smiled, and said, "You know, that's what I like about you people. You cut right to the chase. To the fucking bone."

Kad wondered how much the girl had changed in the three years since they had sat around that kitchen table drinking plum brandy, making plans through long-distance and third-party communication with the Colonel. Or whether she had really changed at all. Were any of them capable of further change? The transformation was complete, as far as he was concerned. From what he had started as, what he had become along the way, and what he was right now—it was a complete metamorphosis. Psychological, physiological, biological, spiritual. He had been a boy once, yes, the little boy who worked and played at his grandfather's farm. The smell of animals in winter, hay wet with the stink of piss. He remembered the boy sometimes, though rarely, and always within the distorted context of fractured memory. For Kadro was dead, the death certificate filed in a municipal office. He was dead, and his brother was an orphan. It was the irony of this strange arrangement—they had to die in order to be re-born for this.

"Let's go," Kad said.

"I'll give you the directions," Turner said. "Drop me off at the subway."

Kad gave him a look.

Turner said, "What, do you want me to hold your hand? This is it for me. I'm done. Over and out. You reach me in the event of catastrophe, period."

Turner opened the garage door, and they both squinted against the flood of light. He slammed the door shut behind them, wiped his hands across his pants, and they got in the car. Kad turned the ignition and put the car in gear then said, without looking at Turner, "Your eye. What happened?"

Turner sort of smiled and said, "Left it in Bosnia."

*　*　*

Kadro dropped Turner off at a small parking lot kitty corner to the York Mills subway station in the north of the city. There was a brick building about the size of a large garden shed, stairs leading underground and connecting to the station across the street. Turner opened the door and stepped out. It was a good late summer day, warm enough for the diehard cyclists to wear their shorts as they careened in and out of traffic.

"Good luck," Turner said, his hand on the door.

Kad looked over and gave a small nod.

"Get back on the highway up here," Turner said, pointing north.

"I know how," Kad said. The grid map of Toronto was burned into his brain like a cattle brand. The hours they had sat pouring over maps, being quizzed as though his life depended on it. And it did.

Turner closed the door, walked to the brick building and slipped inside. Kad waited a minute then pulled out of the parking lot. He made it a block before pulling into a Petro Canada station. He bought a newspaper and four scratch-and-win tickets. He sat in the car and used a penny to slowly scratch each ticket. He blew the crinkled bits of foil from his lap. He didn't think about anything when he was scratching these cards. Nothing. The world around him closed down for a few minutes. He won ten dollars on the last ticket. He went back inside and showed the clerk the card, and the kid took it and hit a few buttons. The lottery computer made a whirling and ringing noise as though he had won a trip around the world. The teenage clerk didn't seem too excited over the windfall. He handed out two fives, and Kad flashed his first smile in a year. It wasn't a big smile, but it was something.

He drove east across the top of the city then south down to the woman's apartment building near the railway tracks. Unit 801. He parked on the street and looked at his watch. It was going on four o'clock. He got out of the car and went into the building. He pressed the buzzer for her unit and waited. He pressed it again, holding it this time for fifteen seconds.

"Yes?" came a woman's voice. "Who is it?"

"Kadro," he said. "From home."

A pause. A long pause. As though she were thinking. This is what he thought as he stood there. It would be naïve to assume every facet and angle of the operation would roll out exactly as planned. People changed their minds. Soldiers talked with bravado and offered up promises of infinite courage while drinking on the eve of battle. When the bullets and the mortars started to fly, it was another story. He knew about people and their limits. This is why one had to be adaptable, ready to transform within the moment. He waited, looking at some flyers scattered on the floor of the vestibule. Full-colour pictures of pizzas and buckets of chicken. Delivery to your door so you didn't have to get off your ass and walk down to the pizzeria. The pizzas looked good and hot. His stomach growled. Then the door buzzed. He opened it and stepped inside.

*   *   *

They had assembled in that kitchen those years ago, around that long wood table. Back home. Would she ever see home again? It seemed like a lifetime already lived in this new country. At first the plan was easy to follow, the directives and the drills running your body as though you were on automatic pilot. The paperwork was handled through the Colonel's unseen contacts, and she'd entered the country with a suitcase and a number to call. The one-eyed man she met through the immigration support centre, everything made to seem natural and quite by circumstance. The man got her the job as a seamstress in the little factory in the fashion district. She kept her head down and made dresses, or parts of them, and the women around her were all immigrants from some other place: Cambodia, Vietnam, and yes, Bosnians too, working for this Serb manager (though she had lied about her background and her hometown to get the job). She worked and she watched and she made notes. She saved some money and moved to that small apartment away from the guns and the gangs of Jane and Finch. She took the night course in English. Her only social time away from work, out of the apartment.

The teacher. This was her mistake. The Canadian with the sad eyes. The good heart, the small smile. She never should have gone for coffee when he asked. And then asked again. But it felt good to talk to someone—even if she felt her English made her sound like a grade school student. This was her mistake. She had lost so much, it seemed like a small gift she could allow herself, a simple coffee with a good soul. First you lose your village, then you lose your family, and finally you lose yourself. You die or choose to be born again. There had been something in the eyes of the sad Canadian, this teacher who made bad jokes about words they looked up in the dictionary—something there, yes, within the sadness a tiny spark of life. A flash of hope. And this was her mistake...

Donia Kruzik opened the door of her apartment. She stood there for a long moment. Kad stared at her, blinking. She opened the door all the way, and he stepped inside. An awkward moment as they stood there, each deciding on the proper greeting. Finally he moved to embrace her, but she shrank, and stepped back.

"Friend," he said, "it has been a long journey. From there to here."

He spoke in his native tongue, and it brought her back to who they were, where they had come from. She went to the tiny kitchen and put the kettle on to boil.

"I will make tea," she said. "Are you hungry?"

He stood there. Watching her. He knew, and she knew that he knew. She took two cups down from the cupboard and got a box of Red Rose from the shelf. Something had changed. However small.

"I met the man. I have the tools," he said.

He watched her. Then he moved to the kitchen and put a hand on her shoulder from behind. She froze. His hand was strong, and he held her there, rooted.

"Are you ready?" he said.

"Ready?"

"To do what we have sworn to do," he said. "Have you forgotten already, sister? Has your time in this country erased the past? Have you lost your appetite to avenge our people? Please tell me this is not so."

She bowed her head and nodded. "I am ready," she said. "It's a surprise, that's all. You plan for the day for so many months and years, and then it is finally here. I apologize for not welcoming you. It was wrong of me. Please, come and sit."

He moved his hand from her shoulder to his side but sensed the change in the weather, within the hesitation. This was the inherent risk for those sent to conduct surveillance prior to operations—a settling in, an assimilation of sorts. He would kill her if it came to that. If she was unwilling to follow through. It was her choice. That was his directive. All of them shared the same directive. The only way this would work is if every link in the chain remained connected, solid—and every link in turn knew it was expendable in the name of the cause. Hesitation or gross misconduct was to be dealt with in the most extreme manner. There was no half measure. They had signed their oath in the blood of their forsaken kin. Those who had fallen in the fields, in the rows. He had not come this far to turn away. Their trust was sacred.

She put a cup of tea in front of him, and he sat at the two-seat kitchen table. She sat with her cup and blew across the steaming water. Their eyes met and held for a long moment. They saw each other as they had been, younger and wounded, not as they had become.

"Can you share your work with me?" he said.

She went to the bedroom and returned with a single file folder. It was letter-sized, blue, and bore no writing or identifying features. She placed it on the table in front of him. He opened and began to read. The first page contained the photos of the two targets, their names typed beneath:

BOJAN KORDIC

GORAN MITOVIC

Then followed several pages of tiny notations—dates and times and tracked movements of the targets. Their home address, their work address, phone numbers, the names of their spouses and children and the schools they attended, their lives reduced to a series of comings and goings. She had done good work. The information was concise, invaluable in ensuring the two main criteria were met: that these were in fact the bona fide targets; and that it would be possible within the scheduling and routine of their lives to make contact and retreat with limited collateral damage or liability to the cause.

"Well done," he said and set folder aside.

"I have worked hard," she said, "getting to know the people at work. The woman who works outside the manager's office, this Bojan Kordic. His executive assistant. She keeps his schedule. We share a cigarette outside during break."

"There will be time to talk of our plans," he said. "It has been what, three years?"

"Almost," she said.

"You look good. Healthy. This country agrees with you," he said.

She caught his eyes, and he held her there, and she knew what he was looking for. Some sign that she had forsaken their plans. The first thing the Colonel had instructed in bringing them together for this: the greatest threat is not death, for we all died a long time ago. No, the greatest threat is that those of you who are sent abroad will succumb to the liberties and luxuries of your new country. Shopping malls and fast food drive-through restaurants, and women and men who lie down with anyone at all after a single dance in a night club. There will be those of you who forget in time why you are there in the first place…

"What do you think of this country so far?" she asked.

"It is new," he said. "Like it just opened."

And they shared their experiences. The first landing. Pearson International Airport. The language. The faces from around the world moving freely on the streets. Everything open and free. And new, so new, as he had said. Some things were better, yes, but many things were not. He thought of telling her about the money he had won, but he kept it to himself.

He excused himself and went to the bathroom. When he came back, he said, "Will you miss this place?"

He watched her.

"Some things," she said. "I suppose, yes."

And then it happened, just like that, just as he was sitting there. Like a narcoleptic zoning in mid-sentence, Kad forgot where he was. Blinked. Somewhere else, the damp and moldy basement of a house in the hills, the shells walking in yard by yard, the artillerymen of the enemy forces well-trained in this after the first days of war in Croatia. They walked them in, they drew lines, and they created walls of exploding shells.

"Getting closer," he said. "Listen."

"What is getting closer?" Donia asked. She looked at him.

Kadro flinched, as though he had heard a noise that was inaudible to her. It frightened her. He stared at nothing at all for the longest moment, then, as though a hypnotist had snapped his fingers, turned and looked at her. And he blinked.

"Are you all right?" she said.

"Good. Yes."

He finished his tea and thought something stronger would

ease the strangeness that had fallen between them. She had cried in his arms all those years ago. In that kitchen where the Colonel's man had brought them together, the sun coming through the window and catching the dust in the air, the little kitchen warm from their bodies, warm from their collective hatred and grief. He had not had a drink in more than two years. He knew men back home, men he had fought with in the fields and the hills, good men who were drunks now, drug addicts. Needles and pills. They did not work, they could not work. Men in their late twenties and early thirties who drank vodka and brandy and cheap strong beer, hoping the next drink would be the drink to numb them just enough, to ward off the memory of the things they had done. It was not an easy thing to live with nightmares when you knew they were real.

"What is his name," Kad said.

She looked up. Caught in the headlights. The accusation.

"This man. This man you have become friends with. Please. Don't lie to me."

"There is no one. I have…I have a friend, that is all he is. He is…"

He closed his eyes. He was not unprepared for this. And so he thought: rather than her, I can erase the trace of this man. A small grace, it would be his little secret. That there could be no compromise of their work, this was the inarguable fact. That he could perhaps spare her for this indiscretion, he would try.

"Who is he? Where does he live?"

"There is nobody, please. I am alone. Look around. You can see the life I have lived here. Alone. I've worked in the places where I was told to work, I have watched the men I was told to watch. When they drink their coffee, where they buy their lunch, when they go pee… "

She stared at him, unblinking. He considered this and finished his tea and rubbed his hands together. He leaned forward, his eyes shining with that electric intensity she remembered now from their early days, the days of the kitchen table, and it was a look that both comforted and terrified her. She understood that with this man, there was no comprehension of the notion of defeat.

"Do you remember what it was like back then? Do you remember? I remember. I remember what it was like to be gone from my village for months that seemed like years, to have been gone so long that I became an animal. Yes, capable of things that only an animal could be capable of. But righteous. In our cause, in the blood we shed. And I remember what it was like that July to come home to find the bastards had rounded up the men—our brothers and fathers and husbands and cousins and grandfathers and uncles—and they had lined them up and shot them…"

"I remember," she said. And she was steel now, or ice. She stared, and she said, "Don't tell me what I remember or don't remember. My husband. I remember my husband. Who he was and where he came from, what he stood for. A good man. But I can't remember his face sometimes. At night, when I wake up with the dreams of the bombs and the guns. I search, and there is nothing. I can't remember his face… "

She did not cry, for the reservoir was long emptied. This, this was something she had shared with the school teacher. The burden of the survivor.

"Tell me," he said, and reached into his jean pockets, "if these belong to your new Canadian lover."

He held a single key attached to a plain metal key ring.

"From my purse," she said. "What right—"

"You are moving," Kad said, and stood, slipping the key back in his pocket.

"When?"

"Tonight. Your tracks here are compromised. We are moving you immediately."

Their words turned into an argument. It was the stress of the days behind them and the days that lay ahead. The high emotion of their shared past. After the neighbours called to complain, and the super stopped by to check in, Kad left her there to pack her clothing. She could bring one bag only. Men would arrive after dark, he explained, to wipe the unit clean so there would be no trace of her life in this small apartment.

"I will pick you up at midnight," he said.

"I'm sorry," she said.

"Remember," he said. "Remember why we are here."

*   *   *

It was the next afternoon when Kad returned to the apartment to take one last look for anything they might have missed. To ensure the movers Turner had brought in had not somehow forgotten anything—for you could not trust anyone these days to complete a mission simply as assigned. He was in the apartment unit when this man entered. Looking for her, for Donia. Calling her name. A friend of a friend. Oh yes, you have a new friend—*a boyfriend*?

So then. She had made her mistake, and now he had made his. He had to see the place with his own eyes to know the job had been done. And by chance, sheer circumstance, he had been there when this man had come looking for her. Their work not yet begun, and already the operation was compromised. After running from the apartment, Kad sat thinking in the car outside a convenience store. He took the roll of golden dollar coins from his pocket and held them in his right hand. The knuckles were already swelling, chafed. He wrapped his fingers about the roll of coins and squeezed. A line of blood leaked where a thin sheaf of his flesh was torn from his knuckle. The man he'd struck, it had been a good hard shot. But he should have finished the job. Instead he'd run. What a fool. Forgive me, my people.

He opened the door and walked into the store. He set the roll of coins down on the counter. The clerk had long hair and hadn't shaved in a few days. Kad wanted to slap the sleepy look from the young man's face. Such disrespect. Running a shop with his shirt stained, untucked.

"Scratching tickets," Kad said.

"Huh?" the clerk said.

Kad made a scratching motion with his thumb and forefinger. "Scratching tickets," he repeated.

"Which one?" the clerk said. "There's like nine different kinds, man."

Kad shrugged. "One of each," he said.

FIVE

McKelvey was perched on a stool at Garrity's, squinting at his raccoon eyes in the dark mirror behind the bar, a good golden pint of Steam Whistle working with the pain killers to produce a new brand of unfailing optimism. It was something one could just never take for granted, this peace that settled in marrow-deep. Yes, if the feeling had a colour, it would be the blurry soft yellow of squinting through a summer's day. The draft beer was cold, and it was brewed just down the street in the old roundhouse where the trains had converged and merged for a century. McKelvey was now officially marked absent from his pain, and it was a good thing. His nose was swollen to almost double its size across the width of the bridge, the pouches beneath his eyes turning the hue of eggplant. A series of blood vessels had apparently imploded in his right eye, resulting in a grotesque black cherry splatter across the whiteness of the orb. He wondered about the employment of some utility beyond bare knuckles.

"I've been punched in the face before," he told Huff Keegan, "but not like this. No, sir. This guy knew how to throw a goddamn punch. That, or it was brass knuckles."

"They say Gordie Howe had one of the hardest punches in the game," Huff said.

"You knocked out a few teeth in your day."

Huff shrugged, and it was like a ripple moving along a

mountain range. Two hundred and thirty pounds of corded muscle rolling in a tectonic shift. But the last two years away from the game had taken its toll, and Huff's body was less toned and more bulky now, his stomach starting to show early signs of the eventual paunch that he would pat while telling stories of his gladiator days to his grandchildren.

"One night you're the guy doing the feeding, the next night you're the guy getting fed," Huff said. "It all evens out in the end. I had my nose broken three times, lost four teeth. I had my orbital bone fractured, right here under my right eye. Broke my left hand twice. Two of the knuckles on my right hand are fused together from hitting helmets. I scored six goals a year on average, and most of those were flukes. Two thousand penalty minutes."

He held his hands up in front of his face, turning them over, thick bricks of permanently swollen and scarred flesh and bone. They seemed a marvel to him that they should still work after the way he had treated them.

"Spent a lot of hours after games with my hands in a bucket of ice," he continued. "Sitting there while the pretty boys and the scoring leaders were out having beers or grabbing a steak—or grabbing a piece of something else. It was the job, you know. It was just the job."

Huff had played a few games up in the big leagues with Buffalo and Detroit, just enough, McKelvey supposed, to give a man a taste of what he was missing. Down in the minors of the American Hockey League, in the dead-end steel towns and the factory towns of the north and northeast, Huff Keegan had been an icon who'd carried his own duffel bag, slept four to a room, and grown old by his late twenties.

"Miss it?" McKelvey said.

Huff shrugged, and said, "Shit yeah. Every day, man." After a beat, he said, "You miss the job?"

McKelvey smiled and said, "Every second day."

He drank his beer and thought of the unexpected visit to the emergency department that morning. The twelve-year-old doctor confirmed what he already knew, that his nose was broken. It was not set off kilter, so it required no setting—the good news of the day. He was taped across the bridge and handed a scrip for yet more pain killers, McKelvey pretended he had never before listened to the spiel about the seriousness of the drug, the constipation and stomach cramps, the responsibility that came with that piece of chicken-scrawled paper. Now his mind was already playing through the next steps here. The partial plate number, the basic description of the vehicle and the man—the fridge magnet in his pocket. He ran through his call to Tim Fielding from the payphone in the emergency waiting area.

"Oh my god, Charlie," Fielding had said, "there's no choice now. We've got to call the police. The apartment was empty? I mean, what the hell is going on here? She wouldn't just…"

McKelvey had calmed the younger man over the phone, cotton shoved up his nostrils making his own voice sound like a cartoon character. Convinced him to settle down, to shut his mouth, to keep it to himself. The police weren't interested in someone who had moved, whatever their reasons. And anyway, Christ, he needed some time to think it through, find this guy and break his nose in return.

"We need to be careful here, Tim. I need some time to figure out a few leads," McKelvey said, as though it made all the sense in the world. "Don't talk to anyone, okay? Don't even answer your phone unless you see that it's me."

"We should do what you wanted to do from the start, Charlie, and call the police. I don't want to mess around. Donia could

71

be…don't you think we should get some help?"

"If this is a love triangle, or if this guy is out of his mind with jealousy or whatever, we don't want to be fanning the flames by dragging the cops into everything, you understand? I'm going to talk to a few people," McKelvey said. "Listen, you brought me in to this, and I just got a nose job. You owe me that much, Tim. A day or two, that's all I want. I'll be in touch."

He hung up. And then he called Detective Mary-Ann Hattie with his list of favours. She seemed beyond the point of asking questions. Perhaps "exasperated" was the word.

"You know they can monitor this sort of thing now. It's not 1973 any more, Charlie. It's not the card catalogue system. You know, Dewey decimal. They use phrases like 'abuse of privileges'. They have all these pesky privacy laws. The douchebags in Professional Standards salivate over these little indiscretions."

Her sarcasm made him smile. He knew she could run with a line for a week and a half, find new ways to insult or bend the humour, squeeze every last drop of life from it. Sometimes he thought if she hadn't become a cop, she would have made a good standup comedian. Other times he looked at her and saw her leading a Grade Two class, her dress powdered in chalk dust.

He said, "You know as well as I do how to open a locked door."

"What the hell are you doing anyway?" she said. "Thinking of renting an office, maybe buying a fedora and a .38 Special? Hang a shingle, 'Private Detective, Charlie McKelvey'?"

"I'm just doing a favour, looking into a few things. Listen," he said, "I need to see you, Hattie. Come on. It's been what, a week and a half? I've got the girls coming Saturday night. Why don't you come over on Sunday. You could stay."

There. He'd said it. Caught in a moment of vulnerability, his head smashed in, brains turned to pillow stuffing. He blinked through the silence that rang from the other end. An announcement over the public address system in the emergency room gave him a start. Code Blue—which he knew meant someone had stopped breathing. McKelvey thought, *Could be an asshole or a saint, it hardly mattered in the end, did it?* They worked just as hard to save the assholes from dying. He opened his eyes, refocused through the ringing in his ears. The hospital waiting room was full of puking kids latched to bleary-eyed mothers, and a gaggle of young college-aged men who had apparently been involved in a fracas of some variety, bruises and lacerations across their young faces.

"We'll see," she said. "Hey listen, I've got to run. I'm working a double today, filling in for Teckles. The guy's sick again."

"Probably got cramps. They never should have transferred him up from Traffic Investigations. He can't stand the pace in Hold-Up. Needs to have everything mapped out with his measuring tape."

"Yeah, well not everyone is as adaptable as you, McKelvey," Hattie said, and he took it the way she intended it. That east coast fisherman's daughter passive-aggressiveness coming through loud and clear. Oh, Mary-Ann Hattie, his redhead beauty with the longshoreman's mouth and those green, green eyes. She was slipping from his grasp like an old dory cut from its mooring. The thirteen-year age difference which at first had seemed hardly a topic of discussion seemed now like an ever-widening chasm. How was it that he always seemed to find himself standing on the other side, the wrong side? *You were not born for these times, Charlie McKelvey.*

"I appreciate you running those numbers," he said.

"Take care of yourself, Charlie," she said. Then she was gone. His mind turned to the magnet he'd lifted from the refrigerator

73

of Donia's apartment. Upon his return from the ER, carried on the wings of the newly prescribed Percocet, he had sat and held the thing and closed one eye to focus.

The magnet had a graphic of a bridge spanning across the continents. It said: Bridges: Bosnian Immigrant Support Centre.

Beneath that was a phone number, address and website link, and beneath that was a line of italicized writing in a foreign language, presumably Bosnian.

So then. Beyond the assault, there was no crime here. In fact, McKelvey was the one with a stolen fridge magnet (Theft Under $5,000). None of it made sense, though, and all of it rubbed him the wrong way. Perhaps it was a simple case of unpaid rent and a midnight escape. But he doubted it. And the first person he needed to speak to in the morning was the superintendent of Donia's building. That was the logical starting point. Find out who the woman was, where she'd gone.

"Last call in a few minutes," Huff said.

"How about a Jameson's on ice for the road," McKelvey said, and he knew it was a bad idea this late into a busted-face day, but what the fuck. He finished the last of the beer in his glass, the taste distorted to a lick of old pennies thanks to the bloodied cotton stuffed in his nostrils.

Huff set him up with a shot of the amber Irish whiskey on ice. It was smooth, then it burned just a little, but he missed out on the taste of peat and toasted barley, the sweetness that lingered within the melting ice. As he set the glass down, he glanced in the mirror and caught the eyes of a man he'd noticed a few nights earlier. He didn't miss the fact the man seemed to be checking him out this night as well. A husky fellow with shaggy black hair, and a thick goatee in need of a trim. Dressed in jeans and one of those long canvas riding coats that seemed always to be slicked

74

with oil. McKelvey stared back via the mirror until the man, who was sitting at a small table near the back, turned away.

"That guy back there, the big guy," McKelvey said, "you know him?"

Huff was removing glasses from the small dishwasher beneath the bar, setting them on a shelf above his head. He looked over in his practiced bartender's way so as not to draw attention. He looked back to McKelvey and shook his head. "Been in a couple times the past week. Sits alone, has a beer, maybe two."

McKelvey knew a rounder when he saw one, and this guy was a rounder. Perhaps somebody he had put away a few years ago. Who knew. He stood and held the bar for a moment while his neurons and synapses began to fire in sequence, sending signals to his feet and ankles, knees and hips. Move. This way. Left, right...

"What's the damage, Huff?" he said, digging in his coat for his wallet.

"On the house tonight, Charlie," Huff said. "You've had a tough day."

McKelvey slipped his wallet back in his pocket and nodded in appreciation. "You're a good man, Huff Keegan."

It was, in the end, all that a man could ask for: a good bar and a good bartender waiting for you at the end of a ball-busting day. I hope heaven is a little like this, McKelvey thought. A stool waiting for you, a bunch of guys with no need for in-depth conversation about household accessories or other impractical and confounding subjects. It made McKelvey miss the locker room at shift change, the warriors in from their patrols, all the swagger and the bullshit.

"I've got to hit the all-night grocery," McKelvey said. "My granddaughter's coming to visit me tomorrow."

He liked the sound of that. And despite the broken nose,

despite this new hangnail of Donia Kruzik throbbing in the back of his brain like an unsolved case he had failed to close years earlier, he felt good. It was in the pills, he knew, this false sense of ease. A little bit of paradise crushed to powder. As he made his way out onto Front Street to the twenty-four Dominion store, the night clear and cut open with city lights and sirens, he thought he might perhaps even buy a package of Krispy Kreme donuts for the little girl with the dark curls.

SIX

Kadro was standing in line at the concession stand at the mid-town theatre. He was watching the sloppy teenagers behind the counter fill cardboard boxes with popcorn, shuffle to the butter dispenser, pump a few shots across the top, then shuffle back to the counter. One boy's uniform shirt was dirty with stains, and it was untucked. Another boy's hair was a rat's nest, and this one kept trying to make a couple of the girls laugh with his sarcastic jokes rather than serve the line of customers. Kad gritted his teeth until his molars ached. How grateful he'd been at their age to earn a few dinars mucking the pens of the farmer down the road, to shovel shit for pocket change to buy candy and a comic book. It seemed everything had changed within a generation. There was no respect, for self, let alone for others. Too many fat people, too many lazy people. Where, he wanted to know, was their sense of pride in service? What would these assholes do if their country ever called upon them to fight in a war, a real war?

As he moved up in the line, he kept his eye on the silver-haired man in the adjacent line. The man was out with a younger woman and a girl of five or six. The woman had brown hair cut short, she was pretty but wore no makeup, and the little girl had brown curly hair and wore a dress with what looked like new black shoes. The man kept his hand on the back of her head, as though to have contact with her at all times in a public place gave him a sense of comfort. Kadro did not need to stare at the man in order to confirm his identification. This was Bojan Kordic, Donia's manager at the dress factory. Bojan Kordic, leader of the rogue unit that had come through the village that summer, staying just long enough to round up the men and the boys, the young and the old and the crippled alike. Driven to a farm field. Lined up. Shot.

Kad had been following the man for two hours now. Thanks to the fastidious notes in the file made by his sister in this, he had everything he needed, the address of the man's home, the license plates of his two vehicles, grainy photos taken on a cheap disposable camera of the home and the cars, of the man and his family walking in a park. Kadro had sat outside the home to get a lay of the land, then the garage doors had opened, and they had come out, heading first to an A&W for burgers and onion rings, then on to the theatre for an early afternoon show. It was true that every life was, in effect, simply a series of habits and routines played out across the days and weeks and months of a life. We fall into patterns that make us easy targets for those who might wish us harm. This man's life was no different—the same coffee shop each morning, the same route to work. His life was put down in black and white, and Kad smiled at Donia's good work when he read the notes about how the man left the office early every Wednesday to go and screw a woman who worked in Payroll.

Here they appeared as any other family. Kad wondered if the woman, this man's wife, knew of her husband's past, the violence of which he was capable. Beneath the suit, beyond the minivan and the suburban home with a two-car garage, the soccer games and the ballet lessons. Did she ever catch of glimpse of the monster beneath the surface? He doubted it. *We are all capable of wearing masks,* he thinks, *of minding our manners when the sign tells us to act this way or that way.* Civilization is based upon this basic principal or unspoken agreement. If you shoot someone on the street, or say in this movie theatre, it is murder, a senseless act of violence. Even if there is a root cause and effect, even if that cause is righteous. It makes headlines in the newspaper. Shocking. And yet, if the same players are lifted and carried to a war zone, any war zone with any number of geo-political roots and causes and righteous notions, then we say, this is simply war; this is boys being boys, it has been this way since the dawning of the first sun.

When the war is done, when the politicians have stood for photos and the signing of peace agreements, then it is back to the rules again. The switch is thrown, and you wash the blood from your hands, and you smile and wave at your neighbour again, the same neighbour who raped and killed your sister, the very same neighbour you had in your rifle sights only a month earlier—how you fired and missed, the physics of fate. Yes, you are told to forgive and forget, to drive within the lines on the highway, to wait your turn in the queue for bread. But nobody can ever completely forgive and forget. That's why the wars are fought, then peace is called, then the wars are fought again. Because there is always a germ of the cause left untreated. Grandfathers tell their grandsons stories of the war, of the old days, of what is right and wrong. And the seed is planted. And it germinates like a speck of rust.

The man purchased two boxes of popcorn, soft drinks, and a bag of red licorice. With his hand again on the back of the girl's head, they walked through the foyer and down the hall towards theatre number 4. *Lilo & Stitch* was playing. Kad waited a second at the door, gave them time to choose seats and get settled, then he slipped inside the theatre. It took his eyes a moment to adjust to the darkness. He went up the stairs with his small bag of popcorn, scanning the rows that were two-thirds filled, and found them close to the middle, over to the right-hand side. He went one row up and settled in just behind and to the left of them.

The previews came on, and Kad settled back and ate his popcorn. It was stale, and the butter tasted of chemicals. Yes, everything had changed. Movies were ten bucks and the popcorn was shit. Gary Cooper was dead. No more simple Saturday afternoons at his uncle's house, the TV playing old movies, then he and his cousins acting them out in the barns and the fields and the woods, those days of wide-open wonder. He looked over to the family every now and then, and he watched them, the back of the man's head, and he wondered what the man would be thinking right now if he knew that he would be dead in a matter of days.

SEVEN

The brain is a yolk that floats in a sea of cerebrospinal fluid—that briny flotsam of all we've learned and tried to forget. McKelvey woke the next morning with his circuits misfiring: bits of grade school math questions, the combination to his high school locker, the faces and names and rap sheets of a hundred criminals. Reminders to pick up milk bread eggs, everything spun together inside the swollen globe of his fragile skull—shaken and stirred. He was alive, of course, but he figured there must be a good part of him left on the grille of the truck that had hit him, backed up and run over him again. He lifted his head from the pillow and knew instantly that the day would require him to meet and exceed the limitations of his physical and spiritual capacity. He stayed in the shower for thirty minutes, the hot water a balm of sorts against the intense swelling pressure that threatened to stretch his face to the point of explosion. His teeth ached at their very roots.

He was gingerly running a razor down the silver stubble on his chin when the phone rang. He wiped away the creamy lather with a hand towel as he moved across the condo to the single phone on the desk by the window.

"Nineteen ninety-five Honda Accord registered to Ontario business B-10078837," Hattie recited in the voice she reserved for testifying, for reading the facts as presented. "And yes, I had a pal at the provincial records office check into the business registration before they closed for the long weekend. It's a garage in Rexdale. Jarko's Automotive."

McKelvey scribbled the information down on a note pad. "Thanks," he said.

"Hey, no problem," Hattie said. "Listen, if there's anything else I can do to help you get me demoted or suspended without pay, don't hesitate. We have operators waiting to take your call."

"Hattie," he said. And that was it, the best that he could do. His mind was already working through the next steps here.

"About tomorrow," she said.

"Right."

She sighed and said, "You forgot, didn't you? You forgot about inviting me over. Jesus, I'm such an idiot. This is like the third time you've done this in a month."

"I didn't forget, Hattie," he said, recovering, coming back on line. "Dinner tomorrow night. I'll make some macaroni and cheese. With the crumbs on top."

"As long as it's not out of a box," she said. "And remember, I caught you last time. I have these rather sharp deductive skills."

"I love you," he could have said. Or even "Have a great day, sweetheart." It was there, it was on the tip of his tongue, always on the tip of his tongue, these best of intentions. He laughed instead and made some joke about soda crackers and the kind of cheese that came in a spray can. As soon as he hung up, he reached for the Toronto phone book. McKelvey remembered how they used to try and split the behemoth in half with their bare hands standing around the change room after a shift, a bunch of young beat cops full of piss and vinegar with too much to prove.

*   *   *

82

The superintendent was a human cliché. He was in his early fifties, but he already owned the look of a man resigned to a life of cheap rent in exchange for waking at all hours to a mind-numbing and seemingly infinite flow of requests. Change the light bulb, fix the fridge, repair the leaky faucet, do something about the goddamned bed bugs. He was perhaps five-six, a hundred and forty pounds, and his t-shirt was stretched across a tight, round belly that was the direct result, McKelvey surmised, of the nightly six-pack of budget beer consumed while sitting in a tattered recliner to watch, hopefully uninterrupted, as Vanna White stood there flipping letters in exchange for a seven-figure salary.

"Help you?" the man said. He held the door open just enough. He had what appeared to be a fleck of corn flake glued to one corner of his mouth.

"Name's McKelvey," McKelvey said and handed the super one of his old business cards. He had a stack of them in his sock drawer. He had crossed out the office number and neatly printed his own number beneath it, fully aware of the legal implications of that simple action.

"Hank Chinaski," the super said. He took the card and read it. "Hold-up Squad, eh?" He shrugged, scratched the back of his hair then adjusted his testicles like some old man out in public. "You looking for one of the losers lives in this crap hole? Lotta old people on pension, maybe one of them robbed a bank?"

"Donia Kruzik. Single woman lived up in 801. She moved out. What can you tell me about her?"

"The Polish chick?"

"Bosnian," McKelvey said.

"News to me if she cut and run," Chinaski said. "Wouldn't be the first midnight move around here. We don't have what you'd call a service elevator, you know, with the option to put it on hold while you move all your shit. They woulda had to hold it up manually. Then again, she didn't have much stuff, now that I think of it."

Chinaski sighed, opened the door all the way, and turned towards the kitchen. The place was a mess, the roost of a slovenly bachelor. He picked up his set of all-access keys and shrugged at McKelvey. "Let's go take a look," he said.

In the elevator, McKelvey asked what the woman was like as a tenant, quiet or loud, on time or late with the rent. Any information was better than none. It was how any cop drew a picture of a suspect or a victim, by asking questions. In McKelvey's experience it was often the detail someone else thought of as insignificant that helped close a loop.

"Yeah, well you know, she kept to herself pretty well. Wasn't here that long. Six months I guess, maybe not even quite. She had a job, far as I could tell. I went up there just the once to fix her shower head," and here the superintendent sort of smiled to himself at some real or imagined memory.

"Guy like you running a building like this, you must get some good opportunities," McKelvey said, an old pal here, the detective's job to find common ground, wink wink.

Chinaski bared his teeth, yellow from cigarettes and coffee and no dental plan. "Time to time. 'Course, not nearly as much as I'd like," he said. "Hey, it's shit pay for a shit job. People yelling at you all the time. No respect, man."

"Sounds familiar," McKelvey said. "So listen, you didn't get anywhere with Donia. Maybe you tried a line or two, but she wasn't interested."

"She seemed, I don't know what you'd call it, preoccupied." Chinaski nodded to himself, satisfied with his word choice, as though he had finally summoned the question to one of Alex Trebek's answers. "The apartment was set up pretty basic, nothing homey. She seemed serious, is what I would say. Guess the Europeans are like that."

"She was quiet, never had any issues?"

"Sure, yeah. Until recent. There was a loud argument in her unit a couple of nights ago, people called to complain. It's got to be pretty loud for folks to bother calling me on a noise complaint. When I got up there, this guy was just leaving."

"What did he look like, you remember?

"Tall guy, pretty big in the shoulders. Buzzed hair. Not to be fucked with, you know. I mean, he was pretty hard looking. He just brushed right by me like he didn't even see me. And then she was alone. She said her friend had left, and she promised there would be no more problems. But I could see that she was very upset, whatever had happened."

The elevator stopped, and the doors slid open. They walked down the hallway and stopped at the unit. Chinaski selected the right key from a couple of dozen on his belt chain, inserted it in the lock, and before turning, and out of habit, called out: "Superintendent. Coming in."

The super held the door for McKelvey. As McKelvey stepped inside, Chinaski motioned to his eye with a few fingers, and said, "Mind me asking what happened?"

McKelvey said, "Getting clumsy in my old age."

The apartment was exactly as McKelvey recalled. Empty. There was a smell of stale, closed air. The place still held the vibe, however, of expended kinetic energy, the invisible buzz of human activity. Something had happened here. An occurrence. It was a sense that was impossible to explain to someone who had never set foot in a crime scene. The corner store with the owner sprawled amidst the bags of chips and cheesies, two holes in his chest, blood pooled and already turning dark as cherry juice—and it was here now, despite the silence of the scene, this residue of limits exceeded in the pursuit of evil deeds.

"Well, shit on a stick," Chinaski said, nodding, taking it all in. "Must have been some quiet operation. Oh well, no loss. They was fully paid up for the month. Sure as hell didn't need to be moving out in the middle of the night like that. Goddamn got to rent it again now, go through the waiting list of jeezly losers."

That word "*jeezly*" reminded him of Hattie, one of the many east coast bastardizations she threw out now and again. The super must have been from the Maritimes. He wasn't alone in the city. There was a standard line about there being more Newfoundlanders in Toronto than on the island of Newfoundland.

McKelvey said, "You'd have her cheques on file?"

"She paid cash month to month," Chinaski said. "That is, after she settled first and last and the damage deposit. I'd have that one on file for sure."

McKelvey felt the familiar tug that ran from his crotch to this throat, the rush of a connection forming. Not to put too much stock into it, but it was something. "Can I get a copy?"

"Don't see why not. But listen, it'll take me a few hours. My office is kind of a shit show, if you know what I mean," Chinaski said.

"I understand. Listen, you have video cameras in the lobby?" McKelvey said. He wanted to run through the tape, capture an image, anything—even a grainy profile of the man who'd jumped him.

The super shrugged. "Thing is, they're not actually hooked up."

"What do you mean, not hooked up," McKelvey said.

"The owner didn't want to pay for video tapes and all that

shit." Chinaski shrugged again. "He's a real cheap asshole. I think he's Ukrainian."

"You have my number there. If you can let me know when you find the cheque, or remember anything at all, give me a call."

"Is this for your cellphone?" Chinaski said, indicating the number scrawled in pen beneath the scratched-out office number.

"Home number," McKelvey said. "I'm sort of working from home these days."

"Geez, that's all right. Everybody's working from home these days. Didn't know they were doing that with the cops now."

"All sorts of perks," McKelvey said, and moved for the door.

*   *   *

The taxi bills were piling up. Hassan had been waiting for him at the curb outside Donia's building while he spoke with the superintendent. Sitting there in his cousin's big car, the meter running, McKelvey's private chauffeur. This was an expense that would never be expensed. Because he wasn't working for anybody; Christ, he wasn't working, period. But McKelvey was getting used to the driver and his old fashioned manners, the way they were slowly starting to share the banter of two old friends sitting on a park bench. Sports and talk radio, the burgeoning war in Afghanistan, the price of gas, the weather.

"This war on terror," Hassan said once, "will never end. It will last a century. Like the crusades you studied in school, yes? This peace we want so badly, it is like trying to squeeze water from stones."

"We've got to try, don't we? What's the alternative," McKelvey said.

"It is just what we do, what we have always done, my friend," Hassan said. "Poking the hornet's nest with a big stick. It is pouring gasoline on a fire. We watch the flames grow. The trouble with settling things with guns and bombs, you see, is that with every death you create a new reason for your enemies' children to hate you. The wheel turns and turns. If you don't listen to the news, if you don't watch the CNN, then how do you know what goes on around the other side of the world? Maybe we all sleep better at night if there are no TVs and we mind our business."

"My father was in his late twenties when he volunteered to fight in Korea," McKelvey said. "Never really talked about it much, but I know it had at least one lasting impact on him. He swore he'd never eat Chinese food in his life. And he didn't. Not even an egg roll. Wouldn't even set foot inside a Chinese restaurant."

Yes, the taxi bills were mounting, but he wasn't hard up. The pension he drew was sufficient to cover his modest living expenses, his draft beer at Garrity's, a pack of cigarettes rationed to last the week, the two sacks of groceries he lived on. The splitting in half of his lifetime with Caroline—the house they'd bought in that neighborhood known as "The Beach" long before it was trendy and overpriced, the retirement savings plan the police association representative had convinced him to buy into in his early twenties, every shred of their lives auctioned off—it had allowed him to pay cash for the small condo and still put some money aside in a trust fund for his granddaughter.

Still, he had already totaled close to a hundred and twenty dollars in taxi fares working on this Donia Kruzik angle. He gave Hassan the address for the garage over in Rexdale and sat back, watching the traffic on the Gardiner Expressway as they headed west then northward on Highway 427, crossing Highway 401—the busiest highway in the country. He wondered what he was doing. That simple, just a question in a moment of honesty. So, Charlie, what are you doing? He heard Hattie's words about him hanging a shingle, wearing a fedora, all that shit. Like he thought he was some sort of private detective. Not even being paid, for god's sake. So what did that make him? Something even more pathetic. Everything everybody had said, everything everybody was still saying about him, was probably true in the end: this was killing him. *Retirement.* And yet he was too old to go back. They wouldn't have him anyway. Not after Duguay. Having come out of that by the skin of his teeth, the grey area of the unregistered handgun he'd kept locked up all those years. The fact that Duguay had entered his home armed and with the intent to cause injury was his out in the eyes of the law. Self-defense, plain and simple. But his boss, Detective-Sergeant Tina Aoki, knew the truth. And so did Hattie. Hell, everybody did. Charlie McKelvey had lost his way somewhere in there. After Gavin. Took a few wrong turns, got blinded by his grief and his guilt—that was the truth of it, his guilt in turning the boy from their home, and the end he met out there on the streets. In the end they let McKelvey slip away without a parade or a retirement roast at the steakhouse.

Did it matter that he had no plan formed here? Did it matter that he was simply putting one foot in front of the other? What was he supposed to be doing, anyway? Fly fishing? God, how good it felt to live like this again, to wake and already find yourself in motion—*propelled.* There was a trajectory here, an arc across the skyline—he would land, eventually, or crash, but why worry now? He had an engine again, all systems firing—the rush. That big bastard in the apartment had knocked some sense into him. Brought him back to life. Means to an end. *I'm coming. I'll find you...*

They rolled past Mimico Creek to the right. The Woodbine Racetrack was to the left, where horses ran and troubled men lost their paycheques to whims of chance on the legs of pure muscle and momentum. He knew a few horse bettors, this sub-genre of the gambling world. They were a class unto themselves. Old guys like Priam Harvey, who could quote Faulkner in one breath then in the next piss his pants sitting at the barstool while circling his picks in the racing form. They were for the most part honestly dishonest men who from time to time gave up the name of a fence or a guy who might be in deep on the ponies, motive enough to rob a mini-mart. You might want to talk to so-and-so, they would say.

They turned onto Rexdale Boulevard, headed east. They were in the midst of low-rise, congested industry. Garages, industrial units, tool and die shops, minor manufacturing—places around here made fasteners, brass and copper works, plastic and composite moldings for some unknown supply chain. Named for the developer Rex Wesley, Rexdale was low income, blue collar, salt of the earth. The homes were older and smaller, and the men went to work, for the most part, with lunch buckets instead of leather briefcases.

"Do you like me to wait?" Hassan said. He had pulled off Rexdale Boulevard onto Brydon Drive. He parked the car a dozen metres down from the garage, concealed against a hedge line. McKelvey liked the man's line of thinking.

"Ten minutes tops," McKelvey said.

Hassan nodded and adjusted the dial on the radio. The disembodied voices of talk radio filled the car. Someone was calling in and saying how Canadian troops should be *peacekeepers*, not *fighters*. The host cut right in, and said, "Listen, this peacekeeping racket is a myth that we've all bought in to. Plumbers are trained to plumb and combat soldiers are trained to fight…"

The garage was showing its age, probably constructed in the

late 1950s or early 1960s. White stucco siding and a red metal roof. McKelvey went into the small office attached to the four-bay garage. There were guys in the bays working beneath a couple of vehicles up on hoists. In the office were two waiting chairs set against the window, a desk facing them stacked and cluttered with invoices, and an old Coke machine against a wall with a handwritten note taped to it: *Quarters Only—No Loonies*. Behind the desk was a shelving unit with different brands and grades of motor oil, all of them covered in a thick coat of dust. There was nobody in the office, so McKelvey went to the door that opened onto the bays and stood there for a minute until one of the mechanics, a guy in his forties, stopped his work. He came over to the doorway, wiping his hands on a brown rag.

"Can I help you?" the man said. He had an accent. Eastern European.

McKelvey fished out a business card and handed it over. The mechanic stuffed the rag in the back pocket of his blue coveralls and took the card with his grease-stained fingers. He studied it a moment then moved past McKelvey into the office.

"No holdups here," the man said. "Maybe you are thinking of Mac's Milk down at the corner. Gas station there gets hit two times a month." He started to look through the invoices and work orders on the desk as though he had suddenly remembered a crucial piece of accounting.

"You the owner?" McKelvey said.

He watched the mechanic. Wide neck and big hands, thick dark hair greying at the sides. His face reminded McKelvey of one of those dogs, the kind with the face pushed in a little.

"Owner, yes. Jarko Automotive. You see the sign, yes?"

"You own a silver 1995 Honda Accord?"

McKelvey watched for it. It was there. Taken by surprise. It was a lifetime of questioning suspects, knowing what to look for. The eyes, the small gestures.

"I have a few cars, loaners. For my customers," Jarko said.

"How about a silver 1995 Honda Accord?" McKelvey said. "Plate number APVB 319. I can come up with the Vehicle Identification Number if that helps jog your memory."

"I have to check, you know, my files. Some ownerships, they are in my lock box. I need to look around. So much paperwork, it takes time."

"I'll wait," McKelvey said, and moved to sit in one of the chairs by the window.

Jarko put his big hands on the desk and leaned forward. He stared. He wanted to react physically right here and right now. McKelvey could sense it. "Why you want to know about this car?"

"Do you know a woman named Donia Kruzik?"

Jarko straightened up and folded his arms across his chest defiantly. He shook his head, but McKelvey had seen all he needed to see.

"I don't know what you want," Jarko said, finding his legs now, "but maybe you should talk to my lawyer. He knows my business, maybe he help you with all of your questions about cars. You have warrant?"

McKelvey smiled. "Warrant? Why would I need a warrant? I'm just asking you a few questions. You own the vehicle or you don't. You know this woman or you don't."

"You didn't show me your police identification. Your badge number."

McKelvey raised both hands, palms out. He said, "Hey, I'm just a guy asking a few questions is all."

"Please, I will ask you to leave my business," Jarko said.

McKelvey nodded and took a few steps to the door. He turned

and said, "Listen, you wouldn't happen to come across any used Mazda pickup trucks in your line of work, would you? I've been looking everywhere."

Jarko's face folded in on itself, flesh and wrinkles. He squinted and shook his head.

"Guess I'll find what I'm looking for eventually," McKelvey said. "Always do."

EIGHT

Jessie Rainbird covered her mouth that Saturday evening when the door opened to reveal Charlie McKelvey in all his bruised and swollen glory. He smiled to mask the fact he felt like Toronto's beloved George Chuvalo after going fifteen rounds with Muhammad Ali. Busted up, but still standing at the final bell.

"Jesus, Charlie, what happened to you?"

McKelvey looked down at Emily standing there with a stuffed giraffe clutched under her arm, her eyes wide. Then she grabbed Jessie's pant leg and began to cry.

"Shhhh now," he said, smiled and got down on a knee. "Grandpa's getting clumsy, that's all. He fell and got a booboo."

This seemed sufficiently probable to the little girl. She shook off the initial fear and wandered past them into the back room, where she knew McKelvey kept a stash of books and toys that Hattie had helped him pick out.

"Charlie, honestly. What happened?" Jessie said, setting her suitcase down.

"It's a long story. Honestly, it's nothing. Do you want a coffee? Tea?"

She watched him move to the kitchen island as she took a seat at one of the breakfast stools and stared at his back until he could feel the heat of her eyes drilling into him. He set the kettle on the stove. He turned to her, a lopsided smile on his face.

"Besides my aunt Peggy, you do know that you and Caroline

94

are Emily's only real family?" Jessie said. "She's going to need to have family in her life. I don't want her growing up the way I did. Bounced around. Alone."

"Message received."

"Whatever you're doing, promise me you'll be careful."

He raised two fingers. "Scout's honour, Jess."

"Speaking of family, I just talked with Caroline last week. She's thinking of coming out this Christmas to visit, or maybe even in the fall. She hasn't seen Emily since last spring. She was asking about you. You know, how you're doing and all that."

"Still checking up on me," he said.

"She still loves you, Charlie. Men just don't get it. She asked me what I thought of the idea of her moving back to Ontario permanently. I think she's had her fill of the west coast. She misses the city. She misses you."

"Caroline never did like the rain."

"You're impossible," she said. She smiled and shook her head. "Shit, never mind."

McKelvey looked at this young woman, the last soul to love his son—how close they had come to carving a life away from the drugs and the streets and the violence—and he was suddenly overcome with a desire to give her the keys to his home, access to his savings and pension. She could make a better life for her and the little girl with the meager bones of his own corpse.

*   *   *

After dinner, Jessie cleared the plates while McKelvey gave Emily her bath. He was unpracticed and over-cautious in his handling, his big hands fumbling as though it wasn't a child in the water, but rather a model ship he was attempting to fit into a bottle.

He was soaked and had to change his shirt by the time they were finished. The girl giggled when he took a handful of bubbles and spread it across his chin like a beard.

"Santa Claus," Emily laughed.

He crossed his eyes and stuck his tongue out at her. Jessie watched them laughing and playing from just outside the door.

He said, "Grandpa loves you, you know."

When Emily was in her pajamas and tucked into bed in the spare room, he leaned over and kissed her forehead and breathed in the smell of Johnson's No Tears shampoo. Straightening, he looked down on her for a moment and saw that she was looking more and more like her mother, the olive complexion and the coal black hair. But there was enough of his son mixed in there, too, the set of the eyes and the line of the mouth. In a world that short-changed you more than it overpaid, McKelvey felt a rush of gratitude for this living reminder of his boy. "Sleep tight," he whispered and closed the door with the night light plugged in.

He found Jessie flipping through the channels in the living room. When he came into the room, she clicked the TV off and set the remote aside. She had showered while he read to Emily. The little girl could listen to three or four books before she fell asleep. He saw in this a resilience or stubbornness, and it was something he could name and appreciate. This was the blood of his blood.

"You really should upgrade to the full cable package," she said. "Thirteen channels, God, I'd go insane."

He could see that she was working through something, knew her well enough now to measure the depth of her moods. It was ironic, he thought, how she viewed herself as a mystery too dark to be cracked, when in fact she was all there to see if you looked hard enough. Sometimes you just had to squint to see things for what they were, or maybe turn them upside down.

"Do you think I'm doing an okay job, Charlie?" she said. Curled up there in his chair, she seemed what, fourteen, fifteen? She looked it. Her wet hair pulled up in a towel. She was so young.

"You're a good mother, Jessie," he said.

He took a seat on the sofa across from her. She looked at him, and he saw that she wanted to believe him. This was the place where he always found himself on rough terrain with this girl. Something inside her made it impossible for her to see herself in all of her strength. There were things you could tell a person and things a person had to find out about themselves all on their own.

"How do you know?" she said. "I mean, how can you be so sure?"

He said, "I know. I've seen it. Gavin's mother. My own mother."

"But you don't think you were a good parent."

He looked at her, then he sort of tilted his head to one side, a poker player trying to make up his mind on how to play out this hand.

"Why are you so hard on yourself?" she asked.

"I figure I was tougher on Gavin," he said.

"Okay, why were you so hard on him then?"

He said, "He reminded me." He stopped for a minute and thought of something. It stuck in his throat. "He reminded me of myself."

It was the conundrum of the ages, McKelvey figured. How we tried to kill the things in others that reminded us of the worst in ourselves. Killing this ugliness. From father to son, and so on and so on. It wasn't fair, not at all, because a man couldn't be a good father until his own father had passed and he stood there staring into the void that was left. How many nights had he dreamed that Gavin was alive, really alive, that it was all just a big mistake—only to wake to the cold reality of that empty space. But there was a moment in there, upon waking, wherein he felt the greatest rush of gratitude for a second chance to take a run at this thing. *Fathering.* It was something.

"Gavin was very stubborn," she said and smiled at some personal memory. "Both of us, really. Most of the kids living on the street are what you'd call extremely independent. Strong-willed. Something happened, and it pushed them out—usually abuse, right—but it's their own stubbornness that keeps them from accepting help. That's the truth of it, Charlie. Gavin knew in the end what he had done, the home he had left, and the chances he was blowing. It's why he was getting help and trying to get away from the Blades."

"You should counsel kids," he said. "You could reach them. God knows the cops have no effect. They see us as the sharp end of the system, we're the bad guys. After a while you get tired of giving people the benefit of the doubt. You see through the bullshit."

"I'd rather cut hair," she said. "I've had enough of that life. I don't want Emily to ever know about all of that. Will you promise me that you'll never tell her about my past, Charlie?"

"That's your call," he said.

"I don't want her to think of me that way. The way I was," she said.

"When you're a little older, and Emily's a little older, you might see things differently. How your past can be an asset. You know, show your daughter how you turned your life around. It takes guts, Jessie."

She sighed and shifted in her seat. "It's hard sometimes," she said. "Staying clean."

"You're tough," he said, and felt stupid for it. He wanted to tell her that it was more than that, that he looked up to her. Her knew

98

about the short stick she'd drawn in life. The early abuse and the childhood fire that had claimed her father, all of the dark days she had stared down alone. It was the easy thing to do, to give up. Everybody was doing it these days. Fuck it. Someone will come along and look after you, help you find a cause for your blame.

"It's funny, because I got out of one scene and found another one. It just changes shape. The girls in the salon, a lot of them are into clubbing. They go to these after hours bars in the east end. Out by…what am I saying, you know where I'm talking about."

"I know exactly where you mean," he said. Oh yes, he'd walked through his share of after hours bars, among that crew of the living dead, the cursed ones caught in that godawful crack between midnight and dawn. Looking for some kid from Jane and Finch who'd dropped out of high school in Grade Ten, who'd just committed his first armed robbery at the Gas-n-Go, on the fast track to the pen.

"I went with them a few weeks ago to this warehouse. It was the music and the crowd, the lights. The whole scene brought everything back. It was horrible. I almost puked, Charlie, I was that scared. Scared that I was in a dream, that this life I'm living right now was going to be taken away from me."

He waited for her to bring out the rest. And he knew there was more to all of this. It was no different than his years on the job, sitting across from a perp in an interview room. You could coax and pull a little here and there, but for the most part the story had to play out to its own rhythm.

"I wanted to leave. I knew I had made a huge mistake. My NA sponsor told me she'd fire me if I so much as stepped inside a bar. But you know how it goes. You're there with a group of people. I've been doing my placement with these girls for two months. I didn't want to pull up lame on them."

Again she paused, and again he waited. He had all night.

"Some of the girls bought Ecstasy from this guy I sort of recognized from around the salon. He knows one of the girls there, Sasha. I bought a few hits from him… "

"Did you drop them?" he said.

A single tear squeezed itself from the corner of her eye and rolled down her cheek. It was all she was willing to give, for she quickly sat up and dried her face with the back of her hand. "No. No, I didn't. I got my head back on and tossed the shit out the window of the cab I took home. Now this fucking asshole Devon comes around the salon and keeps mentioning how I owe him for the pills. I wasn't born yesterday, right? I know a thing or two about how it works on the street. This guy throws out names, these heavyweights, the Crips this and that. He's a wannabe gangbanger. I don't want to tell him that I know the score, I've been down that road. It'd ruin my name in the business down here. It's a small circle, Charlie."

"It's probably not worth very much, but I'm proud of you," he said. And he knew he should move to her, put his arms around her. He sat there for a long moment, too long, remembering all those cemetery nights his wife had cried alone while he stood there, a statue in his own living room. He got up and crossed to the girl, and she stood to meet him, and she closed herself inside his arms, and she was a child again.

"You don't need to worry about all of that," he whispered. "You go up to the Island and enjoy your vacation. Don't think about the city, Jessie. We'll get everything worked out, I promise."

McKelvey was already visualizing his approach to this thing, his jaw set tight. Five minutes with this Devon character, and he'd have him re-oriented in his life path.

"I don't know what I'd do without you, Charlie," she said.

100

In McKelvey's mind it was the other way around. For Jessie and Emily represented the only points of light flickering in the distance. The horizon was murky otherwise. They shone there up ahead through the nights of loneliness and regret. There were days wherein he truthfully wondered how he would reach the end of the month, to say nothing of the decade, stretching things an hour at a time. He circled job ads for security guard positions at least twice a week but never followed up. He went to the coffee shop near the police headquarters on College, hoping to accidentally on purpose run into a few old colleagues. There was a sense of things winding down, of being outside the realm of real activity and function.

"Well," he said, looking to make her smile now, "I think we should eat those Krispy Kreme donuts, since Emily's mother won't let her have any. Cruel and usual punishment."

She pulled back and slapped his shoulder. The sight of her red and puffy eyes made him want to carve a hole in his chest to put her inside, lock it tight. Her and the little girl both. The city was a tough show at the best of times, even more so for an ex-addict walking the line. And then, as though on cue, a police siren wailed across the top of the night.

*   *   *

As usual, McKelvey wakes at just after two. This sleepy-eyed, shuffling nocturnal routine. He stands there at the toilet with his boxers pulled down, willing the trickle. The stop-and-go. Standing there in the dark, in the quiet. The flow of his output is of some mild concern of late. Then again, he is old. Or just about. This is the simple, unalterable fact of the situation—he is no longer on the lip of the threshold, rather he has passed through the archway and is well along the path. How many pisses taken in a lifetime? A million? So it is to be expected, he guesses, this middle of the night stopping, starting. The infrastructure of the plumbing showing its wear and tear.

When he is finished, he closes the lid and makes a mental note to flush in the morning so he won't wake the girls. He pats warm water on his face and looks at himself in the mirror. At his bloodshot eyes, into his eyes, beyond them. Sees something there to be reckoned with, an outstanding account on the books. He opens the medicine chest, finds the bottle of pills. He opens the top and sprinkles the remaining tablets into his hand. He opens the lid of the toilet with his foot, tosses the pills in there with the dark golden pee. He flushes with a mild sense of loss and closes the lid. Perhaps the narcotics, he thinks, once entered into the Toronto water system, will assist in softening the sharp edge of a society already on its knees.

Goodnight, Toronto…

NINE

The next morning, after Jessie and Emily had left, the *Sun* tabloid carried a page 8 story about a blaze at a Rexdale garage. Fire crews called out in the middle of the night. The place burned to the ground. Jarko's Automotive. A photo of the smouldering brickworks, the roof collapsed in a pile of rubble. There was a quote from the responding platoon captain: *"Trucks from West Command arrived on the scene within four minutes. We found the structure fully involved. The fire marshal is conducting an investigation into the cause of the fire. We are having difficulty locating the owner of the business at this time…"*

McKelvey's phone rang as the news was sinking in, and it startled him. "McKelvey," he said.

"Good morning, sunshine. We're going for a drive, you and me," Hattie said, and he could tell from the rush of sounds that she was driving, already on her way over, perhaps even idling at the curb. "I'll be there in five minutes. You've got some explaining to do."

He was dressed in jeans and a well-worn button-down dress shirt left untucked. He stood on the sidewalk and smoked a half cigarette he'd found in the pocket of the shirt. Stale as sawdust, but still. It was a gift, akin to finding money in your winter coat the first time you wore it for the season. The day was grey, a cloudless pewter, but it was still warm as summer. He would take what he could get.

Hattie pulled up. On duty, at the wheel of an unmarked unit. He popped the door and got inside. She did a quick shoulder check and gunned it into the traffic, swung a quick turn and got them headed across King then down toward the waterfront. He immediately felt at ease inside the cruiser. The radio, the screening between the front and back seats, the smell, the history.

"So," she said, "what's up?"

"Oh, you know," he said, "a little of this, a little of that."

She shot him a sideways glance. "Smell like you just had a cigarette," she said.

"Half a cigarette," he said. "A little gift of the gods."

"Still smoking at your age," she said. "Shame, shame."

"I'm on a ration system."

"Now there's an excellent idea," she said. "Bet nobody ever thought of that one."

They stopped for a red light. She waited half a beat, reached out and hit the siren so it squawked once and the dashboard lights strobed. She checked both directions and rocketed them on through the intersection, down beneath the overpass and out the other side. McKelvey shivered as they passed through, knowing his boy's body had been thrown beneath the concrete of the expressway overpass, thrown there among the weeds and the trash. His boy had lain there a full day before someone had found him and reported it. All the while the city continued on above him, flies buzzing at his closed eyes, and his mouth.

"Can't stand those friggin' lights," she said. "Sit there for half a day. Anyway, about your face. I have to admit, there's something strangely attractive about a man with bruises. I always had a soft spot for those hockey players with their black eyes and their missing teeth."

The human body was a wonder all right. His nose had deflated considerably in the past twenty-four hours, but now his eyes were ringed in darkening hues. The pain had shifted gears as well, from that apocalyptic first morning wherein he'd risen as Lazarus, every cell sounding its own alarm bell across the valleys and the mountains—to this place now where he could actually move his head without needing to clench his eyes tight to stop the buzzing drone.

"You should see the other guy," he said and smiled his boyhood smile for her.

She pulled into a vacant lot behind an abandoned warehouse along the railway tracks. The big box of a building sat there with its brown bricks painted in rainbows with the personalized signatures of a hundred different graffiti taggers, its rows of small square factory windows cracked or smashed or missing altogether. Detroit or south side Chicago, could have been anywhere. She turned to him.

"Charlie," she said, "what the hell is going on?"

He exhaled a long breath and gathered his notes, collected his thoughts as he'd done a hundred times on the witness stand. "My friend Tim Fielding—you remember Tim."

"The school teacher," she said.

"He called the other day, very upset. This woman he'd been seeing a little from his night class—he's been teaching English as a second language at nights to get out of the house—she just sort of disappeared. He wanted me to check into things."

"Of course," she said. "Why leave it to the police, right?"

"Anyway, I went over to her apartment. Guy ambushed me. Caught me with my back turned," he said. "Thing is, there was nothing in the place. She'd already moved out. No trace."

He gathered the facts together for her like putting place settings at a dinner table. In doing so he was able to hear his own voice, to look at things from a new perspective. How they had tracked the vehicle down to the garage in Rexdale. How he had questioned the superintendent and the owner of the garage. How the garage had burned to the ground.

"Couldn't be a coincidence, could it?" she said.

"You should have seen this guy at the garage when I was questioning him."

She looked at him for a long moment. Working through something, he could see it in her eyes. She looked at him, and he saw that something had changed there. Something. He couldn't put his finger on it.

"Tell me," she said, "in what capacity you were questioning this individual."

"As a private, tax-paying citizen," he said, "who got his fucking nose broken by somebody driving a car registered to this asshole's business."

"Hmmm," she said, thick with her east-coast sarcasm. "And that same night the garage burns down. Very interesting. What are you thinking on this, recently retired detective McKelvey?"

A good question. What *was* he thinking on this? He sat there in the car in silence, watching pigeons flutter around the roof of the old building, coating the overhang with the poison white waste of their urban hell.

"Me, I'm thinking one of two things," she said. "This chick was playing with Tim. She had a boyfriend or maybe even a husband all along. This would be the gentleman who tried to put his hand through the back of your head. Maybe the guy found out about his woman's indiscretion and decided to pull a midnight move. You know, get out of Dodge."

He turned and looked at her. The plain beauty of her face like a girl from the country, the milky flesh and the red hair and the freckles on her nose. Good god, those green eyes that pulled and pulled. Just the smell of her. He longed to be with her again. Close. Now.

"Or," he said.

"Or else you just stepped into the middle of something really bad. Either way, I think you should stop playing private eye. You want to press assault charges, you know who to call."

"I'm not interested in pressing any charges," he said.

"What are you interested in exactly?"

"It doesn't make any sense. I could buy the part about her having a boyfriend or a husband. It's what I assumed from the get-go. But now I'm not so sure. The connection between the car and the garage. This guy, Jarko, he wasn't above board. Something was off. When I went into Donia's place, it's not like I didn't announce myself. Said I was a friend of Tim's."

"And now the paper says they can't locate the owner of the garage," she said. "They're leaning towards arson. I made a couple of calls this morning to a friend of mine in the marshal's office. She didn't take too kindly to being woken up on a Sunday."

She sighed, settled back in her seat, and they both sat there looking at the scarred face of the building as though they were teenagers at a summer drive-in waiting for something to happen.

"Well, the one good thing is, if you have in fact stepped into the middle of a shit storm, you might not have to go looking for these people. They might just find you. That," she said, "or maybe they'll find Tim Fielding first."

Something dropped inside his rib cage, fell like a stone to the pit of his belly. He said, "I was just thinking that very thing myself."

TEN

Kadro sat eating a bowl of Lucky Charms cereal at a small table in the sparse apartment in the east end of the city. It was a dive, an anonymous and inexpensive safe house located atop a Vietnamese noodle takeout restaurant in a grubby neighbourhood strip mall that also housed a pawn shop, a twenty-four convenience store that had been robbed six times in four months, and a dry cleaning depot that was on the verge of bankruptcy. Turner had accepted his call and made the arrangements—with admonishments and warnings to stay focused, keep the mission on track. Get it done and get gone. There were only so many contingency plans, variations to the schematic. Kad had bit his tongue and let the Canadian swear at him. This time. But he was growing weary of the man's condescension. *Take the butt of his rifle and smash and smash and smash, bone and flesh giving way to the heavy wood of the stock...*

Donia came into the kitchen dressed in the clothes she had slept in. Jeans and a sweater, her brown hair tied back in a pony tail. Her face was thick from a night of poor sleep, tossing and turning. She did not want to stop their work. She wanted them to pause and talk, to think things through, to be strategic. She had not changed her mind. But other things had changed. This place, it was not so simple. Nothing was black and white here in this country, at least not as black and white as during the long days of war she had known. Here there was much grey to be considered. The many different colours of faces that walked the

108

downtown streets, they lived in peace and harmony, at least for the most part, having left their political and religious baggage at the airports and train stations.

"Where did you go last night?" she said, speaking in their native tongue. She moved to the stove and put some water on to boil for tea. The apartment was lightly furnished and stocked with only the bare essentials, canned goods and non-perishables. "I heard you leave, but I didn't hear you come back."

"I just came in an hour ago," Kad said. "I was fixing our mess. The mess you caused. It is a big mess, let me tell you."

She smelled the stink of smoke on him, but she dared not ask. He set the bowl aside and looked up at her. There was a dribble of milk on his chin, and he wiped it with the back of his hand. This is what the city children ate, bowls of sugar and marshmallows because nobody had time to cook. Everything was already finished when you bought it—cooked or baked or fried, nothing left to do but consume. In his village, back when he was a child, all of the mothers knew how to take the seeds and the scraps and to stretch them and twist them into tables full of food for the working men. Fresh baked breads and dried meats and cheeses, vegetables still tasting of the rich fecund earth from which they'd been plucked. The old country, the old life, the old ways—gone now, bombed to shit.

"A big mess for us to clean up," he went on. "This man friend of yours, he has a friend on the police. I caught the policeman looking around the apartment."

"What did you do?" she asked. But she did not want to know, not really.

Or what had *she* done? And why had she brought these innocent people into this?

"Did you kill him?" she asked.

She had to ask, because he just stared at her. Something in him perhaps enjoyed this punishment. The place of the woman and the place of the man. Theirs was not an equal partnership, not here and certainly not back home in the world they had come from. She had her role, and it was an important role, but Kadro was in charge. Make no mistake.

"Yes, I should have killed him," he said. "But I did not kill the man. I did not have the time or the tools to properly dispose of him. Somehow he tracked the vehicle to our contact, Jarko. A friend of the cause. Just a good and simple business man who came here even before the wars in our land. He called Turner to tell him this man, this cop, had been asking questions. Now this friend of our cause has no business, and he has been sent away in hiding. His life in this country is finished."

She sat down at the table, her legs suddenly weak. "Is all of this necessary?" she said. "To send this friend away because of this police officer? What will they find? There is nothing to find, Kadro. Turner can deal with these details, he can make anything go away. Please, we can still do what we have come to do. This week. Tomorrow even. And then we can go back home. We will have kept our bargain, but there is no sense in taking risks. I have done the work that was asked of me. I have the files and the logs, everything is there."

"The work that was asked of you? This is work you volunteered for," he said.

"Yes," she said. "I volunteered, and with a glad heart. My family was taken by these men, too, not just your family. My husband. I have as much at stake here as you or anyone else, and yet from the moment you came here you have acted strange, as though you are in charge, you are the only one concerned with finishing the work. I'm telling you, Kadro, there is nothing to find. These are all good and simple people who have nothing to do with anything."

"Are you out of your mind?" He stared at her, and his eyes held her in her place as though her feet were bolted to the floor. "We are here to kill two men, my sister. We can leave no trace of our involvement. All strings that come back to any part of this must be cut. Do you not understand this? That was the directive from the Colonel."

She fully understood the ripple effect from this stone she had thrown in the water.

"Listen," he said. "Before this trouble with Jarko's Automotive, I went to a movie. Bojan Kordic brought his perfect little family. I am ready now. And so tomorrow this man faces justice for what he has done. But first, my sister, first we have to do some cleaning."

"What are we going to do?" she said.

"A little mopping up. This boyfriend of yours. I need to speak to him. But first," Kad said, digging into his pants pocket, "first we need to return your keys to your landlord. I forgot to leave them on the kitchen counter as we discussed. My mistake."

*   *   *

The superintendent opened the door a few inches and made a face a that said *'What is it? Which one of you assholes needs a lightbulb changed now?'* He was unshaven and his eyes were red, perhaps roused from sleep. It was possible, Kadro thought. After all, it was early yet, quarter after eight.

"I have keys for you," Kad said.

"Who are you?" the super said, still holding the door. He had failed to notice the blue medical gloves on the hands of the man at his door. And then recognition clicked, the morning fog lifted. "Wait—you was the guy up there the other night with the Polish

111

chick. Hollering like a couple of teenagers."

"The Polish chick," Kad repeated, amused.

"She pulled up stakes, 'cause I told her to keep it down?" Chinaski said.

Kad did not have the patience to work this aspect with dialogue or reasoning. Time was a luxury he could ill afford. And so in one bullet-fast motion, he raised his booted foot and kicked the door with the force of a battering ram, so quick and so sharp that the superintendent had no sense that it was even coming. He was simply on his rear end looking up from the carpet, his forehead bleeding a trickle where the corner of the door had struck him.

"What in the hell—"

Kad slipped inside and closed the door behind him. He reached down and pulled the superintendent up with one hand behind the man's neck, the other wrapped tightly around the gathered ball of filthy undershirt. Kad flung him towards the junky recliner as though he were a small boy, and the superintendent landed squarely in the chair with such force that both his feet flew up and the chair sprang back to its naturally reclined position.

"First," Kad said, "does building have cameras?"

The super's eyes were stretched wide now, and the line of blood had dribbled down to his chin, dripping like melted chocolate ice cream onto this undershirt. He shook his head slowly. "Why's everybody want to know about video cameras?" he said.

Kad said, "Everybody?"

"Cop was around here asking the same thing. You mind telling me what the fuck is going on here? You come in here kicking my goddamn door—"

Kad leaned over and slapped the super across the face, hard. The sound rang in the silence of the apartment. The super's cheek went scarlet. Kad stared into the man's eyes until he looked away.

"Focus," Kad said. "What cop? What is his name?"

The super was shivering now, his body unable to process the overload of adrenalin, the shock. It happened, Kad knew. It was nothing to be ashamed of. Grown men pissed their pants, or worse, shat themselves in that moment of challenge. Fear stripped even the bravest of their dignity.

"I got his card," the super said. "Over there, on the kitchen table."

Kad walked over to the grungy little kitchen. The stove was splattered in thick globs of white grease built up from years of frying bacon. The fridge was plastered in work orders and to-do lists, coupons for take-out food. The table itself had no open space available, stacked high with invoices and rental applications, empty beer cans, old tabloid newspapers folded in half. Kad spotted the business card on top of the pile of paperwork and slipped it into his pants pocket. He paused, regarding something else on the table, then he picked it up and turned back to the super.

"What is this?" he said and held out a rental application form with a photocopy of two cheques.

"Well, that's your friend's cheque, her first and last. A copy of it anyway. The cops…well, come on, man, read it for yourself."

Kad folded the paperwork and shoved it in the back pocket of his jeans.

"That's my only copy," the super said. "Head office'll need that for income tax purposes. Give me a break, will you?"

Kadro looked over to the kitchen table and saw something else. He got an idea. "Here," he said and threw the pornographic magazine.

The superintendent caught the magazine on instinct, the

pages curled from being thrown. His face reddened further, and his lips began to quiver as his mind attempted to decipher the strategic plan at work here. His eyes darted between the intruder and the cordless phone receiver on the cluttered coffee table.

"Won't make it," Kad said. "Relax, please. Everything will be okay."

Kad reached into the pocket of his jacket and produced the eyeglasses case to which he had transferred the syringe that Turner had supplied. He had intended its use solely for his official targets, but there had been complications, and if he had learned anything from war, it was the need for adaptability, decisive action under fire. The barrel was already loaded with a quarter CC of the clear juice. His fingers worked nimbly while the superintendent struggled over his shoulder to see what the intruder was fiddling with. Kad tapped the barrel with a flick of his middle finger and used his teeth to slip the safety cap. As he turned back, Chinaski surprised him by making a bolt for the phone, but the super was at a serious disadvantage, as he first had to swing his raised feet to the floor and pull himself from the chair, a rush of momentum he was never quite able to manage. It all happened so very fast, he hardly felt the needle dart in and out of the back of his neck. It was milder than the fast and clean sting of a wasp.

"What'd you do?" he said, his hand moving to the back of his neck.

And then it was upon him—as though a pair of vice grips were squeezing his heart. The pain was acute, a knife's thrust, and his eyes rolled back in his head, one leg stabbing at the air. The superintendent eased back into his recliner, his eyes already half-closed.

"She's Bosnian," Kadro said, holding the man's head as the

chest pumped once, twice, then failed to re-inflate. There was a soft sigh, the rattle of a last breath.

Kad set the man in the recliner with his pants undone, the magazine on the floor as though it had dropped there. He took a couple of the empty beer cans and arranged them around the chair as well. A drunkard is prone to bruises and all sorts of cuts from cupboards and doors and other objects which suddenly lunge from nowhere. It was a loose end, perhaps, but best managed as though it was something the superintendent himself had dealt with. Kad went to the bathroom, which was even filthier and more cluttered than the kitchen. There were multiple pairs of threadbare boxer shorts balled up on the floor near the tub where the super had slipped from them for his presumably weekly shower. Kad picked through the medicine chest until he found a box of bandages. He cleaned the small cut on the man's forehead with a wet tissue then applied a Band-Aid, something used for shaving cuts or slivers. He took the bloodied tissue and went to the kitchen, opened a cupboard door, and smeared a bit of blood on the sharp corner. He left the wrapper from the Band-Aid on the counter in the bathroom, which seemed in keeping with the man's character. The bloodied tissue he put in his coat pocket to take with him.

Kad studied the scene before leaving. It seemed quite plausible. He was certain the man's reputation was widely known among the building's tenants. Sad end to a sad man's life. Too much drink, too few vegetables. He paused to inspect the door and its frame to ensure his boot had not caused any visible damage. It was clear. He opened the door and moved his hand down the edge to wipe away any residue of the man's forehead cut. He waited a beat and scanned the hallway before stepping outside.

When he got back to the car, Donia asked him if the

superintendent was upset with them for leaving the way they had, in the middle of the night.

"He's not overly suspicious, is he?" she said.

"He understands completely," Kad said.

He turned the engine and sat there for a long moment. She understood they were at a crossroads. The school teacher, her loose end. She wanted to tell Kad that nothing would come of this, that Tim Fielding would try calling her, would most likely scratch his head at the situation then move on, none the wiser. No, she thought. Who was she kidding? She was breaking the man's heart. This gentle man who had lost his wife. Their shared bond. Her dead husband and his dead wife, the ghosts of their past. And that was the magnet that had pulled them together that first stupid night she'd broken her rule and gone for a coffee after class.

"Where does he live?" he said. He did not look at her. He stared straight ahead.

"It's not necessary," she said. "There is no need for—"

He turned and looked into her eyes. And she saw darkness there, always the darkness, but something else as well, yes, something new that made him a stranger to her. For the first time since they had devised the plan, created the missions, drawn up the roles and responsibilities, for the first time since they'd gathered at that kitchen table in that farmhouse those years ago, she doubted his stability.

"I'm not going to hurt him," he said. "We need to talk, is all. For me to explain you are my sister, and you had to go back home, and thank you very much, here is an address where you can send love letters. No loose ends. Remember."

"Promise me," she said. "This man doesn't know anything, he doesn't deserve this. He is a good man, a school teacher. He is innocent."

116

"Innocent? Who is innocent?" Kad said.

"Promise me," she repeated.

"I promise," he said.

She told him the address, and Kad pulled the car into the stream of traffic.

ELEVEN

Maxime Auteuil adjusted himself in his economy seat on the KLM flight from Lyon to Toronto, quite thankful for once that he was five foot seven, for it was obvious the airlines were maximizing the ratio of space to passengers these days. He doubted a man of any significant height could make the transatlantic journey without serious discomfort, cramping, perhaps even the affliction of blood clots you read so much about these days. There was an especially corpulent man a couple of rows up, and when Maxime had passed him as they boarded, he'd felt a rush of sympathy both for the man and those who would be seated in his proximity. He himself would rather sit near a mother with a newborn baby than spend eight hours leaning to one side as a stranger made vain attempts to contain his excess flesh.

He was as comfortable as he could be, having finished the somewhat decent meal of chicken Kiev and a good cognac, and now he was reading a book about the meaning of names, their roots and their histories, their imagery and connotations. He was about to become a father, no simple undertaking at the age of forty-six. He was a young forty-six, people were always saying, with his jet-black hair that was only now beginning to trace with grey, the lack of wrinkles that was a family trait, and he was slim and wiry, compact. And anyway, it had taken him a long time to find the right woman, or any woman, that is, to

118

convince him to settle down and, well, even to consider reading books like this about baby names. His had quite literally been a love at first sight. Well, if not literal first sight, then within hours. He had met his wife, Angelique, at a large chocolate exposition in Paris, the largest event of its kind in the world. It drew the top chocolatiers, who performed miracles, these white-clothed magicians who turned raw slabs of cocoa into works of art. This was their instant connection—for he himself came from a long line of chocolatiers and hoped one day to own his own shop. And she, the copper-haired Angelique, had recently graduated from France's top school for the culinary arts. While she was currently working as a sous chef in a Lyon bistro, she too had aspirations to create magic from chocolate, to deliver that very distinct smile to the faces of her customers that came only from that first taste of the unexplainable, the mysterious, this gift of the gods.

If it was a boy, he was thinking Gabriel. A girl, perhaps Laetetia after his dear mother, rest her soul. Names were not unique, yet they meant everything to their owner. So did titles. He had learned that lesson while on the police force in his hometown port city of Marseille, working the underground gangs and arms and drug traffickers, all of his cronies anxious for promotion, to earn that extra stripe. The back-stabbing and careerism had been a genuine shock to him, for he himself believed that what was earned, what was due, would come in time. How naïve to think this way, to believe such a cumbersome, goliath civil service machine could ever apply the principles of rightness to any degree of accuracy.

And so he had retired from the cops at age forty, burned-out and jaded, and with his eyes set on taking over the chocolate shop on Rue du Paradis in Marseille that had belonged to his grandfather then his father—called simply *D'Or*, of gold. But life is life, and it didn't work out that way. While Maxime came to the end of his last year on the force, his mother got sick, and his father, to whom the wife meant everything, let the store fall into debt and disrepair. While Maxime toiled eighty hours a week on too many cases, his family business went down the proverbial toilet. The most loyal of customers stopped coming as they grew tired of the shop either being closed at the wrong hours or in a state of disarray, the father unshaven, dark-eyed and surly from his late-night vigils at the hospital. It was to be Maxime's greatest regret to carry, that he had not paid more attention to his parents as they floundered through this trying time—it was, quite simply, unforgiveable, and in the end he felt he deserved the taking away of this personal dream, this family heirloom. The shop was bankrupted, and Maxime stood on the curb across the street while the men removed all of the equipment from inside, the counters and displays, sinks and signage, everything gutted for auction, stacked it in a white van and carried away. His mother gone to heaven, and his father long since retreated in exile and shame. A friend asked Maxime why he would do that to himself, stand there and watch the dismantling of the family dream. All he could think to say is that he wanted to make sure the movers were gentle, that they did not break anything, that they performed the operation with dignity and grace.

Requiring a paycheque and some sort of meager pension, Maxime had spoken to friends of friends and made the move to Lyon, to the glass and stone museum-like headquarters of Interpol. These days his title was very long indeed, as evidenced by the five lines taken up on his business cards:

Maxime Auteuil
Specialized Officer—Criminal Intelligence

Crimes Against Humanity Branch
General Secretariat
Lyon, France

Maxime's background in undercover work cracking international drugs and arms traffic through the port of Marseille had been of particular interest to his superiors as the organization developed a specialized unit dedicated to the investigation and persecution of genocide, war crimes and crimes against humanity. They were looking for candidates with experience in the milieu of conspiracy, tracking multiple points of origin to one nucleus, able to think for themselves in the field—those less inclined to sit behind a desk, to shuffle the endless papers of the bureaucratic mill. In Maxime they had found just the right candidate, for the work offered him the best of both worlds— the freedom to operate at arms length, to the extent that this was possible within the matrix, but most importantly the knowledge that the mission was righteous. It was, in fact, the highest calling an officer of the law could receive—to track and investigate and bring to justice those who had perpetuated some of the most heinous, most cowardly acts imaginable to the human psyche.

Now he set his book of names inside the seat back, stretched his feet and closed his eyes. He would need his rest for the days ahead, of that he was certain. This was to be the last of his adventures, the tying of a final knot, before he was to announce his retirement from the strange work they called international policing. Yes, if he had thought the force in Marseille was mired in the complexities of bureaucracy and careerism, well, Interpol was a world, perhaps even a universe, unto itself. There were so many lines, so many levels, so many jurisdictions, so many codes and always, in the forefront, the awareness of one's actual authority in the mix. Interpol dealt primarily in intelligence-sharing and high-level cooperation with police agencies representing sovereign nations in the pursuit of justice. But right now, on this flight from Lyon to Toronto, Maxime Auteuil had all the authority he would need—an Interpol Red Notice: *to seek arrest or provisional arrest of wanted persons with a view to extradition*—as issued by the Secretariat General.

He drifted off as the lights inside the cabin dimmed and his fellow passengers settled to sleep as best they could, and his mind played through the work that lay ahead, the snaring of the Colonel.

TWELVE

Hattie dropped McKelvey off in front of Union Station beside a line of yellow cabs. The drivers were standing outside their cars in front of the iconic station that owned a full city block with its grand arches and pillars. It was sunny and warm again, and the drivers were smoking and talking in a dozen different languages, waiting for trains and subways to bring them business on a slow Sunday morning.

"I'd drive you up to Tim's myself," she said, "but I've got this pesky job thing going on. The triads were busy last night turning over the after hours bars in Chinatown. I've got to go by and pick up Anderson, see if he's out of bed yet, the little pisstank."

McKelvey had met Stu Anderson a few times. He was a kid on the Hold-Up Squad, the new breed. He had seen way too many cop shows on TV. He was thirty years old if he was a day, and he wore his blond hair spiked with gel, a snarly-lipped rock star. He was single, and he was still hitting the clubs to dance and troll for women, dragging his ass into work with bloodshot eyes, smelling of that strong cologne he apparently bathed in. Anderson was always toying with his facial hair, growing these razor-thin lines across his jawline, or these goatees and handlebar mustaches, fads that lasted a few days at a time. McKelvey wasn't prone to jealousy, but this morning the thought of Hattie and Anderson driving around together rubbed him the wrong way. He knew the sorts of conversations that took place between partners working long hours together, sharing all these soul-deep secrets about life. Fortunately for him and Caroline, his partners had been for the most part chubby men with dandruff and bad breath. At least until Hattie came along. There had been sparks there from the beginning, the first time they'd worked a case side by side. How his stomach flipped a little when he was around her. Like now, how his hands were getting sweaty. Some pimple-faced kid at the high-school dance, for God's sake.

He opened the door and put a leg out, his hand up on the roof. He turned and smiled, but he didn't say what he wanted to say—which was something along the lines of "come over, I want you, I need you"—because he saw it there on her face and in her green eyes. She was pulling back, cutting herself a little space, doing some figuring. Okay, he thought. Fair enough. Forget Stu Anderson and his fucking spiked hair. Hattie was a big girl.

He got out of the car, then leaned back in. "Don't work too hard," he said and immediately felt like an idiot, some dolt standing on her step with a bouquet of wilted daisies and a string of clichés.

"Charlie, listen," she said, "I'm serious. Don't let this thing, whatever it is, get out of control. They've got this neat system now; you pick up the phone and call the police for help."

"Right," he said. "What's that number again, I can never remember."

"You got a pen?" she smiled.

He pretended to flip open a pad and click a ballpoint.

"Nine-one-one," she said, speaking slowly as though to a child.

"Got it."

He nodded, still smiling, and closed the door. Hattie hit the gas and was gone. McKelvey stood there and felt the good morning sun breaking through, warming his battered face. He looked across at the grey façade of the Royal York hotel with its long-coated doormen on the sidewalk at the ready. Hot dog vendors were setting up their carts on opposite ends of the arches to the train station, the smell of their boiled dogs and grilled onions already filling the air. A great Sunday for a baseball game, for a walk along the beaches, for a pint on the patio of the Bier Markt down on The Esplanade, just to sit there under an umbrella and watch the beautiful women walk by. He thought briefly of popping a half tab of the pills, but shook his head—they were gone anyway, and good riddance. He had responsibilities, no time for a rocket ship ride to the moon. Tim Fielding, he thought. Why hadn't he just told the kid to call the cops? What an asshole, Charlie. You and your goddamned pride.

He had a cell phone, but it was at home on his dresser in need of a new battery or some other incomprehensible electronic part. He went inside the station to a bank of telephones across from the VIA Rail ticket counters and tried Fielding's number. There was no answer. He hung up. He waited a few seconds then tried the number again, thinking Fielding might be screening his calls. Still, there was no answer. Out for a Sunday morning walk, most likely. Or sleeping in. Still, he had to be sure. He pulled Hassan's card from his pocket and called the driver.

"Yes?" Hassan answered on the third ring.

"It's McKelvey," he said. "Are you working today? I need a ride."

"Always working," Hassan said. "Where are you, Mr. McKelvey?"

"Just inside Union Station."

Hassan laughed. "Go look outside. I just pulled up."

McKelvey hoped this flash of serendipity was a sign of good things to come, but he didn't really believe it. That wet wool blanket was hanging around his shoulders again, the sense of impending doom, the understanding that he was responsible for everything from here on out because, as Hattie had been so willing to remind him, he should have enlisted some help from the beginning. Like the police, she had said. The *real* police.

*　　*　　*

McKelvey had Hassan wait outside the building in a visitor parking space while he ran up to check in on Fielding. On the drive over, he had worked it out in his head. Without causing undue alarm, he would suggest Tim come and bunk with him for a few nights until Donia Kruzik turned up, her jealous husband or boyfriend had time to calm down, or the whole thing otherwise blew over. It would be a chance for them to live like a modern day version of Felix and Oscar, the Odd Couple. But in truth, he sensed it wouldn't be quite as easy as that. As he played through the key facts to date, the potential coincidence of the garage, the broken nose, the empty apartment—he suddenly remembered the magnet from the fridge. The immigrant support centre. A lead he needed to follow up, one he had almost let slip through his fingers. Out of practice, out of the game—was this the first trace of rust settling in? It was amazing how much of the job remained with him, the way he watched people, the small things he noticed as he walked the streets or talked with strangers—and yet also startling how quickly he had dulled at the edges. It was his age, and it was living alone and it was being "ex" this or that, the whole jarring experience of retirement. It happened so quickly. As though you were driving along the highway at eighty miles an hour and someone suddenly reached over and pulled the emergency brake. Here, pal, why don't you hop out here and go sit on that picnic table over there and let the people who still matter go on by?

"What do you think of these Blue Jays?" Hassan said, glancing in the mirror.

"I think they need to win another World Series," McKelvey said. "You get sort of used to it, you know, the parades and the street parties. Seems like a long way off these days. Hard to believe that was only seven, eight years ago. Be nice to even make the playoffs for starters."

"My wife says they need a woman to manage the baseball team. Only a woman, she says, can stand back and see the whole picture. In my country, Mr. McKelvey, in my country she would be shot for saying something as foolish as that. But here, in my kitchen, she tells me what she thinks. Oh, does she tell me what she thinks. Are you married, sir?"

McKelvey went to respond in the affirmative—the old habit of prattling off police codes or his Social Insurance number, it was that automatic. *Married?* What exactly were he and Caroline, besides about three thousand miles apart? Neither one of them had mentioned divorce in the nearly two years of their twice monthly phone calls. It was all cordial updating on life's little wins and losses, the new muffler for the car, the weather and what was going on in the news, and of course their shared joy in measuring the growth of the only grandchild, Emily. They were legally separated, the details of their arrangement set out in pages of legalese. But to the question, at least in legal and technical terms, yes, they were married. It was strange, McKelvey thought, how they had stumbled and fumbled through the past thirty years to end up in this strange place, this new and uncharted landscape. It was then that he realized how much he had missed her these past few years. Even before the trouble with Gavin, even before all of the grief, he had stopped trying. To talk

127

to her, to listen, to reach out and touch her sometimes for no reason at all. To hold her. The things that would not have cost him at all, the things that seemed so easy in hindsight.

"We're separated," McKelvey said, "by three provinces."

And a Y chromosome, he was going to add. He caught Hassan's quick glance in the rearview, and he couldn't hold the man's eyes. He turned to the window and watched the city rushing past. Here he was again, yet again, in the centre of a mess of his own making. He imagined Caroline slowly shaking her head, perhaps even smiling as she said something like, "Here you go again, Charlie... Why don't you ever ask for help?"

McKelvey, the Blunderbuss.

"Good ones are hard to find," Hassan said. "Remember that."

"I'll remember it," McKelvey said.

Hassan smiled and said, "I can't forget it, because my wife tells me every day."

* * *

McKelvey knocked at Fielding's door and waited. He leaned in to listen, but, unlike the cheap door at Donia Kruzik's apartment, this was solid wood reinforced with steel. You get what you pay for. He tried the doorknob without expectation and was surprised when it turned in his hand. He pushed the door open and felt his heart in his chest, this mess of wires connected to his ribs, and he closed the door behind him.

"Tim," he called out to an empty apartment, for the second time in a week.

Goddamn, he thought, and he knew in his gut that something wasn't right. He looked around, over at the kitchen and the island bar, the living room. Nothing out of order. He walked over to the

128

two-piece bathroom off the living room, pushed the door and looked inside. Then he walked over to the master bedroom. The door was closed. He put his hand on the doorknob, hesitated, uncertain now whether he should walk back out and call Hattie, or maybe just sit on the couch and wait for Fielding to come back from his walk or his trip to buy fresh bagels, wherever the hell he was. But it was just fear, something he had to get past. The same brand of certainty that had brought him over here was telling him now that what he had come for was behind that door, waiting for him. He took a deep breath, turned the knob, and eased the door open to reveal the body of a woman sprawled face-down beside the bed.

The room was in chaos, the mattress askew, sheets torn off, books and magazines and a reading light knocked from a night table and scattered on the floor. He went to the closet on instinct and pushed the doors open, then went to the master ensuite bathroom and did the same with the shower curtain, even the doors on the vanity, knowing from experience how impossibly small a human could make themselves when it came to the necessity of hiding from the police. And he wasn't about to get blindsided twice in the same week, a shadow springing from behind a shower curtain with a butcher knife. He reached out and felt the towels that were hung, and they were damp. Fielding had showered that morning, he had been in the apartment. Or someone had, at least.

I'm fucked, he thought, easing back into the bedroom. Fucked six ways to Sunday. First witness on the scene is the first suspect. Without adjusting her body, he bent over and touched the woman at the carotid artery with two fingers. There was nothing, and she was somewhere on the colder side of lukewarm, her flesh already beginning to turn the blue-grey of early death.

What, a couple of hours? She was about five foot six, maybe a hundred and forty pounds, her dirty blonde hair shoulder length. One arm was tucked beneath her belly and the other was outstretched, the hand reaching for something, perhaps the light or a cordless phone, a last desperate clutch at faint hope. He squinted and noted that between the strands of tousled hair there appeared to be darkened flesh. He gently moved the hair and confirmed it. The neck was dark with bruising, the deep purple of strangulation. Hands or a ligature, he couldn't tell, he wasn't an expert in these matters—the crime scene and forensics folks would take photos, measure, create diagrams and schematics. But given the width of the line of bruising, his money was on a ligature of some fashion. He looked around the room, around the floor, for anything that might have been employed in the task—the belt from a bathrobe, a tie—but there was nothing that he could see.

He stepped back out of the room and stood there for a long minute. Fielding was gone—either of his own volition or against his will. So then, think. Play it through. Okay, Fielding finally makes contact with Donia Kruzik. Maybe she comes by and they get into a heated argument. She admits she has a husband or a boyfriend or turns tricks every third Wednesday, and Fielding loses it, strangles her, and he bolts.

No. Jesus.

Not Tim Fielding.

McKelvey understood it was a cardinal sin of police work to discount from the get-go, to let personal feelings or judgments blind you to the cold, hard facts, but he knew the man. His nature, the stuff that he was made of. Just not possible. No, there was something at play here, and Fielding had found himself at its rotten centre. What had Tim found out about this woman?

Who she knew, where she was from? Was his body somewhere as well, or had he been taken, set up as the fall guy for the murder? Christ, was the dead woman even Donia Kruzik? Who *was* Donia Kruzik, for that matter?

It didn't look good, not for McKelvey, definitely not for Fielding. All the connections, the dotted lines that could be drawn. He had called the apartment twice before coming over. From a payphone, but still, they could and would make that connection. Hassan was waiting downstairs, had driven him straight over after he had made the calls. The superintendent at Donia's building could confirm that yes, this ex-cop had showed up looking for her. Passed himself off as a cop on active duty. Jesus. He felt dizzy for a minute, his chest tight. What sort of half-assed, half-rate hack would bumble through something like this? What a fucking fiasco...

He found the cordless on the coffee table and dialed Hattie's cell phone.

"Detective Hattie," she said.

"It's me," he said. "Where are you?"

"With Anderson. On our way to an address in Scarborough to get a few hammerheads out of bed, see if their mommas can vouch for their whereabouts last night. This after-hours bar got turned over for the cover charge take."

"There's a situation," he said. "At Fielding's apartment."

"A situation," she repeated. And she waited.

He drew a long breath and exhaled slowly. He closed his eyes and shook his head at nobody in particular. "A body," he said. "I think there's a pretty good chance it's Donia Kruzik."

"Jesus and Mary."

McKelvey said, "And Fielding's missing."

"Sit down and don't even think of moving," she said. "I'll

131

make the call, Charlie. You're in enough shit." He heard her turn to Anderson and say something, then she came back on the line. "My very understanding partner here has offered to bring me around once we finish up our stop. Shouldn't be too long. They'll be all over you by then, but I'll try to be quick."

"Thanks," he said.

She didn't answer, she was simply gone. The dial tone. About what he deserved. He walked over to the kitchen bar and sat on a stool, trying to focus his thoughts on the facts, the details of the last few days.

Hattie called it in from the road—a 10-45, dead body—and patrol cars arrived on the scene within six minutes. Two patrol officers entered the apartment with their sidearms unstrapped, hands at the ready—modern-day gunslingers. McKelvey could tell right away they were young on the job, at least the first one in the door who caught sight of McKelvey at the kitchen bar. This kid held a hand out in caution, the other hand hovering at his holster.

"Don't move," the cop ordered. "Hands up where I can see them."

The rookie's oxymoron—don't move, but put your hands up. McKelvey slowly raised his hands to shoulder height and said, "Vic's in the master bedroom face-down on the floor. Female Caucasian, mid-thirties. Signs of trauma to the neck. Secure the scene and don't touch anything."

"He's the cop they said was here," the second officer said to the first.

"Ex Hold-Up Squad," McKelvey said and slowly lowered his hands.

The first patrol officer nodded and stood in the centre of the room to secure the scene while the second officer ducked

132

into the bedroom to clear the rooms and then check for a pulse. McKelvey heard the officer making a call on his radio. He sat there with his hands on his lap, lightheaded and in serious need of a pain tablet. Christ, even a half tab. Why had he flushed them in a moment of guilt? He wasn't an addict; he was simply looking for a window to let in a little light.

THIRTEEN

Hattie hung up and tossed the phone on the seat between her and Anderson. They were headed east on the 401, the King's Highway that cut across the very heart of Ontario. It was a line of two, four and six-lane asphalt spanning 820 kilometres from Windsor in the southwest corner, to the far eastern border with Quebec. One section of the freeway in Toronto alone carried more than 400,000 vehicles on an average day, giving it the distinction of being North America's single busiest stretch of highway. For three hours each morning, and for three hours each afternoon, it turned into the country's biggest parking lot. Today, a Sunday, traffic was light and moving well.

"Anything you want to share?" Anderson said.

"Goddamned McKelvey," she said then unleashed a string of Maritime expletives, which included multiple references to saints and fishermen, many H's and Mary's.

Anderson whistled, and said, "Trouble in paradise." He ran fingers over the short stubble on his chin. "He's too old for you anyway, you know. You've got what, like a fifteen-year age difference?"

"Shut up," she said.

"All I'm saying is he's old school," Anderson said.

"What the fuck do you know about old school?" she said, turning to look at him, his young face without even a hint of experience beyond the late nights he kept. He owned the tight and showy physique bought in a fancy gym, where they handed you a clean towel on your way in, but she still figured she could take him down with a good solid shot to his pretty little nose. Her brothers had taught her how to fight the same way they had taught her how to tie a dozen different seaman's knots.

Anderson shrugged and said, "Don't take it the wrong way. I think McKelvey's cool as shit, I mean, Jesus. He shot that biker, he fucking took care of business, you know what I mean? The guy has balls the size of pumpkins. I'm just saying, if you're looking for, you know…someone who's going to listen and understand, then…"

"Then maybe I should turn to someone like you, someone who really understands the complex inner workings of a woman," she said, smiling now. "Well, whatever his faults, I can tell you, McKelvey never once even contemplated frosting his fucking hair."

Anderson went to say something but turned to the window instead, and Hattie gunned them towards their destination, her mind stuck on Charlie, Charlie, Charlie. She knew she had a decision to make. They both knew it had been coming for some time. She was up for a promotion to the Homicide Squad. It was a very real possibility. Homicide in the biggest city in the country. She needed to keep her nose clean. The closer she was affiliated with McKelvey, the less her chances were of making the grade—it was that simple, the politics of his exit from the force, the cloud surrounding his dogged pursuit of Duguay. It made her sick to her stomach to think this way, some sort of careerist, but goddamnit, she was forty-two years old. She had herself to think of for once in her life. Well, maybe twice. Leaving Halifax, and her ex-husband, and two hundred years of ancestral roots, had been the first time she'd really thought of her own desires and aspirations over all else. The decision to leave a lifetime

135

of fishing and fiddles, kitchen parties and long winters of her husband sitting at home drinking and waiting and watching *The Price is Right*. It was strange, because she had loved her ex in much the same way that she loved Charlie, meaning she had stuck around too long waiting for the results to change simply because her heart won out, because she was in deep. She loved Charlie, but it was getting to the point where a shared future seemed like the dream of a naïve girl. Just when she seemed to catch the glimpse of a beacon of hope on the horizon, some notion that he might take up golf or surprise her with a sudden trip to Antigua—anything that signalled an investment in himself or their shared future—McKelvey retreated to his view of the world as this failed experiment that was long overdue for a cancellation of its funding.

"You're not going to tell McKelvey what I said," Anderson said. He sounded like a young boy now. He turned and looked at her, waiting for a response. "I didn't mean anything by it. You know me, I take every opportunity I can get. I'm sick that way. It's a disability, probably even chronic."

Hattie laughed and shook her head.

* * *

Detective Mary-Ann Hattie arrived just as the crews from Homicide and Forensics were pulling into the parking lot of Fielding's building. McKelvey knew that in an hour the place would be stuffed with evidence experts dressed in their white space suits, scanning the place with their blue lights, photographers taking still shots and 360-video of the scene, recording and measuring everything. Even the Homicide dicks had to wait for the evidence geeks to get in and do their job, crime scene preservation trumping all else. The nerds could take as long as they damned well pleased. They had all been patrol officers at one point, which was their saving grace. There was a shared understanding of roles and responsibilities.

"Detective Leyden has agreed to take you to headquarters," Hattie said. "No cuffs, no fuss. And listen, Charlie, they're going to ask you a lot of questions. You know how it works. Be patient, for god's sake, and let them do their job. I told Leyden I can corroborate the events leading up to you being in Fielding's place to check in on him."

"Sounds like you don't have much faith in me," he said.

"I have an unmovable faith in the fact that you don't change," she said. "Cooperate. You know the process at play here. You're working within the parameters of the system, whether you like it or not. You're a *civilian*, Charlie… "

Leyden drove him to the police headquarters on College Street. McKelvey rode in the front seat like a partner riding shotgun, and it brought him back to those better days, those long ago days of youth and midnight shifts and locker rooms boiling over with bravado and bullshit. Back then, back when life seemed either black or white, everything was boiled down to its purest essence: a code in the police book, a 216 or a 61, and you could drink half the night and swagger at the bar after pulling a twelve-hour shift. The police work back then had perhaps been rudimentary when compared with today's science and digital voodoo—and a lot of the officers had been rough around the edges, to be sure—but they had worked cases based on their heads and their guts and a thousand hours of experience working in the blood and the filth of the streets.

Leyden was perhaps forty-five, a lanky man with a build that made McKelvey think of a ball player, long limbs and lean musculature, broad shoulders and a narrow waist. He had a Marine-style crew cut buzzed to the bone on the sides so that you could make out every small nick or cut the man's scalp had earned in a lifetime. Very little personality, McKelvey thought, and something about the man made him think of Clint Eastwood, all squints and grunts. He looked like a cop, if one could look like their occupation. As though as a kid Leyden had practiced in front of a mirror. McKelvey gave him a sideways glance and wondered if he himself had that same look. Perps and rounders recognized a guy like Leyden a mile away. The sport coat and the too-short tie, the never-smile, that look on his face that declared: Police, Police, Police.

"Anybody call Aoki on this?" McKelvey said. He wasn't nervous, not yet, but a little help from his old boss on the Hold-up Squad couldn't hurt. Last he'd heard, Aoki was in line for a jump to Homicide, the Holy Grail in copland. He understood she had finished her Master's degree in criminology through night school.

"Don't know," Leyden said.

"Was your father a duty sergeant over at 51 back in the day?" McKelvey said, trying to make conversation.

"Fifty-one, that was my uncle," Leyden said. "My dad was on patrol for twelve years, hurt his back wrestling a guy he was taking in to the Don Jail. Got put on permanent disability."

A police family. The best and worst kind, McKelvey thought. How each generation came at the job a little harder, something to prove. He saw Leyden as a ten- or eleven-year-old boy, his old man at home on disability. His father must have been bitter at the world, reliving the old days, the lost potential. It would have been hard on a kid, then as he grew older, there'd be little choice between college or the cops.

"Tough on the family," McKelvey said. "The association look after you guys?"

Leyden nodded and drove on in silence. McKelvey could respect a man of few words, yet at the same time he understood why perps were always yammering away out of nervousness, looking to fill the space, and it was only the most controlled and measured con who knew enough to keep his mouth shut. Everything you said in the presence of a cop was fair game for the record. Sometimes the adrenalin ran, and you just couldn't stop it.

On any other day they would have driven into the garage, the heavy door closing behind them. McKelvey well understood this territory, the geography of the police. The walk to the back doors, the duty officer waiting to sign you in, the hand off to the processing officer. This was the case for perps, but here, today, this was simply a conversation to straighten out how it was that a former police officer had come to be in a residence with a dead body, the tenant nowhere to be found.

Leyden parked the unmarked cruiser out front, and they went up the walkway past the stone flower beds, the marble swept and tidy as though the place was a library and not the headquarters of the country's largest urban police force. Leyden checked him through and left him sitting outside the bank of interview rooms. These spaces wherein McKelvey himself had squeezed the balls of countless crooks, the holdup crews. In his early days on the force, these rooms at the old HQ over on Jarvis Street were choked blue with cigarette smoke and, in fact, cigarettes were used as a bargaining tool. Some perp sweating like a bastard, facing a few years in the joint, could spill his guts for the discount price of a few smokes. But not now, now everything was clean and proper and sterile and recorded as part of the process of democracy.

"Be me and Detective Kennedy," Leyden said, and with that he headed, McKelvey assumed, up to his desk in the Homicide Squad where he would confer with his partner on the facts thus far. Which were few and far between, McKelvey knew. They wouldn't have ID'd the victim yet. There was nothing. Just a whole lot of questions and curiosity.

A young duty officer came over to where McKelvey was sitting.

"Can I get you a coffee?" the officer said. He was thin and looked too studious to be a cop, glasses and bowed chest. Perhaps like Leyden, this kid's father had been on the force, and the son's life had been decided for him. It had been the same with McKelvey's father; the man toiled and bled in the mines, cursed and swore about the crappy pay, and yet he didn't speak to McKelvey for three years after his son left Ste. Bernadette to become a Toronto cop. Rather than feel happiness at his son making a break from the dead-end life in a dead-end town, McKelvey's father had never quite forgiven him. McKelvey had the nagging sense, however, that it was generational jealousy rather than anger.

"No thanks," McKelvey said. "I remember what the coffee was like here."

"We've got pop, water, juice. Just let me know, okay?"

The kid sort of smiled at him then opened the door to one of the interview rooms—or *interrogation room* as the old guys referred to them. The kid would have been told that McKelvey was ex-cop, they would have passed on that information as a professional courtesy, and he seemed a little embarrassed to be escorting this man who had been throwing the cuffs on bad guys a hundred years before his entry into the world was even mulled.

"You don't have Steam Whistle on tap, by any chance," McKelvey said.

The kid laughed, shook his head and walked away with his shoulders stooped.

McKelvey slipped inside. There was a conference table and four chairs, two on each side. A strip of fluorescent lights overhead bathed the room in institutional white, and within the light fixture, McKelvey knew, there was a video camera. He waited in the interview room for forty-five minutes, his mind going back to specific days when he'd sat here, right here, turning the vice. The fundamentals of police interrogation had not changed in a hundred years. It was only the degree of pressure, or more precisely the application of said pressure, that had been fine-tuned over the years thanks to liberal courts and the asserted rights of the individual to not be walloped across the head with the Yellow Pages. The act remained, at its very core, all about control. The copper must be seen to be in charge from the moment a suspect was pinched on the street. Handcuffed, thrown in the back of a cruiser, taken downtown and made to wait. The atmosphere, a room too hot or too cold, the mood, access to fluids or solids, sleep or a place to shit, it was all in the hands of the interrogator.

McKelvey himself had in his prime been a master of this game. He would sit down across from a suspect and chat awhile, perhaps ask if they were hungry or thirsty or in need of a good long smoke, then he would tell them that he would pop out and see what he could do about their request. Later—maybe an hour, maybe two—he would come back in and get right at the questions, completely forgetting whatever it was he had promised. Come at them with questions like artillery salvos, boom boom boom—where the fuck were you at seven o'clock last night, who is your girlfriend's mother's sister, where did you go to school, what make of car did you say you drive…

Leyden and his partner finally came in, each holding a styrofoam cup of coffee. Wisps of steam rose and curled from

141

the cups. The same diarrhea-inducing sludge McKelvey had put through his system for years, the brew bubbling in the squad room for six or seven hours at a time, black and thick as dirty oil. That and the poor diet of cops on the fly had almost killed him. How many of their brethren had been felled not by bullets but by cholesterol and stress and cigarettes and caffeine?

"Bob Kennedy. Sorry for the wait," the younger investigator said as they came in, his hand out for a shake. He was a thirtysomething with freckles and orange hair parted on the left, the sort of aggressive hair colour that caused a kid to be teased without mercy. He looked to McKelvey like the sort of person who was always sunburned in summer, always red-cheeked and peeling. He was a thickly built man with big hands, knuckles swirled with curly blond and red hair. He owned the perpetual face of a boy, and it looked to McKelvey like the man probably didn't even have to shave every day.

"You been around, eh?" Kennedy said, pulling up a chair, smiling like an old pal. "Finished up your tour in Hold-up. I hear you had some good collars in your day. The Royal Bank Bandit. I remember reading about that. I was working for the Barrie Police back then. We thought he might have been good for one of our bank jobs, too."

Ah, McKelvey thought, small town cop makes big city detective. He pictured Kennedy in a photo with his mother on the day of his swearing in, goofy kid with a goofy grin. The whole while Leyden sat there picking at a nail, his head down as though he were sitting in algebra class and couldn't wait for the bell to ring.

"We had our days, that's for sure," McKelvey said.

"I bet you did," Kennedy said, and McKelvey could tell the man wanted some stories, tales of the good old days.

"How'd you hurt your eye there?" Leyden said. He didn't look up. And it wasn't so much a question as a declaration.

"Too much Irish whiskey one night, tripped on my laces," McKelvey said.

Leyden smiled a small smile and nodded once.

"I'm sorry about your son and all of that business with Raj Balani," Kennedy said, almost blurting it out, looking glad to have said it and now it was done. "Balani was a good cop at one time, from what I understand. Not the first guy in the Drugs Squad to get in over his head. Dirty business that stuff. Anyway, you know how this goes. We're covering bases here, just ticking off the boxes. We appreciate you coming in like this so we can get you out of the way. So how do you know Timothy Fielding, and how did you come to be in his residence?"

"He's a friend of mine. I went to check on him. He's been worried about his girlfriend. She wasn't returning his calls, and it looks like she up and took off a few days ago," McKelvey said.

"This girlfriend, you know her?"

"Never met her."

"She the dead woman back there on the floor of his bedroom?"

"I don't know," he said. "I never met her."

"No idea who the dead woman is?"

"Not a clue," McKelvey said.

"Did you kill her?"

McKelvey started to laugh, but he stopped himself. The techniques, the catching the perp off guard. Get him revved up, squeeze some emotion out of him. Kennedy was trying too hard, not a natural at this, coming in too fast and clumsy. What did they expect, he'd be curled in the fetal position and sucking his thumb within the first five minutes?

"Like I said, I went to check on my friend. He wasn't home. I found the woman on the floor of his bedroom. I called it in right away. You should probably write that down."

Kennedy shot him a look as though he were both angry and hurt by the comment. He flipped the page in his notebook and scribbled a few lines.

"Okay," Kennedy continued. "All right, so your friend's girlfriend, you were never at her place or vice versa, never bumped into each other at his place?"

A sticking point. But at least for now, for now it was something he would skate around. No good could come from prattling off the whole strange story. Admission of his innocent checking in on Donia Kruzik's apartment would keep him in this box for a day.

"I've never met her," McKelvey repeated. "They haven't known each other long."

"About how long is that?"

McKelvey shrugged. "He said a month, maybe six weeks. Something like that."

"So you stopped by to check in on your friend, your friend who has been having troubles with his girlfriend of a month or so..."

"I didn't say he was having troubles, Kennedy. What I said was, he was worried because she wasn't returning his calls, and she had missed a class. They met through his English as a second language night school course."

Leyden made a few notes in his black pad but seemed otherwise disinterested.

"So you went in—you have a key?" Kennedy said.

"The door was unlocked."

"The door was unlocked?"

"Correct."

"Hmm, okay. Did you find that unusual?"

144

"I can't speak to my friend's habits with regards to security," McKelvey said, "but yes, I made a note of the fact."

"So the door is unlocked, you go in and you look around as you said, and boom, there's a dead lady on the floor. Holy shit. You must have panicked. I mean, where's your friend, Mr. McKelvey? Where is Tim Fielding? Any ideas?"

"Wish I knew," McKelvey said.

"We'll find him," Leyden said without looking at him, still cleaning a nail. "Be better if he came in on his own to help clear things up. Doesn't look good for him. 'Course you know how it works."

"If I hear from him," McKelvey said, "you'll be the first to know."

"Right," Leyden said.

It went like this for a while, perhaps an hour, Kennedy asking the routine questions, then doubling back and trying to catch McKelvey in a lie. At least it seemed that way to McKelvey, and he had to wonder what stories had been told about him in the months that followed his shootout with Duguay. The off-hours investigation into the murder of his son, the implication of a dirty biker squad detective. The limits he had exceeded, the boundaries pushed. It didn't matter that McKelvey had been a good cop, at least a decent cop, working his way up the old fashioned way: a seeming lifetime in patrol cars across four divisions until he cracked enough good cases to make the move to the Fraud Squad, which is what sealed his distrust in appearances, then finally, and until the end, the domain of armed robbers and crackhead gas station jackers in the Hold-up Squad. All those hours logged, those miles walked, those collars made, mattered not at all when your career ended beneath a cloud.

"How did Fielding meet his girlfriend?" Kennedy asked.

"I told you. He was teaching a night school course. English as a second language. She was enrolled in the course. She was a student. They went for coffee or something like that, and they hit it off."

"We'll need the name of the school and all of that, if you have it."

"I know where he works days," McKelvey said. "They'll have what you need."

"One question," Kennedy said, and he ran his hand over his orange hair, then his red face, which wore a combined look of reticence and bewilderment. "Why didn't you just tell your pal to, you know, wait it out a few days, cool off. How is it he knows there's something wrong with this girl he's been seeing what, a month?"

"I went easy on him," McKelvey said. "He's a widower. Lost his wife a few years back to a drunk driver. I guess I didn't have the heart to be an asshole. I figured she was stringing him along, maybe even a husband at home. I was trying to protect him."

Leyden cleared his throat.

"How about you, detective? Anything else?" Kennedy asked his partner.

Leyden shook his head.

"Well, thanks for your patience, you know, as we run through all this shit. You know how it is. We'll have your prints on file," Kennedy said, and put a hand inside his shirt pocket and produced a swab kit. "Be good to get a DNA sample, get you excluded from the get-go. You don't have a problem with that, do you, Mr. McKelvey?"

McKelvey almost corrected him—had the words formed and on his lips. *That'll be Detective-Constable to you, Freckleface.* How quickly we forget. He was indeed Mr. McKelvey now. And for always.

146

"Swab away," McKelvey said and hooked his cheek with a finger.

Leyden came to life, sleek in his movement, as though he were simply sitting one minute then standing the next, shoulders squared. Something about the man bothered McKelvey, as though Leyden didn't see himself as one of them, a brother in blue, but he couldn't quite put his finger on it. There was an air of superiority, the feeling that Leyden would never go for a beer with the boys after work. A perfect candidate, McKelvey thought, for a gig in Professional Standards, some asshole willing to investigate the real or imagined trespasses of his own kind. Leyden leaned over and set his business card on the table in front of McKelvey.

"Call any time," he said and left the room.

"Not the most talkative guy," Kennedy said after the door closed. "I don't mind most of the time, you know, but imagine a twelve-hour stakeout with that guy? Jesus Christ, it's like watching paint dry."

FOURTEEN

Maxime was to be met at customs by a sergeant from the Royal Canadian Mounted Police. Sergeant Robert Marshall was the liaison officer within the Toronto office of the RCMP's War Crimes and Special Investigations Enforcement division, which was headquartered in Ottawa. Maxime followed his fellow weary travellers down the ramp and through the tunnel, stretching and yawning as they hefted laptops and handbags, shuffling like the living dead. In the terminal, he shouldered his suit bag and scanned the throng of people lining up for customs. He spotted Marshall off to the far right, a tall, balding man with a thick black mustache standing there with a cardboard sign that said "Auteuil".

"*Bonjour*, hello," Maxime said, and set his bag down.

"*Bonjour et bienvenue*," Marshall said.

The men shook hands.

"You must be tired," Marshall said. He walked Maxime over to a specific kiosk, where a Customs agent was waiting like a judge on his perch.

"It won't hit me until tomorrow," Maxime said. "The airport is very busy. It seems I have come during your holidays?"

Marshall had set his thin leather attaché case on the counter of the kiosk and was searching for paperwork, declarations and legal notes.

"Labour Day," Marshall said. "Last long weekend of the summer. It's a holiday."

148

"Ah, yes, well," Maxime said, "every day is Labour Day in France."

Papers were presented, stamped, and returned to the RCMP officer, who appeared to Maxime just a few years shy of retirement. There was a gentlemanly nature to this officer, a sort of distilled patience, and he reminded Maxime of someone's grandfather. Once Maxime had been processed, they headed through Customs to the RCMP detachment located within the country's busiest airport to file papers and retrieve Maxime's handgun.

"Welcome to Canada, officially," Marshall said, and he handed Maxime a sheaf of papers for his safekeeping. "Keep these with you at all times. They're your marching orders. You are now legally entitled to carry on your police work on Canadian soil."

"How long have you been in war crimes and crimes against humanity?" Maxime asked as they walked through a maze of hallways in the terminal.

"The RCMP got into this game back in the late Eighties after amendments to the Criminal Code provided Canadian courts with the legal jurisdiction to try war crimes and crimes against humanity," Marshall said. "Me, I transferred in from criminal intelligence and international training after a tour in Rwanda and then Bosnia."

"You must have seen your share over there," Maxime said.

"Mind-boggling, actually. Life-changing. I was in shock when I came back from Rwanda. The sheer scale of the death. And then I shipped off to Bosnia, thinking I could make a difference this time. I went through a depression and a divorce after I got back from that tour. All the things you see and are helpless to change. You have to focus on the few things you do that make a difference, they say. I transferred over to war crimes investigations as a means to hunt my own ghosts, I guess you

149

could say. But it's pretty much the same deal here as every other division, more paperwork than policing."

"I know exactly what you mean," Maxime said.

Marshall entered a pass code to unlock a door then held it open for Maxime. They entered a small reception area that opened onto a series of cubicles and offices. The place was empty. Marshall went over to a counter with a coffee pot on a burner, a jar of powdered coffee creamer and a bowl of sugar cubes. He took two styrofoam cups and poured coffee. Maxime could smell the burnt brew, and it turned his traveller's fragile stomach.

"And what about you?" Marshall said. "You career Interpol?"

"City police, Marseille. Eighteen years. I was undercover the last seven, working the arms and drugs dealers mostly. The same men who committed war crimes in the Bosnian War, once the fighting stopped, found work in organized crime. Serb mob, Croats, Russians, they run all the ports, the longshore unions. I think of all the boxes of guns that made it to the Taliban, and now we find ourselves fighting over there. The loop just grows bigger."

Marshall stirred the creamer into the coffees and handed a cup to Maxime, who wondered how he would drink the stuff without offending his host. The notion of powdered coffee cream, of cheese slices not made from cheese, sugar donuts and hot dogs and drive-thru fast-food restaurants, it all was his idea of North America, a vision of pot-bellied masses waiting in line to consume garbage dressed up with fancy logos. His chocolate shop was to be the antidote to all of this corner-cutting.

"These two targets in Toronto. I've been reading the briefs your office provided. It's hard to believe with all of our coordinated efforts that these assholes can still buy their way into a new life," Marshall said, leaning back on the counter and blowing across the top of the coffee. "We work with Border Services, Custom

150

and Immigration, the Justice Department. Like you said, the harder we work, the loop it seems just gets bigger. These killers are laughing while we're filling out paperwork."

Maxime took a couple of quick sips of the acrid brew and nodded. "The loop is closing on these two, of that I am certain," he said.

"You'll need to check in to your accommodations, get freshened up," Marshall said. "What's the plan from there? Did you want to get started right away, meet with my liaison on the Toronto Metro Police?"

Maxime casually set his coffee cup on a desk at his side. He was beginning to feel the onset of the jetlag that would, within the next twelve hours, fully bloom into a foggy-headed, bleary-eyed stumble. He did not want to involve the local police, not yet. He wanted to do some poking around on his own first, the lone wolf in his character the only detraction from his career as an international police officer; in his world, partnerships and collaborations were not only expected, they were a requirement of law. But this was his case, his final case, and he would do it his way. He wanted forty-eight hours.

"To be honest, Sergeant, I would very much like to rest for a day or so, catch up on my sleep. Perhaps it's best if we meet our local police liaison after the holidays? These men, they are not going anywhere," Maxime said.

He saw the look of relief on Marshall's face. A holiday was a holiday. "As you wish. You have my number," he said. "Now let me get that sidearm of yours. Though I doubt you'll need it. We're a gentle folk, except when we play hockey."

FIFTEEN

McKelvey turned down Detective Kennedy's offer of a ride back to his place and instead walked out the front of the station, turned left and ducked into Fran's famous diner at College and Yonge for a grilled cheese and a Coke. He was starving, guts growling. The place was busy with brunchers enjoying oval platters of huge pancakes, fried eggs, sausages and home fries. The restaurant was a throwback to the 1940s, red leather booths and mile high pies, milkshakes served in frosted stainless steel mixing containers, lunch specials of meat loaf, mac and cheese, liver and onion. It was Hattie's favourite place for a cheeseburger and fries, her every-payday treat. McKelvey thought of her as he sat alone and ate to fill his gnawing stomach, wondered how much or how little to tell her. He knew that despite her comments about the Homicide crew being elitist assholes, she had taken her courses, she had written her papers, she was on the precipice. It was what every cop wanted, after all, to reach the pinnacle of police work and to be a dick, a shamus. If he leaned on her too heavily, if he continued to press her to dig up intel, help him connect the dots, well, he'd be responsible for the consequences. He decided that he would ease up on her. Sure. Once he got her to reach out just a little more, he would really let up on her.

He finished the last of the Coke and left cash on the table. He crossed Yonge Street, intending to grab the subway the two stops down to King Street Station. From there it was a short walk south and east to his place. It had turned into a perfect day, and the streets were busy with people on their way to brunch or to shop, to buy flowers or veal or lamb for Sunday dinner. In a few hours the patios and pubs would be filled with long weekend cheer, pitchers of draft beer. McKelvey had a sudden urge to swallow a tablet, feel himself lifted from his boots, lifted from his skin for a little bit—that glow he got at the top of his scalp. Maybe have a cold beer and talk hockey with Huff at Garrity's, then crawl into bed and pull the covers over his head, wake up in the spring with a big beard. He realized how irresponsible he had been with the prescription, popping them out of boredom perhaps, or pain that was more spiritual than physical. The ages-old story of every loser who ever got stuck under the thumb of that shit. Too smart for it, that's what everybody thought. *It won't happen to me, I won't get stuck.* Still, he saw himself flushing the pills after Jessie had confessed to him her struggle with the demons of addiction, and now he both congratulated and cursed himself. Not that any of it would matter in the grand scheme of things. Look around, Charlie, at all of these millions of people, life swirling on with or without you...

He stopped at the stairs leading to the underground labyrinth of tunnels which had been carved beneath the city in the early 1950s. He looked up to the sky, and he wanted to scream. Fucking McKelvey. He'd done this, he'd brought them here, Fielding and himself. Tim Fielding. School teacher. Widower. Jesus Christ, where was the kid? He had no right to be sitting on a stool at Garrity's. He needed to follow up on the magnet left on Donia's fridge, the immigrant resource centre—Bridges. This was perhaps the only line to Donia Kruzik or her people or her past—whoever and whatever the hell this woman was.

He went down the stairs to the subway, crossed the threshold of the underground and was immediately embraced by a blanketing wave of stale, fetid air. Sometimes that initial waft was so strong, the taste of sulphur on your tongue, it turned your stomach a little. Especially if you had been drinking the night before, your belly already in a precarious state. He pulled a ten from his wallet and went to the dispenser against the wall, bought two tokens and took the rest in change. He pushed his hips through the turnstile and went left towards the northern line. He had the address memorized from the magnet. It was an easy haul up the Yonge line to St. Clair.

He waited behind the yellow caution line, looking up to the video feed of weather, traffic and the latest news ticker of headlines. There it was, the update on the murdered woman and the missing tenant of the apartment, as yet unnamed. But McKelvey knew it wouldn't be long before Fielding's face was on the front page of every newspaper. A train whooshed in, and he got in and took a seat. It was just one of about seven hundred subway cars running daily on the Toronto Transit Commission's three subway lines, moving hundreds of thousands of passengers beneath the city. Unlike many of the large urban subway systems in the U.S., Toronto boasted a good safety record on its trains. The transit cops were both uniformed and plainclothed and had basic police authority within the jurisdiction of TTC property. It was one of the jobs McKelvey had contemplated as he wrestled with the early days of retirement. But he knew himself too well, and figured he would eventually shoot some gum-smacking teenager. It was another idea best left untested.

He picked up a copy of the *Globe and Mail* folded on the empty seat beside him and scanned the headlines. The newspapers were filling with personal testimonials, commemorative pullout sections more than a week in advance of the anniversary of the attack on the twin towers. Everybody was trying to find a way into this thing, to have the light shine on them for just a few moments, like the day John F. Kennedy had been shot—where you were and what you were doing suddenly seemed to matter. Gatherings were planned in every major city across the country. Canadians would stand shoulder to shoulder in a reflective moment of silence. Journalists now referred to the fateful day simply as "9/11", as though it were a branded trademark. Conspiracy theorists filled the airwaves and newspapers with their strange deductions, drawing lines to JFK and Martin Luther King and the Skull and Crossbones, Osama bin Laden and the Russians, and how the man on the moon had been filmed in a production set in California. McKelvey had watched with a sense of mild trepidation as his ally to the south gathered its army to invade Afghanistan. He was hopeful for a decisive and righteous victory, and yet somehow too cynical too really believe it. It seemed that nothing would be easy to figure out ever again.

For the first time since the Vietnam War, newspapers featured daily photographs of combat set against the red rock and dust of that ancient place. The Gulf War at the turning of the last decade now seemed little more than a toe in the water, with its nearly harmless Scud missiles, oil fires blackening the sky, its made-for-TV ending. The television news these days began each broadcast with a body count. Eleven U.S. soldiers were killed when their transport helicopter went down on a spiny mountain ridge on the other side of the world, some obscure place named Spin Boldak. There was an ambush waiting for the rescue party, and those soldiers were lost as well. The president said the nation ought to steel itself for many more days of bad news to come. Years, even. This was to be a fight of biblical proportions—good versus evil.

If the world had seemed an unpredictable place a year earlier, it was now entirely incomprehensible. McKelvey sensed a shift at the axis, an internal adjustment to their collective cognition. People now spoke openly of their anxiety in riding the subway, that great potential tunnel of death. Movie theatres and shopping malls, patio bars and outdoor concerts; any place of human congregation now seemed suspect. Business travellers of non-white descent drew the weary and suspicious gaze of their fellow passengers. At the bottom of McKelvey's stomach sat a coiled knot that told him this had been waiting for them all along. It was their number.

As with the murder of his son, and the eventual implication of a fellow detective in the death, there were things for which a human being simply could not prepare. Any parent worried about their child crossing the street or talking to strangers, but this, this was beyond the scope of comprehension. The late night phone call notification was the first of many sucker punches thrown in the dark. McKelvey had caught the jab square on the jawline, and his knees had buckled—but he'd stayed on his feet. As the president down south kept telling everyone, it always seemed darkest just before the dawn. And it was a cliché, but it was true, at least in McKelvey's case. There was the identification of his boy at the morgue, the wax grey face of his child with the little hole in his forehead the colour of black cherry. There was the push to keep the stalled investigation active; pushing hard, for he sensed his boy's lifestyle on the streets had relegated his case to the background. There was the chase for Duguay, the shooting in that darkened hallway, the ensuing investigation by the dumbasses in Professional Standards...

Right now McKelvey was listening to a young man tell his girlfriend how the subway was actually the best place to be if there was a terrorist attack.

"How do you figure that?" the girl said.

She looked to McKelvey like she was maybe seventeen. A high-school student with hair bleached to a blinding white, pierced nostrils. The boyfriend, too, had facial piercings, two long studs on an eyebrow that resembled bones. The sight of this hardware always gave McKelvey a desire to reach out and twist them, just to show the wearer what sort of opportunity he was providing to a potential foe. Darwin and all that business.

"We're underground, dude," the boy said. "They probably have like reinforced concrete and everything, like a bomb shelter, oxygen they can pump in or something. Like in that movie, right, how the people down in the subway were the last people on earth after the nuclear war."

The train sounded its stop at Rosedale, a neighbourhood of money and old families. The doors chimed and opened, and the two kids got up and shuffled out. McKelvey watched them slip away as the train moved on, and he was glad they were gone, because he had an overpowering urge to lean over and tell them the truth about their collective predicament. He imagined the look on their stapled faces when he said, *"It doesn't matter if you're upstairs or downstairs when the whole fucking outhouse blows up. Have a nice day."* He wondered what they were teaching kids at school these days.

The thing he liked about the subway was its steady thrum, this comforting sense of being in motion, moving beneath the city blocks when traffic was gridlocked. On more than one occasion in those days of his recuperation following the shootout, if truth be told, McKelvey had put tokens in the turnstile just to ride the thing back and forth to kill a few hours, to watch people in their habits, to get lost in the anonymity of public transportation. He would sit there listening to the train cars shooking on the tracks, or screeching through the tunnels with that sound that made you shiver and cringe. Sit there and try to think of nothing at all, least of all the future trajectory of his life, the great burn of his prime now fizzled and ebbing. It was something he would never tell Hattie, or anyone else, this aimless subway riding. Now he set the paper down and read the advertisements along the top of the subway car, ads for condoms, one for a college program in graphic design, a poster advertising free testing for STDs at a health clinic near the Ryerson University campus.

McKelvey got off the subway at St. Clair and went above ground, hit Yonge Street and walked the two blocks to the address. It was wedged between a European deli and a flower shop, the sort of leased space that appeared to have been a storefront at some point in its history, with a floor to ceiling front display window that now featured posters in various languages promising access to career counselling, assistance finding accommodations, basic transit maps and schedules. To his surprise, the lights were on, and there were two or three people in the back standing around a long table. It looked as though they were stuffing envelopes, collating sheaves of paper. He stepped up and pulled the door handle, but it was locked. The sound of his rattling caused the heads inside to turn towards the door. A woman in her mid to late twenties turned, looked at McKelvey for a minute, said something to her colleagues, then came towards the door. She unlocked it and opened it.

"I'm sorry," she said. "We're closed."

McKelvey worked quick on his feet. He feigned severe disappointment, sighed and looked down the street, shook his head then looked back to the woman. "Shit, I knew this would happen. I told them at my office that you'd be closed with the long weekend and all. I'm a lawyer from Ottawa," he said, "representing an immigrant in a deportation case. I only have until tomorrow, see, or...oh well, it's not your problem."

The young woman stood there, the door ajar, and regarded him. She was dressed in plain khakis and a blue-grey wool sweater—or perhaps it was hemp—and she sported a nose ring. Her brown hair was curled together in tight rolls. McKelvey knew the word for it, it was on the tip of his tongue—dreadlocks, that was it. She looked, at least to McKelvey, exactly like someone who volunteered at a place like this should look. *How unique we strive to be,* he thought, *and the harder we try, the more we fall into cliché.*

"I'm sorry," she said. "We're in here doing a mailing for our annual fall fundraiser. The executive director's not in. We're all volunteers."

She shrugged, and McKelvey caught a glimmer of possibility. He tensed and got his shoulder ready to push through the door of opportunity. "This woman I'm representing, Donia Kruzik, she's going to be sent back to Bosnia if I don't provide proof that she came through here, that she was provided assistance by your centre. It's a long story, lots of legalese. I just think of her kids here."

He watched for it, but there was no immediate recognition of the name he'd thrown out there.

"I don't know what we could do to help," the woman said, and she looked over her shoulder to her colleagues, who were interested now, absentmindedly stuffing envelopes. "I mean, with the privacy laws and everything, we can't get access to any personal client files anyway."

"I understand," he said. "It's not your fault. It's the government."

"Don't get me started," she said, smiling. When she smiled, her face changed, and she was prettier than he'd first thought.

"Right," he said, "they get to make their own rules as they go. They can follow immigrants around and tap their phones and kick them out of the country on a whim or a rumour, but we've got to play by the rules."

She looked back over to her colleagues then held the door open. "Come in," she said. "I can at least give you some of our brochures."

"Anything would be a help," he said.

He stepped inside and smiled over at the other volunteers, a woman and a man. They were both in their mid-twenties as well, and McKelvey pictured them all sitting on the floor of a Queen Street West apartment, smoking pot and talking politics and civil rights. He hadn't gone to university himself, or college for that matter, and so he'd always thought of the world as containing two sorts of people: those who thought about things, and those who rolled up their sleeves and got things done. It wasn't accurate or fair, perhaps, but it was a philosophy which had served him well going on six decades.

"I didn't get your name," she said.

"Leyden," he said. "Dick Leyden. I appreciate you opening the door. Listen, I should apologize for my face. I took a tumble off a ladder last weekend."

"I'm Pamela," the woman from the door said. She turned to her colleagues and relayed the story McKelvey had provided. "I know we don't have access to any personal files, but I figured we could at least give him some of our brochures, our annual report. It's something at least. I feel bad that you came all the way from Ottawa."

The young man had been eyeing McKelvey. He said, "It is a

long weekend. Why would you assume we would be open?"

Smart kid, and confident, too, McKelvey thought. A good catch—why would an intelligent lawyer travel all that way without a confirmation?

"Guess my clerk got her wires crossed," McKelvey said with a shrug. "She called here the other day and spoke to somebody, I know that much. Maybe they forgot it was a long weekend. Anyway, I took the chance. I don't really have many options left at this point."

The younger man nodded, satisfied, and returned to his work. Pamela went over to a shelving unit that displayed dozens of publications, brochures and leaflets and fact sheets. She picked a few, came back and handed them to McKelvey.

"I'm really sorry I can't be of more help," she said.

"This is a start," he said.

"The executive director is Peter Dawson. I know he checks his messages even when he's on holidays. He's pretty dedicated to his work. I can leave your name and number if you like."

"That would be great," he said and gave his home number. "I'm staying at that number while I'm in town."

It wasn't until he was on his way out the door that he remembered the name he'd given. He would have to keep that straight. He was Dick. Dick Leyden. He smiled as the door closed behind him.

SIXTEEN

Kadro drove the new junker Turner had acquired for him south towards the green-blue lakeshore. The vehicle was a 1996 white Toyota Corolla that smelled of wet dog hair and stale cigarette smoke, probably stolen, Kad surmised, from some social housing parking lot. Turner had left it in the parking lot of the Scarborough Town Centre with the keys under the lip of the wheel well. Kad stopped only once—to exchange a winning twenty-dollar ticket for a new set of scratch and wins. He selected two five-dollar tickets for a game called "Keno" and two others for "Bingo".

He sat there in the parking lot of the mini-mart and used a nickel to scratch all the tickets, brushing the foil flakes from his jeans and his hands. He didn't need to do this, he didn't even really want to. It wasn't something he could necessarily explain to anyone who might see him sitting parked outside a convenience store—he just wanted to win, knew that unlike in war, the odds here were controlled by the printing of tickets. There had to be so many winners per box of tickets, of that he was sure. He had to look at the tickets very closely, to read the English very slowly and be sure he had not lost when he had in fact won. It was a fear, that because his English was rough, he might misread a ticket and throw it in a garbage can. He wondered how many times that had happened, someone reading a ticket too quickly, tossing it in the trash. How many people on the planet were still stuck in their humdrum life when in fact they were undeclared millionaires?

162

Fate and the odds. It was like mortar shells falling from the sky, launched by unseen hands across the distance, the trigonometry of death. The luck of the draw, they said. Utterly random. You were standing there taking a piss or else you weren't. Here it hits a bridge, or over here it hits a house with fourteen children huddled in the basement. The further you were from your target, the greater the odds of missing. How he had been standing not four feet from a fellow soldier when the man's head suddenly exploded from a sniper's shot—like a watermelon, the skull simply cracked and splintered, let loose the contents, this liquid so red and rich and putty grey, the taste of it on his face, combing it from his hair hours afterward. It left a man wondering, why me, why him, why here, why now. One second, half a second, not even the blink of an eye. What sort of strange algebra was at play? Born too soon, too late, or right on time.

A man had to discover for himself, Kadro had learned, the difference between the things that he could control and those that he could not. In the middle between those two poles there rested a patch of open space called *"semblance of peace"*. Once he himself had learned this lesson, always the hard way, always through death and guilt and bloodied hands, once he had learned this lesson, he was set free. The war was no longer something to be feared, for bullets and mortars and bombs and mines were entirely beyond his control. The only things over which he had perfect dominion were his own hands, his head, his heart. If it was his will to kill, then so be it. If he was told to take the point in entering a village controlled by the enemy, then so be it. Come what may, come what may, there was no sense in pretending he had any say in any of this. That moment of realization was, Kadro believed, like being born again.

"Try again," he said aloud. "Fuck you," and he tossed the tickets to the floor.

He was careful not to speed or take sharp turns, lest he draw undue attention or scramble the precious cargo in his trunk. The school teacher, with hands and ankles tied expertly with military knots, would scarcely have noticed a bumpy ride, however, as he was still partially unconscious, breathing in shallow gasps in the dark, tight space. The teacher had been easy to subdue, as easy as Kad would have guessed, for the teacher, like most of his contemporaries in this soft and new country, had never known war, had probably never even as much as thrown or received a punch in anger. Knuckles soft, belly soft, jawline out there exposed—snap, and the man was out like a punch drunk boxer. He had placed his hands around the man's chest and dragged him gently into the master bedroom, set him carefully on the floor, tied his hands and legs with a couple of neckties, then went back down and got Donia where he had left her in the car across the street.

"He wants to see you," he had told her, his head at her car window.

"What did you tell him?"

He looked at her earnestly, shrugged and said, "I told him that we have to go back home for a death in the family. He understands. He was worried is all. Please, he wants to see you. And then we are finished and he is free to go."

He jumped in the car, moved it across the street to the visitor parking, then he waited just long enough for her to disappear inside the building. He came up right behind her. She was standing at the door to Fielding's apartment, hesitating because it was slightly ajar. He had hoped, of course, that she would slip inside, but he was prepared to adapt. He came up behind her. She

164

turned. The look on her face seemed to tell him that she knew what was to come. In her eyes he saw confusion and sadness, anger and regret and sorrow—the eyes of his mother when he'd left for war in the hills...

Of course, the operation was not ad-hoc, as Krupps used to say, his old squad leader with the university education in literature, throwing these expensive words and Rimbaud and Kipling quotes out during the heat of a firefight. Nothing Kadro did was ad-hoc, not if time and circumstance permitted. Earlier he had cased this building sufficiently to understand the landscape, the possibilities. He'd hugged the side of the building, bricks to his cheek. At the laundry room door he'd pulled a sample-size of black spray paint from his coat pocket, reached up and coated the video camera that provided roughly, in his estimate, a forty-degree scan from its position.

From there it had been tactical, the collateral damage of battle. His hands moved and his legs moved, and he was bent at the waist, the trees and the fields and the mud at his feet and the stink of death and gun powder, and he heard Krupps screaming at him to hurry up, hurry up, and he pressed and squeezed, then she was limp and he was done, Donia was done. She was gone.

He set her gently on the carpet. His breath came fast and short.

Her eyes staring, lifeless grey.

How the eyes of the dead saw everything and nothing all at once.

There was a long moment wherein he could hear nothing but the rush of blood in his ears as if he were in a firefight, and he stood there in the school teacher's room with his mind playing tricks—like where was Krupps, where were the others?

Then he blinked. He looked down at Donia's body, and

everything was here and now. He untied the school teacher and shoved the neckties in the man's back pockets, not wanting to leave anything behind, and he put the man's head and neck in the vice of his arms and applied a sleeper, ensuring continued compliance. At the doorway, Kad borrowed the man's British driving cap and fall jacket from the hall tree, even put his eyeglasses on, then he left the building by the stairs with the dead weight of his drunken friend wilting at his side. He was sweating profusely by the time he kicked open the exit door on the main level, shuffling with Fielding's hundred and sixty pounds at his side, huffing it across the ridge, to the next hedgerow and the safety of his squad, Boom-Boom set up with his big machine gun.

"Pardon me," an elderly lady said when he bumped into her. She was coming around the hallway towards the elevators, a bag of groceries in her hand.

"My friend is sick," he said and pushed on, down the hall to the laundry room.

Baskets sat atop the working washers and dryers and the room smelled thickly of heat and the false spring scents of laundry detergent, but he got lucky and there was nobody in the room. Out the door and along the wall, he came out to the parking lot from the far side so that any video that did catch them would be difficult to decipher. He set Fielding in the passenger seat long enough to get them out onto the street then in behind a strip mall by a clump of overgrown weeds and saplings near a dumpster. The man was coming around, woozy, and he got sick on himself a little bit, the result of being knocked out. Kad worked fast, with precision, and Fielding was in the trunk and Kad was back on the road in less than three minutes.

Kad had called Turner on his cell and told him they had to meet at once—plans had once again been altered out of necessity—and Turner, swearing a blue streak, had given him directions to Exhibition Place. Edging the lake and bordered by a tall stone wall and triumphant archway, this was the space where, since 1879, the city had annually staged the country's largest fair, the Canadian National Exhibition. In late fall, the grounds hosted the Royal Agricultural Winter Fair, where, as the ads declared, "once a year the country comes to the city".

"Are you out of your fucking mind? I'm spending time with my family, asshole. Do you remember when I told you to contact me only in the case of emergency?"

"This is an emergency," Kad said.

Now the two men were standing in the parking lot of Exhibition Place.

"You've had a goddamned emergency every day. Two targets, that's all you had to look after. Christ almighty," Turner said, hands on his hips. He looked around, taking in the enormity of the exhibition grounds, the sky windswept and cloudless. "Do you appreciate the planning and training, the costs, the sheer lengths that people besides yourself have gone to here in order to make this happen? And you're running around like some sociopath. Didn't I say not to draw attention to yourself?"

Turner's older model Volkswagen station wagon was pulled in beside the Corolla at the far end of the lonely parking lot. The Honda, there was the first mistake. Jarko's Garage. Poor Jarko.

"Jesus, this is like a nightmare or something," Turner said. "I thought you'd be the least of our problems. I thought of all people, this is the guy we don't even need to worry about. You're one of the few who actually served in the Colonel's unit."

There were people out jogging and riding bikes along the lakeshore, and the long blades of the country's first large-scale urban windmill were turning soundlessly in the slight breeze, gulls fluttering around the lot to pick at the last of the squashed fries left from the end-of-summer exhibition.

"So let me get this straight. You've eliminated two people; the superintendent of your partner's building, and now your partner," Turner now said in a low voice, calm and measured. He leaned back against his car, arms folded across his chest, the sun on his face. They could have been old buddies meeting up to throw the Frisbee or smoke a joint and talk about girls from high school. "Two bodies, and not one of them is an official target. All you've done is draw heat and add to the trail that leads back to you and me and everybody else involved in this gaggle-fuck. I mean, you just wacked your partner in this whole thing. The one who just spent months working a dead-end job so she could track and detail and ensure the targets are bona fide. You don't think the cops will track her back to her job then straight to Bridges? What the hell am I supposed to think here? Are you shell-shocked?"

Kad leaned back against his car now, too, and folded his arms. He stared at the Canadian. In this light the man's one good eye appeared grey, like smoke.

"It had to be done," Kad said. "I did not plan this. I am not stupid, I am not a sociopath. I am doing what I came here to do. You talk like the fat generals who ran our war from the back rooms, from the safety of their fancy hotels with their whores and their wine and caviar, while we slept like dogs in the rain and the snow, scrounging for food like goddamned animals, not even enough bullets for our guns. Don't talk to me about my partner, you know nothing of the sacrifice she has made for her people. This will never be forgotten. We all have our roles to play in war. She made a mistake, and I controlled the damage."

"Listen," Turner said, and stepped closer now. "I'm not going to stand here and tell you about the places I've been and the things I've done. I'm no backroom general. My job is to get this back on track before the Colonel finds out and sends another squad over here to clean up your mess and clean you and me up at the same time. You've got twenty-four hours. Find your targets, eliminate them, then call me. I don't want to hear from you until this is done."

Kad exhaled. He turned and walked to the back of the car and he said, "There is still this." He unlocked and opened the trunk. The school teacher was awake inside, bound and gagged, lying on his side. The light flooded in, and the school teacher squinted, turning his head away. He made noises and tried to lift himself.

"What the hell is this?" Turner said.

"The school teacher."

"You're just zipping around town like some goddamned Sunday driver? What if you get pulled over?"

"He is my insurance," Kad said, then slammed the trunk. "This man's friend, he is a policeman. This is the man I met in Donia's apartment when I returned to make sure we had not left anything behind. I should have killed him, but I did not. Now I am cleaning up my own mess. This man's friend is the one who tracked us to the garage then also went back to talk to the superintendent to get answers to his questions. He left his card… "

Kad pulled the business card from his shirt pocket and held it up. "He is the final link to all of this, to all of us," Kad said. "I will tell him he can find his friend safe and sound if he follows my instructions. In the meantime, I am free to finish my work. The police and the newspapers are looking for the man in my trunk. He is the one who killed Donia. It is called, in the military jargon, a diversionary tactic."

Turner nodded, taking it in. "I've got the perfect place for you to store your insurance," he said.

169

SEVENTEEN

Sometimes when sleep would not come, when the burden of his thoughts grew too heavy, McKelvey would find himself walking the streets of old Cabbagetown with only the whores of Jarvis Street and their shifty-eyed johns for company. This was the other side of Last Call, when even the dive bars were emptying of their lost-soul patrons. He knew from his patrol-car days the street whores were for the most part crack or heroin or meth addicts—dead-eyed zombies on the slow-foot shuffle to nowhere, millions of miles accrued in that four foot span of sidewalk. Girls not unlike his Jessie, who shared histories so similar, it was cliché—abused, given too much or too little attention, cast aside, pushed to the margins, stumbling to a place where this was actually a conceivable employment option—handjobs, blowjobs, whatever, whenever, the body as a commodity in the supply chain of human misery. Jessie was strong, stronger than she knew, and she'd made it out before things could bring her to this, the street level. He would make sure she never fell back to the old life.

Regardless of age, they appeared to McKelvey as young girls, pathetic with their leg bruises and their dirty skirts and torn nylons, hair teased and sprayed and stinking. One girl in particular stuck out in his memory. He had arrested her on a cold winter night about a decade and a half earlier, back when he was in the patrol cars. Taylor, that was her name. He remembered how her feet were filthy. Toes grafted with dirt so deeply they were almost black, permanently tattooed. It was the dead of winter, and she was wearing open-toed shoes like she was the maid of honour in a summer wedding. So stoned, so far gone, she hadn't noticed it was fifteen below zero, puffs of her breath in the air like clouds from cigarette smoke. Her eyes dark, so sad and beautiful. McKelvey remembered feeling a sense of admiration for her toughness, this survivor's grit, like they were the same somehow and yet by sheer circumstance happened to find themselves standing on opposite sides of the abyss. He guessed he felt this kinship with the truly vulnerable, not the armed robbers and subway purse thieves and the Saturday night wife beaters, not the social housing thugs. No, there was nothing to be done for that variety of criminal except for the application of punitive repercussions. He understood and accepted as fact, for example, that the majority of armed robbers he put away would end up committing the exact same crime within three to six months of their mandatory release from prison—this is what the prison psychologists called recidivism, a fancy word that meant "chronic fuck-up". These were the incorrigibles who continued trying the same things over and over again until eventually they killed someone in the commission of their crime or got killed themselves, some idiot waving a gun in a video store.

McKelvey didn't have a soft spot for hookers, nowhere near it—for he knew their hearts were long turned black, knew they could summon tears, dredge up the most vile anecdotes of what their fathers and uncles had done to them regardless of fact or fiction—but rather he felt it was something, this commercial transaction, best left between consenting adults. In this regard he was long a proponent of so-called "red light" districts. A block on a street wherein nobody was rolling anybody, nobody was on the take, women weren't owned or muscled by bad men, where nurses and doctors and cops and priests could navigate with equal access. It would make all their jobs so much easier if the boundaries and the rules were set out. The devil's playground, open 24-7.

As for the johns, they were everyman. Lifetime losers on parole, the socially awkward, the sexually addicted, the small-cocked, the deformed and the tormented, or those teased as children—McKelvey knew them all, he knew them as well as he knew himself. How could he not after having spent so many hours in patrol cars driving down those endless streets, the radio crackling, driving and begging for some action to jump across the wire, spending more time with these people than with his own family. In those days he'd been a player sitting on the bench waiting for the coach to call his number, to pat him on the helmet and say *"Yes, we need you, get out there, McKelvey…"*

On those nights when sleep would not come despite the coaxing of the draft beer, perhaps even the extra nudge from a painkiller or two, McKelvey would throw on his coat and hit the street. He was quiet on the stairs, careful to close and lock his door without making any noise, forgetting that he no longer shared a home with a wife and a son, a family. No, he lived alone now in a building where nobody cared what he did or where he went. But old habits die hard. On this night, too, he watched his steps on the stairs. The night air was cool and made him aware of the sweat in his armpits, chilled.

This night he was unable to sleep with his mind working through the mess he'd found and likely made worse, and he walked not so much for escape, but in search of entry. A way into this thing, the little crack that he could squeeze his fingers in, gain leverage, split wide open. The skeleton of something was beginning to form. He had returned from the immigrant support centre to find his answering machine flashing. He hadn't been home in what seemed like twenty hours. It was Chinaski, the superintendent of Donia's building.

"*Yeah hey there, this is Hank Chinaski calling like you asked. Listen, I found that stuff you were looking for. The cheque and the application. I got it here when you want to come by. Looks like a cheque from…* (here he paused, and McKelvey could see in his mind's eye the man squinting to read the cheque) *…some place called Bridges, if that means anything.*"

He had taken that information, coupled with the publications from Bridges, and retreated to Garrity's for a much-needed pint and some space to think where he wouldn't be alone. The confines of his condo apartment, the emptiness, the threat of long days of winter to come, it was too much. He remembered stories his father had told about the mining and logging camps up north, how men went absolutely insane if they were snowed in and alone for a winter. Or worse, locked up with somebody else. Staring across a table at the same guy for months on end, eventually every little thing about him started to drive you crazy.

"I knew a guy, Lucky Lachapelle," his father had told him once, "got his hand chopped off because of the way he scraped his food with his fork. Made a certain noise that drove his cabin mate crazy. Chopped it off with a hatchet, just like that."

The trouble with McKelvey was that he was alone and had only himself to drive insane. He stopped and asked the woman behind the bar, a university student named Melissa, if Huff was off for the night.

"He's sick," she said, pouring a pint of thick, coffee-brown Guinness.

"The flu's making the rounds," McKelvey said.

He passed by the bar and took a small table at the back. The beer had never tasted so good, and he got through two pints and

173

a bowl of mixed nuts by the time he had read the centre's annual report and brochures. The support centre had been founded in late 1995 as NATO bombers brought an end to the wars in the former Yugoslavia. It was initially funded through a series of grants provided by a Bosnian community association which was now apparently defunct—hence the need for fundraising drives. The mandate of the centre was to provide services to the influx of those seeking refugee status (or, McKelvey surmised, those with enough money or connections to make it out of the war zone). A group of dedicated volunteers, mostly final-year students in university social work and international studies programs, provided counselling and advice to the centre's clients on their transition to this new country, this new way of life. McKelvey flipped to the back page in the annual report that featured a photo of the volunteers standing in the middle of the centre with the executive director, a middle-aged man named Peter Dawson. He would call the man on Tuesday and see what he could find.

His eyes paused on a slim and clean-cut man standing among the volunteers with his face turned slightly to the left and downward as though he were shy. It was the man's eye patch that made him stop. It wasn't every day you saw a guy with an eye patch. Like a pirate, McKelvey thought.

*   *   *

Now Garrity's was long closed, and McKelvey was walking and walking, his mind working through the tangle of lines. Tim Fielding was out there somewhere, alive or dead, and McKelvey had to find him. This was his responsibility. He didn't deserve to sleep, to rest, to slow, until he had found his friend and cleared his name. He passed a pawn shop across from the empty benches and dead statues of Moss Park. Guitars and blenders and old TV sets displayed in the barred front window, and at the doorway he saw a guy standing there as though it were a perfectly normal thing to be doing at this dead hour.

"Got a smoke, buddy?" the guy said.

Hands in the pockets of his sweatshirt. His face was pock-marked, and he had a teardrop tattoo at the corner of his right eye. He had done time, he had broken his momma's heart. McKelvey noticed everything.

"Sure," McKelvey said, and he stopped. "I got a smoke."

He fished a couple of cigarettes from his pack, handed them over. Standing there in the dark on the street, the guy gave a nod, his eyes narrowed to slits. Out here on the street, McKelvey looked everyone in the eye, kept his hands out of his pockets. He felt he was ready for anything, and some nights he wondered if he was perhaps inviting something into his life. *Go for it,* he heard his own heart whisper. For it was only out here on the dark city streets, at the very nucleus of this urban experiment, that he felt oddly in control of the direction of his life—minute by minute, breath by breath. These days especially, with Caroline living her life out on the west coast, with Jessie busy with her school, with Hattie focused on her career, he felt lonelier than he'd ever felt in his life. But out here everything was slowed down, the landscape was familiar, the smells and sounds. He knew there was nothing to be taken for granted, that anything could happen at any time. For better or for worse, this was his space. Where he was alive, where he maneuvered best. It was in these moments he believed he understood why so many retired cops were divorced or suffering from cirrhosis of the liver, or both. Because nothing—paying bills, building model ships,

Tuesday night sex, or fish sticks and minute rice—well, nothing could ever quite measure up to this, the city of sirens.

He turned at the other side of King and came back down Jarvis towards Front Street. As he crossed the street near the St. Lawrence Market, a car came around the corner like a boat swinging from port, and McKelvey saw that it was a ghost car, and Jesus, there at the wheel was Leyden. McKelvey stopped halfway across the street and let the cruiser pull up beside him, a great sleek whale of the night. The window rolled down. Leyden looked at him for a minute, then said, "Late for a walk."

"Needed some air," McKelvey said, "after being cooped up in that box with you and your partner. He has B.O. You really should tell him about it. Unless it's part of the approach, bring the suspect to tears, squeeze out a confession."

Leyden almost smiled, but it was hard to tell with the interior of the car swathed in shadow.

"No word yet on that woman's ID beyond the name we get from her classmates and her co-workers," Leyden said. "We got her forms from the HR department at the garment factory she was working at. Showed the morgue photo to a few classmates and co-workers. Say they knew her as Donia Kruzik. Everything's in order on paper, but none of it checks out through the system. Almost like she's a ghost. We got her last known address from her night school registration, but get this. Place is empty, like she was never there."

"That is odd," McKelvey said.

Leyden leaned across the seat now and looked right into McKelvey's eyes. "And check this for luck. Superintendent had a heart attack sometime this morning. Found him stiff in his La-Z-Boy, so we can't even interview him. His place looks like a bomb went off. Guy wasn't what you'd call on top of his paperwork."

The superintendent. Dead. It gave McKelvey a quick chill. A

coincidence or another link in this obscure chain? The man had not been the picture of vim and vigor, but still. What were the odds at play here?

So then…the guy in Donia's apartment has his car tracked to Jarko Automotive. The garage burns down after McKelvey talks with the owner. The superintendent of Donia's building has a heart attack after McKelvey talks with him about Donia…

McKelvey had a hundred things he wanted to ask the detective, but all of them would reveal that he knew more than he was letting on. It was too late to go back and expand on the answers he'd given Leyden and Kennedy—about stopping by Donia's apartment, about the stranger who was inside and had broken his nose. He would need Hattie to poke around. It was the last time he would ask this of her, put her in this bad spot.

"A real conspiracy of bad luck on our part," Leyden said.

"I'm sure something will turn up," McKelvey said.

"Hope your friend does, too," Leyden said. "Before he gets himself in trouble."

The two men regarded one another for a long moment. It was a strange dance, both of them confident in their assessment of the other, of the situation they found themselves in. McKelvey's mind flashed with an image of the two of them in a schoolyard at three o'clock, a ring of students formed around them, the sun beating down, their hearts hammering as they looked to finally settle something that neither of them fully understood.

"Well, enjoy the air," Leyden said and gave a nod.

McKelvey put his head back and pulled a dramatic inhalation of the city air. "And you enjoy your midnight prowl," he said, then he crossed the street and turned south towards The Esplanade and his condo. He heard the cruiser float down Front Street, then the sound of its engine and tires on the pavement dissolved into the night. McKelvey stopped to light a cigarette. It would put him in the deficit column to start the following day, but what the fuck. The added stress of being tailed by Leyden while he also attempted to find Fielding—while he also wrestled with the realization that Hattie was drifting away from him and there was a good goddamned chance that Jessie and Emily might stay up in Manitoulin or Sudbury—well, it seemed like more than enough justification for a temporary pause in the rationing system.

Back at home, he turned the TV on with the volume off and sat back on the sofa. He remembered the days when most of the channels at this hour were frosted out, but now the flow of entertainment was infinite. He found a number of infomercials. One for a dissolving toilet cleaner in the shape of a hockey puck that featured a guy with a black beard who was shoving the puck out to the camera. He switched the channel to an infomercial for a 1-800 sex chat line, the image on the screen of this young beauty coming out of the ocean in some tropical paradise, dressed in a too-small red bikini, as she flung her wet hair in slow motion, but she didn't seem to have a phone anywhere within reach. McKelvey noted these small details, always pointed them out, and it was something that drove Caroline crazy. Especially if they were watching a cop show or a mystery movie.

"Would never happen like that," he'd say, just barely under his breath.

"Shhh, and just let me enjoy it," Caroline would say.

"Not very realistic."

"It's not supposed to be, Charlie! It's for entertainment!"

He flipped the channel now to the local TV guide that featured the weather and a rundown of the day's biggest headlines and news briefs. He stopped and read:

Night school teacher wanted for questioning in slaying

of student   City cops searching for Timothy Fielding, teacher wanted for questioning in slaying of student. Detectives say all airports, train and bus stations are under surveillance after a woman's body was found in a mid-town apartment. Cops have confirmed the victim was a student enrolled in evening courses for English as a Second Language. The woman's name has not been released, pending notification of next of kin.

McKelvey turned the TV off and tossed the remote to the end of the couch. He sat there in the dark with his head back, wondering where in the world Tim Fielding could be. He had this horrible feeling his friend was closer than he could imagine, nothing to go on but a hunch. He drifted off, without knowing it, and when he snapped awake, the room was dark and silent. Just his heart rushing blood in his ears, then, within the stillness of the off-beat there was the sound through the window of tires rolling by on the street down there. He sat up. He blinked and wiped his face with a hand. Fuck, the mess he'd made. Again. *This pattern, Charlie. Dig it deep then feel like you're alive, really alive, when you're fighting your way back out.* Tim Fielding was in trouble with bad people, and here he was trying to do it all on his own.

You're not a cop any more, Charlie. Get it through your head. Ask for help…

He sat forward, and with his head in his hands, he thought maybe it was true after all. Maybe Hattie was right. Maybe he did have a death wish. Move things along towards the inevitable. Jesus, it was too late to be thinking about shit like that. Or maybe it was too early. He sat there for a long time, listening to the city outside, sufficiently quiet at this late hour for him to be able to isolate the specific sounds of urban activity. It was going on

179

four o'clock when he moved to the little table by the window. He stood there and looked out at the bricks and stones and the darkness washed with false light. He picked up the receiver. Held it for a minute, or maybe longer, then he dialed the number. She answered on the third ring, her voice thick with sleep.

"It's me," he said.

"Hi me..."

*   *   *

It was that surreal time of the day, impossible to tell whether the hazy light spreading across the city was the last burn of night or the first glow of morning.

"Smoke 'em if you got 'em," Hattie said.

She was sitting up with her back against the headboard, her red hair untied from its workaday bun, tousled from their lovemaking. She pulled the sheet to her waist and folded it there. McKelvey liked how she would sit like that, a tom-boy unafraid to show her parts in the locker room, this fisherman's daughter with her curse words and her spitting on the sidewalk.

"I've cut down on smoking after sex," McKelvey said. "I found I was going through too many cigarettes."

He left out the part about the short, sharp pinch of pain at the moment of highest pleasure—the electrical current that shot through his core. The fact it had been happening for a few months now seemed to mean that it was, at some point anyway, something to be addressed.

She turned to him, that smile on her face, those eyes. She said, "How many cigarettes?"

"Oh," he said and pretended to make a count. "No more than two packs a day."

Her elbow hit his ribs, and he let out a groan. He slid under the covers, and his hands found her waist and pulled her down so that they were head to head. His big hand moved up her thigh to her ass, across her back, warming her cool flesh. He kissed her on the mouth then moved down her neck, breathing the smell of her roll-on deodorant, and he kissed her tiny breasts that she so detested and he so loved, and he was back in the game again, alive, alive. She put a hand in his curls and gave a little tug.

"Hey, hey," she said, "I've got to be at work in forty minutes."

He pulled up beside her, and rubbed his face with his palms. She had arrived at his place just after four, an overcoat thrown over her pajamas. Like two kids stealing time together while parents were out of town.

"Is this like a booty call?" she had said, whispering at his door. Her freckles, that bratty smile of hers.

Now it was just after seven, and he wanted to be with her again before she got swept up in the work, and he knew what it was like to be on-call during a long weekend. Everything increased during the holidays—families pushed together, too much drinking and too many grievances left unsettled, too many things to buy and not enough cash. The booze cans were stuffed beyond capacity after the clubs let out, thugs carrying heat looking for a chance to gain some respect. He had wanted to make her a nice breakfast to make up for the last few weeks, the distance he'd put between them, but she said she had a Pop Tart in her glove compartment.

"So," he said, "I want to tell you straight up, I didn't call you over to get information on Tim Fielding's case."

"But since I'm here…"

"Since you're here," he said.

He looked at her and smiled. His boy's smile. She gave him a serious look and shook her head. "I talked to Kennedy late last

181

night. I can tell you that they completed their canvass of Fielding's building. Pretty much a dead end there," she said. "Apparently some old lady saw two guys leaving by the stairwell, which stood out as odd, and one of them might have been Fielding, but she can't be sure. Poor old doll has early-stage Alzheimer's. Surveillance video at the front shows you coming and going on the dates you said, also shows the victim coming in the front doors about half an hour before you got there. Camera on the east side of the building, by the laundry room door—the only other way in or out—was recently spraypainted by some taggers. Could be a coincidence or maybe not. Depends if you're on the team that believes Fielding killed this Jane Doe in a jealous rage, or the team that believes Fielding is the victim in all this."

"Which team are you on?" he said.

Hattie exhaled through her mouth. She shook her head. "I don't know. I wish I could say, but it just... I mean, Christ, the evidence is overwhelmingly against your pal right now. And listen, they can't find out who this woman is. No positive ID. Kennedy said they canvassed a few of the students in her class, showed the morgue photos, and yeah, they said it's the woman they knew as Donia Kruzik. But who is Donia Kruzik and where did she come from, that's what they're trying to find out now."

"No word on Fielding?"

"Our guys are working with the media to keep his face on the front page, keep the pressure dialed up. I don't know," she said, "you know him better than I do. Do you really think a guy like Tim Fielding could elude the police for a few days with this much heat on him?"

It was true, Fielding's story had all the right elements—teacher and immigrant night school student embroiled in an affair, the woman turns up strangled in his apartment, the suspect gone missing…it would be front page in the *Sun* and the *Star* by that morning. Fielding's apartment building was swamped with reporters and satellite vans. Both Kennedy and Leyden would be quoted as saying it was early days yet, that they would need the autopsy results before commenting further. They referred to Tim Fielding as "a person of interest" at this stage. They said they hoped he would present himself to help clear things up.

"He didn't do anything, and he didn't run," McKelvey said. "This woman he was seeing, Donia Kruzik—if that's even her real name—she's tied in with something. I think Tim was in the way or he was a loose end. He's either dead or being held somewhere."

"Jesus and Mary," she said. "She was eastern European, right?"

"Bosnian."

"What are you thinking, sexual traffic, human smuggling? Organized crime?"

"I wish I knew," he said.

He closed his eyes and tried as he had been doing every hour on the hour to bring forth a clear image of the man in Donia's apartment. The head shaved to a dark stubble, six feet or maybe six-one, two hundred pounds but solid and lean, fist like a goddamned snow plow. But the face, it wasn't there…

He went to tell her about the support centre, Bridges, and the lead he planned to follow with the executive director, but he stopped himself. He knew what she would say, where her allegiance would ultimately fall. This case would attract a significant amount of media attention. The sort of file that made or ruined careers. He had backed himself into a corner; to come out now with the information about Jarko's Automotive, the man in Donia's apartment, the connection to Bridges, well, there was no way to come out clean.

183

"I hate to eat and run," she said and flipped the comforter back.

She sat on the side of the bed, reached down for her panties, stood and wiggled them on, then found her socks and stooped to slip them on. McKelvey couldn't help but watch as she got dressed in her pajamas, the sheets all tangled and the room filled with their smell. He was involved again, everything in his being flowing to that centre of demonstration. He tried to hide it by bunching some of the comforter.

"You know I'd do anything for you," she said, "but I have to tell you. I mean it. I have an interview next Thursday with Detective-Sergeant Rowland. I told you I took the tests. Well, I passed. I fucking aced them, actually. My course credits are good, and I've got references stacked from here back to Halifax."

She finished buttoning her pajama top and stood there, looking like a kid. McKelvey saw it then, what he was doing, and the cost of it all, always this cost that others had to pay. My god, she was young, if not by years, then at least by his benchmark. She had a good fifteen-year run left in her career. He couldn't even make the night without getting up to piss three times. He smiled at her.

"You'll be the best homicide dick they've ever had," he said.

"You're just saying that because I let you in my pants."

"No," he said, "I'm not. You're cut out for it. I sure as hell never was, not to play at that level. But you are, Hattie. You've got the stuff to work in the system and still get it done your own way. To walk that fine line, I mean, shit. I never had that talent. The politics."

"That means a lot," she said.

He thought for a minute that her eyes were moist, and he saw again what he had done to her, the compromise he was asking

184

her to make. How selfish it was, because on her own she would never cut the cord between them. He would have to do it, let her go. Homicide Detective Mary-Ann Hattie. He could see it. How proud he would be. But he didn't see himself in the picture standing beside her.

"I'm not going to ask you to do anything that will jeopardize your chances here," he said. "But you can do me one last favour."

She smiled; she couldn't help it. "Go for it," she said.

He said, "Get Leyden off my ass. Guy thinks he's in the Gestapo or something."

She shook her head slowly.

"What?" he said.

"This guy really pisses you off," she said, reaching down to pull on her flannel pajama bottoms, "because he's exactly the same as you, Charlie. You guys could be brothers, for Christ's sake."

He sat up, pulling up on his elbows. She pulled her trench coat over her pajamas.

"What are you taking about? I'm not like Leyden at all. I have some personality, don't I? I don't think I'm an asshole just for the sake of being an asshole."

"He's a good cop because he doesn't give anybody the benefit of the doubt. He doesn't believe in anything or anyone, just the holy trio of motive, opportunity and evidence. He has to see it to believe it. Sound familiar? If it doesn't, well, you have no self-awareness, Charlie McKelvey, and I can't help you there. Look at the facts, the circumstances. I would be keeping an eye on you, too, to be honest. You haven't exactly been as forthcoming as I think they would have assumed a former cop to be in all of this."

There was no point trying to explain to her why Leyden was a dickhead and he himself was simply highly determined to follow a line to its end point.

"If you bump into him, tell he's not fooling anyone. And he can kiss my ass, okay? If he has questions, he knows where to find me. I'm not hiding from anybody, I'm right here. But this following me around, the fucking cloak and dagger act, it's wearing thin."

"It's ironic," she said.

"What is?" he said.

She smiled and said, "Oh, you know. You're asking me to get Leyden off your ass. And last night his partner Kennedy is asking me to reach out to you."

"Reach out to me. For what?"

"He asked if I could talk sense into you, that's all. Pull a favour, he said, and ask McKelvey to stop being such a closed door on this. It's actually called 'obstruction of justice', but that's just the technical terminology. He asked me why you were being such a hardass on all of this. They know you know more than you're saying. You're not the only cop in the room, Charlie."

He sighed and sat up on the side of the bed, suddenly aware of his vulnerability. Here he was naked under the covers like a newborn baby. He reached out, got his khakis and stood to pull them on.

"What a fucking fiasco," he said. "I'm trying to protect Tim, okay? Things look really bad for the guy right now. I take responsibility for that. I need some time to clear a few things up, that's all. A day or two. Just get that hall monitor Leyden off my tail."

"Oh, Charlie," Hattie said.

"Oh, Charlie, what?" he said, zipping his pants.

"You drive me crazy."

He said, "Well, that makes two of us."

EIGHTEEN

It was beyond comprehension, a surreal nightmare. Tim Fielding emerged from the cocoon of semi-consciousness to find himself with his hands tied behind a post or a beam of some sort. Blindfolded. Smells of dampness, wet concrete and something else, a sickly sweetness. Malt or hops. A brewery or a tavern? He began to hyperventilate, and he cried a little until his stomach hurt, then he stopped because there was simply nothing left to do but slow his breathing. Calm down. One step at a time, Tim. One step at a time…

The man at his door. He'd been punched. Then bits and pieces of memory or dream—tied up, carried, and yes, stuffed in the trunk of a car.

Slices of blinding light—arrows in his eyes when the trunk was raised. Too bright to make out the features of the men, or even how many they numbered. Two, he guessed.

Donia. Where was she, and what was her connection to all of this?

Who was she, and what had he found in her?

He thought back to their conversations, their time together. He saw her face, her beautiful and sad face, and the sound of her soft voice that first night she'd surprised him by saying yes when he'd asked her to go for coffee. So out of the ordinary for both of them, they came together in their awkwardness and shyness, found this shared experience of having lost a spouse so early in their respective marriages.

"My husband," he remembered her saying. "He was... executed."

He'd thought in his naïveté that she'd meant as a prisoner, that he had been executed as a criminal. And it was true in a sense, for she had told him—the closest she had come to shining a light on her past—she had told him how he had been murdered during the war. But then, seeming to sense she had betrayed her secret memories, she had closed up again. He told her about his wife and the drunk driver who ran her down on the street as she was leaving work. How everything left you in that single moment when the telephone call startled you. Your whole life draining from you in one rush.

Who was this woman?

There was no clue to her past beyond the meagre facts she had set out: she had lost her husband, she had come to Canada to escape both the memories of her brutalized homeland and to start again. And she wanted to learn to speak and write English better than she could.

"Here I can be anybody I want," she had said. He remembered it now.

He called out, and his voice echoed. A large room then, empty. Factory or warehouse? Sounds of the harbour, gulls and boats—if he listened closely, with intent and focus. He was near the lake, of that he was certain, as certain as a blindfolded man can be.

What were the motives at play here? A kidnapping for ransom? What the hell did he have to offer anyone, besides a teacher's pension? It didn't make sense. It was Donia, something about her. *Who was she?* Charlie had been right, of course. He had no idea who she really was, who he was fooling around with.

He squeezed his eyes shut, wiggled his hands to no avail, and willed with all of his remaining energy to send McKelvey a sign, a signal.

Come for me, Charlie…

NINETEEN

Bojan Kordic brought the razor to the neckline and, with the fore and middle fingers of his free left hand, pulled the skin taut. The razor made its familiar scraping sound as it slid upwards following the grain of the hair, mostly grey now. He paused there in mid-motion, face pasted with rich sandalwood lather, the straight razor which had belonged to his father spread open in its sterling silver "V"—the only piece of home, of his past, that he had carried with him to this new country. Now he owned a new name, a new history.

He paused. He thought he saw something move in the mirror. The slightest ripple of the shower curtain behind him. He slowed his breathing. The tap dripped. He shifted his weight, gripped the razor, then pivoted on his hip, thrashing open the plastic curtain. Empty, of course. A shampoo bottle on the edge of the tub teetered over from the momentum and fell with a hollow clunk. It was getting to him again, the war. Those days, so far removed, and yet burned into his memory for repeat play without advance notice. The images came back while sitting in a meeting at work, or reading to his daughter at night, these flashes, sounds, smells. He had been waking from terrible dreams lately, too, dreams of faces, arms, hands reaching out to him…

After shaving, he went quietly down stairs and ate a bowl of hot oatmeal while scanning the international box scores for soccer in the *Toronto Star*. He did not like hockey, although in order to talk business in this country he kept up on the progress of the Maple Leafs, the player names and trades, even bought tickets to take clients to games, feigning passion when the Leafs scored. He did not like hockey or baseball or basketball, but he missed the old rivalries in soccer, the open air stadiums in his old country. He ate alone in the silence of the kitchen until his wife came down in her robe and put coffee on. And then his daughter, the jewel of his eye, came down the stairs. She came over and asked to sit on his lap while she dribbled Cocoa Puffs down the front of his dress shirt. She was dressed in her new *Lilo & Stitch* nightgown, her new favourite movie character.

"Do you really have to go to work on the long weekend?" his wife said.

"I have paperwork to catch up on," he said, "my sales and inventory reports. I won't stay more than three or four hours. How about we take a hike on the bluffs when I get back this afternoon?"

Then Bojan Kordic grabbed his overcoat and his briefcase, kissed his wife and daughter goodbye, and, with a heart full of gratitude, pulled out of his suburban driveway in his silver Subaru Forester. He did not notice the white Toyota Corolla pull away from the curb a little ways down the street and follow him through his neighborhood maze, out to join the line of traffic on the Don Valley Parkway moving south towards the downtown.

* * *

Maxime Auteuil was quite certain the driver of the white Toyota Corolla was unaware that he was being followed. How interesting—the follower being followed. And it was quite conceivable, he mused, that he himself was being followed as

191

well—this strange chain to infinity. Though not likely. He glanced in his rearview and side mirrors. It wasn't the first time he had done this; he had become something of an expert in the tracking and tailing of people during his days working undercover, tracing the drugs and arms shipments through the ancient port of Marseille, that cavernous underworld of dangerous characters. He had followed suspects for weeks, sometimes even months. He'd watched people shave, shit, shower, shuffle along in the mundane ruts of their life, he'd seen it all and written it down in a notebook for later recall and testimony. The only difference here was the lack of familiarity with the landscape, the lay of the land. He had waited a moment before pulling from the curb, and now he was three cars back on the parkway. It was a beautiful country indeed, and this city, what he had seen in his first twelve hours, was not bad at all. It was no Paris, no Lyon, to be sure, but it had its charms. It was new and clean, for starters, even though the food was horrible and the wine even worse.

He yawned wide and saw the back of his throat in the rearview mirror. Hard to believe he was here, really here, closing the loop on this final case. After leaving the RCMP officer, he had gone to the avenue of car rental agencies. He'd selected a black Hyundai Accent, joined the Gardiner Expressway, and wound his way downtown to the Royal York Hotel. He'd passed on a free upgrade to a full-size car, much preferring the familiarity of a smaller vehicle, which was the norm back home. Even the police vehicles were tiny Renaults. The flats, too, and the hotel rooms, the pant sizes. Here, everything was larger, starting with the sky. The attitude seemed to be "more space, so why not take it up?" But it was his accommodations that he refused to downgrade, choosing wherever he travelled to stay in four-star properties, which was of course covered within the expense claim guidelines as set out in a sixty-page booklet that every agent was expected to memorize—despite the fact the bureaucrats in Financial Control were constantly updating the thing with sub-clauses and fine print to guard against complacency and fraud. Yet another reason he couldn't wait to retire, to leave behind the universe of reports and receipts and statements and testimonials, dotted 'I's and crossed 'Ts'. There would be no bureaucracy at his chocolate shop, *mais non*; as long as he listened to his wife, he expected they would be just fine.

The red wine he'd ordered in the dark and small Library Bar on the main floor of the Royal York Hotel had been half decent, he had to admit, but it still did not compare to the wines of home. He could not be certain if this was a question of quality, which he doubted, or more a question of setting—*les environs.* This was the *je ne sais quoi* of French cuisine, the small miracles of fresh and warm baguettes brought home under your arm at the end of a long day, strong cheeses and red wines partaken of in the middle of the afternoon. He was sure this was the case, as the wine he had ordered had actually been French, so go figure. It just didn't taste the same over here. Not to mention the fact that the waiters didn't know wines from their assholes, even though they pretended to know the difference between a *syrah*—or Shiraz, as the Americans called it in their sensitivity to corporate branding—grown in the scrublands of middle California or in the Rhone Valley of France.

Maxime followed the white Corolla. And the white Corolla followed the Subaru driven by Bojan Kordic. There were two targets that he was aware of: Bojan Kordic and Goran Mitovik. There was no police science to his choosing to begin with a stakeout of Bojan Kordic. It was simply flipping a coin. But Maxime had been a cop long enough to appreciate that strange mix of luck and hunch and a little nudge from the cosmos. He had been sitting slumped down in the seat of the car for just under two hours when his choice to begin with Bojan Kordic had so quickly brought about a promising lead. While there was no way he could be certain at this point that the man in the Corolla was in fact one of the Colonel's operatives—perhaps it was a creditor or a jealous husband or a disgruntled former employee—the odds were heavily in his favour.

That Bojan Kordic had perhaps only hours left to live worried Maxime not at all. It was not his concern, not his place to intervene in the fate of this man. These events had been set in motion years before. His interest was solely in tracking the man in the white Corolla, who would eventually—hopefully—lead him to the man he had travelled across the ocean to find. It was all about working your way up the chain one link at a time.

*   *   *

Kadro followed the Subaru down the DVP, across midtown, then southward to Spadina at Queen. The so-called Fashion District was home to the city's largest selection of garment and fashion accessory producers, custom bridal shops, fabric and leather and fur outlets. Many of the producers and boutiques were housed in renovated former warehouses.

Bojan Kordic pulled into the lot behind his factory, a four-storey brick warehouse with the words "Garbo Garments" painted neatly in black lettering on the bricks above the front entrance. The parking lot was big enough for forty cars, four rows of ten. Today there were only half a dozen cars, and it made the place look all the emptier. Bojan got out and started for the back doors, after a few steps sounding his car alarm with a click of his key fob. Kad pulled in and stopped so that his car was still concealed by the side of the building, not yet visible in the parking lot. As Bojan unlocked and slipped inside the rear double doors, Kad eased back out of the lane onto Spadina. There would be fully functioning video surveillance cameras to catch a one-eighty field of view, of that he was certain.

*　*　*

Maxime slowed down along Spadina just in time to catch the white Corolla backing up the laneway between two warehouses. Maxime was in the flow of traffic and unable to stop, but he glanced over his shoulder and watched as the Corolla pulled out and found a parking spot along the street. He went two blocks farther and did the same. He sat in the car for a moment with his notepad, marking the times and locations, the license plate of the Corolla. He opened his attaché case, which contained his Walther P38 sidearm locked within a smaller case, his files on the two known targets—Kordic and Mitovik—as well as a much thicker file on the operations and known associates of The Colonel. He moved these aside and found the slim black case that contained his GPS tracking device and the handheld receiver that looked like a cellular phone.

While the global positioning system technology had been tested and toyed with by the U.S. government since the late 1970s, it was not until the 1990s that the technology was made available for non-militaristic purposes. With each generation, the technology improved, allowing users to draw an ever closer bead on the exact latitude, longitude, altitude and time of a tracked object. Or, in the case of Maxime, the subjects he followed. The first GPS tracker he had employed during his undercover days following the murky arms and drugs dealers was not provided or even authorized for use by the police force. He had purchased it on his own, seeing this as the future in terms of surveillance tools. The model he had with him now would allow him to trace a subject to within roughly half a block. One day in the not too distant future, he believed the technology would be refined to the point where the subject's exact and precise location would be known to within an eyelash. Good for dropping bombs and finding errant husbands.

Maxime got out of the car, and with his hands tucked inside the pockets of his black leather jacket, he moved down the sidewalk towards the white Corolla. It was a beautiful late summer day, clear sky and warm. In fact, Maxime felt a little conspicuous in his leather jacket. He had come to the country prepared for the worst, all these stories you heard about Canada. Ice floes and Eskimos. He felt foolish now, for he had left his short-sleeved shirts at home. He had even purchased a new black wool toque, which was packed in his bags at the hotel. As he walked towards the Corolla, his mind drifted to his wife and his unborn child, and he thought: *If it's a boy, then, yes, it will be Gabriel. After the angel.*

TWENTY

McKelvey was buttering a toasted slice of Wonderbread—the last piece of bread in the cupboard—when the phone rang. He grabbed the receiver and, on instinct, barked: "McKelvey."

"Oh, I'm sorry," the male caller said. "I must have the wrong number."

McKelvey's mind clicked. "Wait," he said. "Who are you looking for?"

"Leyden, Dick Leyden," the caller said.

"You've got him," McKelvey said. "Sorry, I'm just answering my friend's line. How can I help you?"

"It's Peter Dawson calling. I'm the executive director of Bridges. I got a message from one of my volunteers that you stopped by and had some urgent business."

"I appreciate you calling back so quickly. I'm working on a case that involves a woman named Donia Kruzik. Does that name ring a bell?"

"Perhaps. I think so, yes," Dawson said. "Yes, I remember her. She came to Canada about a year ago. Is she in some kind of trouble?"

McKelvey glanced at his watch. It was closing on noon. After Hattie had left for work, he had drifted off again, his body and mind exhausted.

"Listen, if you've got the time, I'd like to buy you lunch and ask you a few questions. I can't really talk about it over the phone."

"I'm not sure how I can help. Much of the information we collect is protected by privacy laws, you understand."

"I understand," McKelvey said. "Even some background on the centre and what you do would be helpful."

McKelvey hoped the man's dedication to his work, as the volunteer had suggested, would be sufficient motivation to get him out on the long weekend.

"I could do that, I guess," Dawson said. "I'm heading down to the Eaton Centre to do a little shopping this afternoon. I could make time for a coffee."

"Just name the place," McKelvey said.

He hung up and turned back to his piece of toast. It was cold now. It looked utterly pathetic sitting there on the kitchen counter, a pad of unmelted butter at its centre. He couldn't eat now anyway. His body thrummed with the surge of energy that came with each new possibility, each tiny crack that might bleed a little light. He took the piece of toast and tossed it in the garbage on his way to the bedroom to throw on a shirt.

*   *   *

McKelvey removed his black sports coat and hooked it over his shoulder with his forefinger. He stopped walking long enough to light a cigarette, his first of the day, and he smiled as he remembered Hattie's joke about the cigarette after sex. It was too bad about the two of them, he thought. He knew that she wanted him to want her all the way, to live with her without concern for titles or legalities. They had tried it for awhile, it was true, this idea of modern co-habitation. But the thing was, he was getting old. And it was getting too hard to fake, this endless energy, this enthusiasm for new things, new foods, whatever.

That was the cold, hard truth, and it made him think of the last time he had seen his father. McKelvey's mother had died a few months earlier, and McKelvey had gone up north to see if his father was planning to sell the house and move into a senior's home. Of course he knew the answer to that question before he even got behind the wheel of the car to make the eight-hour drive. Caroline had said it was what any good son should do, so he had done it. Images of the old man sitting at the cluttered kitchen table, dust dancing in the sunlight streaming through the window, bony cigarette-stained fingers curled around a half bottle of beer, bits of the label peeled off. The silver hair on top of the old man's head was tinted with yellow, and it was uncombed, his undershirt was dirty, and his muscles, which had once been toned and tight as snakeskin, were slack and soft as baby's fat. McKelvey remembered feeling absolutely staggered by the sudden advance of years in his dad, this shovel in the face. He just stood there, couldn't say a word. There was something terrifying about realizing the truth of mortality.

Now he smoked and walked. The morning chill had burned away beneath a brilliant sun, and now, at noon, the day was fully in bloom—perhaps even a record temperature for this time of year. He walked the few blocks up Yonge to Dundas, the hub of the city. If New York had Times Square, then Toronto had Yonge-Dundas. It sat at the crux of what was probably the country's busiest intersection, right across from the Eaton Centre, which was without argument the country's busiest shopping centre. The five-storey mall drew more than fifty million visitors each year.

The public square was right now under construction as part of a massive urban redevelopment plan to return the area to its former glory as a focal point for open-air concerts, exhibits, receptions, community celebrations. The winning bid for the redevelopment included plans for a large open court comprised of granite slabs, twenty fountains, water and lighting effects, a canopy shelter. While McKelvey's first reaction to news of the upscale redesign was one of trepidation—who wanted some goggle-eyed, sandal-wearing architect to determine the course of the city's very heart, after all—but now, as he passed by the work site, he figured it deserved some benefit of the doubt.

The Eaton Centre had just opened its doors for the holiday weekend crowd, and the place was already filling with tourists and locals both, employees and cleaning staff, those using the centre as a cut-through between Dundas and Queen Streets. McKelvey took the escalator down to the food court level. He was immediately assailed by the strange perfume of sickly sweet cinnamon buns mixed with the fecund scents of freshly brewed coffee, cheesy pizza, pretzels, buttery popcorn, deep fried fish. It was no wonder young people were getting so fat. He saw teenagers hanging around the doors to the mall, pot-bellied and stoop-shouldered as though they were in their late sixties, for Chrissake, stumbling around with gout from a lack of vegetables and fruit. They thought poutine was one of the seven food groups.

He and Dawson had arranged to meet at the Starbucks Coffee island just past the water fountain at the mouth to the south food court. Before McKelvey could tell him that he had his picture from the annual report, Peter Dawson had provided the helpful piece of information that he was "tall and skinny and will be wearing a plaid British wool driving cap". McKelvey joined the queue for coffee and again took note of the number of young teens buying these silo-sized concoctions of froth and whipped cream and drizzled chocolate with a fucking cherry on top.

"Medium coffee, please," he said to the young server.

"Would you like to try our new pumpkin spiced latte?"

"Pumpkin *what*?"

The server must have seen the look that Hattie was always telling him about, this scrunch-faced, slit-eyed squint that came so naturally in moments of confusion or frustration or condemnation. *When you do that to your face,* Hattie had told him, *it makes people literally want to run the other way.*

"For Halloween," the girl shrugged. "Never mind. Mild or bold for your coffee?"

"Bold, I guess."

With the complicated transaction complete, McKelvey went to the condiment stand and stirred in a shot of cream. It was eighteen per cent, thick as yogurt, but the doctors were nowhere in sight. As he turned, he caught view of a man standing off to the side. Peter Dawson. And he wasn't kidding, McKelvey thought. The man was six-six, a hundred and fifty pounds, this plaid wool cap on top of his head as though to guard against the weather patterns at that altitude.

"Mr. Dawson," McKelvey said and went over.

"Mr. Leyden, I presume," Dawson said, and they shook hands.

The joke had gone far enough. McKelvey was wishing he hadn't kept on with the play on Leyden's name. Too late now to turn back without drawing suspicion.

McKelvey said, "Can I buy you a coffee?"

"Sure," Dawson said. "I might try one of those new pumpkin lattes, actually."

McKelvey got in line again as Dawson went and got them a table in the food court. The same server came to the counter, She smiled at McKelvey.

"Pumpkin spiced latte," he said through gritted teeth.

"You changed your mind, that's great," she said, grabbing an empty cup and marking the order on the side with her grease pencil. "Room for whipped cream?"

"Of course," he said. "As much as you can fit."

McKelvey took the drink over to the table. Dawson thanked him, removed his cap and ran a hand over thin reddish-brown hair that was halfway gone. He leaned in and drew a mouthful of the whipped topping then licked his lips. There was no way, McKelvey thought, that a man could drink a drink like this without looking ridiculous.

"Thanks for taking a few minutes," McKelvey said.

Dawson nodded. "I hope you don't mind me asking, but can I see your business card? I mean, *if* you're an immigration lawyer."

If you're a lawyer. McKelvey saw that he needed to show a little goodwill in the domain of truth. That, or risk the man closing up entirely. He said, "I'll be honest with you, Peter. I'm a former police officer."

Dawson nodded as though he had come prepared for this information. "Then I'll be honest as well," he said. "When Pamela called me and gave me the message, well, I'm not twenty-two years old. I figured there was something else to it. I thought maybe it was taxes, some audit of our funders by CSIS. You know, in the wake of 9/11 and everything. So what are you doing exactly? What are you looking for at Bridges?"

"I have reason to believe Donia Kruzik was murdered. A friend of mine was seeing her. He was worried about her," McKelvey said. "She just stopped calling, disappeared. I went looking for her on behalf of my friend. She was gone, but someone was in her apartment. Things have become increasingly complex from that point on."

Dawson drank some of his latte and wiped his mouth with a napkin. He was fair-skinned, lightly freckled, and his cheeks

202

were a little scarred from teenage acne. He seemed innocuous. McKelvey saw the man at the front of a Rotary Club meeting with a name tag taped to his suit coat.

"This is that case that's all over the news, isn't it? I mean, they haven't released the woman's name, but that's why you're here, right?"

McKelvey nodded. He took a sip of his coffee and watched the man's eyes for signs of where this was headed. The man had no obligation to sit here and talk to a civilian.

"I should be speaking to the police, in that case," Dawson said, as though reading his mind. "I mean, whoever is handling the investigation. To keep this above board."

"I can put them in touch with you," McKelvey said. "I'm just hoping for some basic background information. My friend is in a real jam here. Time is of the essence."

"I don't know much about that particular client, Mr. Leyden. What I can tell you is that Davis Chapman was her intake volunteer. And he was our most senior volunteer, in terms of career and background experience. Most of our team members are third or fourth-year university students."

"You said 'was'. He no longer volunteers?"

Dawson sat back. He shrugged and his head tilted to the left. His body language told McKelvey to keep picking. The man wanted to let go of something. "He works for the government. He travels a lot," Dawson said.

"How long did he work with you at Bridges?"

"Off and on since late '97, I guess, somewhere around there. We were just getting up and running, we barely had office space. He was eager to get in and help. And he brought a lot to the organization, to be quite honest. I would say we are where we are today because of a lot of the work Davis did. He got us

203

several grants through the government. He was a whiz at cutting through red tape. The money started to flow our way."

McKelvey finished the last of the coffee then picked a few grounds off the end of his tongue. It beat wiping whipped cream off the end of his nose.

"Why was he so dedicated, do you figure?" McKelvey asked. "What was his connection to the cause?"

"Davis is a very private person," Dawson said, his tone making it clear the character trait was not necessarily a good thing in this regard. "I do know that he worked in foreign affairs in some capacity and that he spent a couple of years in the former Yugoslavia during the war. Actually, he lost an eye over there."

The pirate from the photo, McKelvey thought. *Okay. We're heading somewhere together now.* It was his job to keep Dawson talking. As long as people kept talking, there was a chance you'd discover something new. The trick was in not losing the momentum. It was the fine balance every cop walked when they sat across from a subject—to keep the thoughts rolling, the words coming, everything and anything, while not tipping off the fact that they had just heard something worth writing down. McKelvey played it that way right now. He nodded and turned the cup in his hand.

"Let me ask you," he said, "is covering rent among the services that Bridges supplies its clients?"

His experience of sitting across from bank robbers and hold-up artists, these guys who had all the balls in the world but no brains, had taught him to read body language as though it were his native tongue: the drop of a shoulder, the biting of a nail. He knew at the very core of himself that Dawson was hiding something.

"We had a parting of the ways," Dawson said.

"Over financial matters?"

Dawson looked away. He chewed it. Finally he sighed and

204

turned back. "That was a big part of it, yes. He went way beyond our mandate in terms of providing financial support to a client."

"Donia Kruzik."

"That's right. Including her rent. He said it was a deductible for us, and that we couldn't just sit back and not help these people coming over here with nothing. Some things went unaccounted for, and records weren't kept. We're probably at risk of losing our charitable status. That's all I'm going to say."

"I appreciate you taking the time," McKelvey said. "It's important."

Dawson drank the last of the latte, and McKelvey got a whiff of the pumpkin smell. It wasn't bad, actually. Like pumpkin pie.

*　　*　　*

McKelvey walked past the water fountain on his way back to the escalators. He spotted Leyden right away, sitting there on the cement lip of the fountain with a copy of the *Toronto Sun* held up, some character in a John Le Carre book. McKelvey stopped and drew a deep breath. He swallowed the urge to walk up and slug the guy in the face. He turned and smiled instead.

"Go for a walk?" McKelvey said.

Leyden stood up, folded the paper under his arm and waved for McKelvey to take the lead. McKelvey walked back over to the escalators. Dawson passed them on his way down the mall, and he gave McKelvey a look, perhaps wondering who this second person was.

"A partial print on the doorknob at Donia's apartment," Leyden said, drawing the words out slowly, as though he were trying to make sense of them.

They went up the escalator. McKelvey watched the faces of

the people coming down the escalator on the other side. He wondered briefly what sorts of thoughts were on their minds, wished for a moment he could slip into their stream and simply move through the mall without Fielding's predicament weighing down on him, this logjam of life.

"Whatever her real name is," Leyden said. "Let's call her Donia for now, just to keep things straight. I had Kennedy get the geeks to run your prints. Just a gut feeling. And guess what?"

They got off at the main level. The daylight out on Yonge Street flooded the entranceway. McKelvey stopped short of the doors.

"Go ahead," McKelvey said. "The suspense is killing me."

"A partial print of Charles McKelvey," Leyden said.

"How partial?"

Leyden smiled a little. "Pretty partial," he said. "But still. Seems like a good chance you were there after all, at her apartment. But that's not what you told me and Kennedy the other day. You said you'd never met her before."

McKelvey needed to get away from Leyden so he could track down this Davis Chapman. From there to Donia and the guy who had attacked him in her apartment. And maybe, just maybe, right to Tim Fielding. It was the only connection he had. The "what" was still as obscure to him as the day Fielding had called. But he had a hold on the end of something, and he planned to pull himself to the top.

"I'm starting to think maybe you were right when you said there was no way Tim Fielding could have killed the woman," Leyden said. "Because maybe *you* did it. You know what I mean? You're found in the apartment with the dead body. Your prints are found on her doorknob when you say you never met her."

"A partial print," McKelvey corrected. "Pretty partial."

"You know what, McKelvey? I don't like you. It's true. I think you lasted on the force as long as you did through a combination of luck and balls. But your luck seems to be running out."

"Are you saying you're going to arrest me?" McKelvey said.

Leyden looked at him. They were eye to eye, identical in height. But where Leyden was lanky, McKelvey owned the thick upper torso and broad shoulders of his ancestors, bricklayers and miners.

"Might be getting close to that day. Right now I'm just saying things are starting to match up in a way that makes a man stop and wonder."

"I appreciate the professional courtesy. I wish I could help you," McKelvey said, "but I've got some errands to run."

Leyden watched him walk into the sunlight and slip out the main doors.

TWENTY-ONE

Kadro was parked across from the condo building on the edge of the Distillery District when the breaking news came over the radio:

A 51-year-old has been found dead in Toronto's fashion district. A police source says afternoon cleaning staff at a garment warehouse on Spadina Street discovered the body of the business owner in his office late this afternoon. Forensic and homicide investigators are at the scene. The victim's identity has not been released pending notification of next of kin ...

Kad had run into the twenty-four hour Metro up the street and bought a handful of scratch tickets. It put his mind in neutral, this getting lost in that slow reveal of what lay behind the sheen of foil, and he supposed this was actually the first step towards compulsion. This was probably how it happened. He knew plenty of veterans from the war, these men his own age who shot dope in the bathroom of the garage where they worked, drank vodka with their breakfast toast, stumbling through anesthetized. Or else they were so addicted to the adrenalin surge that had come with every firefight—this knowledge that bullets were aimed at your head, coming so close they sounded like the zing of angry hornets—they forever sought the confrontation and the danger as though cursed with an unnameable affliction. They fell to organized crime, they ran women and guns and robbed and killed. It was as though once tasted, the palate forever craved the distinct flavour of death's sharp edge. Post-war life had been a letdown. They were all still struggling to make ends meet, still meeting in the pubs to talk about the politics and the graft and the broken promises. *At least in war,* Kad thought, *we knew we were alive.*

This operation with Bojan Kordic had been seamless. In and out. The look in Bojan's eyes. That tiny and momentous moment. Kad would take it with him to his own grave. And what Was it there in those eyes, this mixture of fear and acceptance? as though the man had known this day would eventually come, as though some part of him had been expecting it. And yet still he had begged for a reprieve. This was the open door through which Kadro dragged the man backwards through time. To that summer day, to those fields outside Kad's village, to the windswept sky and the sounds of artillery in the distant hills.

"My father," he had told the man behind the desk in his native tongue. "He was in his sixties. And when you executed him, my mother's health suffered. I was off in the hills fighting, and she was left to die alone. July 1995. You remember?"

Bojan did not say anything. His eyes spoke for him. He sat there without moving, a pen held between his fingers, the blood gone from his face.

"That day has travelled years and miles to catch up with you."

"Please," Bojan said. "I have a daughter…"

"This," Kad had whispered—the final words this man would hear in this life—"is in the name of the dead."

Kad got through four of the scratch tickets now—three "try-agains" and one "free ticket"—before he set the them aside and used the cellphone Turner had given him to call the home number written on the business card the policeman had left behind with the superintendent. *McKelvey.* There was no answer. The line kicked into a message on an answering machine. No name disclosed, simply a recitation of the number the caller had reached. Kad hung up and looked out the windshield across the street.

*   *   *

McKelvey darted across Yonge Street and disappeared down the stairs into the subway at the under-construction Dundas Square. He was just in time to catch a train. He slipped into the car, held onto a pole, then got off at the first stop, Queen. All to shake Leyden, though he doubted the man had followed him this time. He came up into the air of the day, darted through the slow-moving traffic on Yonge, then headed south toward Front Street.

He went down the stairs and into the pub in the Flatiron Building at the split axis of Front, King and Wellington. There was a payphone against the wall near the washrooms. He fed the machine with change and waited.

"Hattie," she answered.

"I've got a name," he said.

She said, "Hello to you, too."

"Sorry. I'm in a hurry."

"Well, Jesus, why didn't you say?"

"Davis Chapman," he said. "Apparently he works for the government in some capacity. If there's any way you can run it. I don't know, maybe you need Kennedy in on this. Christ, I just need some space to figure this out."

"Don't you think it's time to turn this over to Kennedy and Leyden?" she said. "You know, make it official? Playing the devil's advocate here, what happens if Tim isn't found alive? You won't look good in all of this, Charlie. You've obstructed justice."

Obstructed justice. He turned the words over like a bad taste.

He wasn't obstructing anything; he was looking after a friend. It was too late to come around now and spout off some breathless admission of the facts thus far. Fuck, he'd be sitting in a cell at Metro West Detention Centre before you could say *obstructed justice*. And the time it would take Leyden and Kennedy to catch up on the facts, well, Fielding would be dead.

"I find this Davis Chapman guy, I can maybe figure out who this Donia Kruzik woman was, where she came from. What was she doing here? He's the closest link I've found."

"What's Davis Chapman's connection?"

"He was Donia Kruzik's liaison through an immigrant support centre. He paid her rent through the centre, covered a bunch of her expenses that went against policy. I met with the director, he said he's half expecting an audit to come down on him."

"So this Chapman guy had personal motives where Donia was concerned. Do you think Donia was brought over here as a sex worker?" Hattie said. "Maybe Chapman was using the support centre as his base for recruiting girls then covering their expenses behind the guise of a non-profit. Jesus, that'd be a pretty good idea."

"I don't know," McKelvey said. "It could be anything. But he's the direct link to Donia Kruzik. My gut says he's involved in her murder and Tim's framing. As for motive, I'm coming up empty at this point."

Hattie said, "Well, your gut has never been wrong before, has it?"

"Once or twice," McKelvey said. "But not this time."

"I'll see if I can tack his name onto some other stuff we're looking at, slip it through," she said. "But I'm also going to share any details of relevance with Kennedy. That's my deal, and it ain't open to negotiation."

"As long as you call me first," he said.

*   *   *

Maxime had lost track of the white Corolla after it had pulled away from the factory, but now he came back to it again by driving with one eye on these foreign roads and one eye on the GPS receiver. It wasn't the traffic here—for anyone who had driven a car in downtown Paris was forever desensitized to the concept of snarl and chaos—but the fact that he was still adjusting to this orderly ebb and flow of things. He wanted to honk his horn and steer around those waiting to make a turn, do what was necessary to move things along. Canadians were polite to the point of frustration. The triangulation of the GPS brought him to within a block of the vehicle. He slowed and passed along Front Street, and sure enough, there it was, parked at the curb. The vehicle was empty. Maxime found a spot on the other side of the road, having pulled a quick u-turn in front of this old building that looked like the Flatirons in those iconic pictures of New York City.

He watched the Corolla from across the street for a few minutes, and the area around the vehicle. His mind clicked through the links in this long chain. Bojan Kordic, whom Maxime had been sent to collect with his red notice, was now dead—of that he was certain. How unfortunate that he had been too late to both save the man and bring him to justice in a proper court of higher authority—this was the line he was preparing for his eventual final report on the matter. In truth, Maxime felt Bojan Kordic had received precisely what he deserved. He would focus now on the second ticket for one Goran Mitovik. He would need to make contact with the local authorities before long and have them put some eyes on Mitovik's house. But this tailing of the Corolla, or more to the point, of the man driving the Corolla, was of paramount importance. It was through this link that Maxime was certain he would make the connection to the Colonel.

The jet lag was settling in now. His body had moved beyond the initial stage of exhilaration, adrenalin-induced alertness—those first glorious hours in which you were as close to full-blown mania as was possible without drugs—and he now put his head back against the headrest, and he yawned until a tear squeezed from the corner of his eye and rolled down his cheek. A coffee, that's what he needed. But not a cheap North American coffee from a drive-thru, weak as piss and ruined with excess cream and sugar. An espresso, dark, strong and deadly effective. *Ah, je m'ennuie de la France!*

TWENTY-TWO

Tim Fielding's body—like that of all humans—was comprised of sixty to seventy per cent water. It was water that was the common denominator of all major bodily functions: from absorption at the cellular level, to circulation via the turgidity of veins and arteries, to digestion and excretion—most everything depended on water to make it work. Tied to a post and blindfolded, Tim Fielding was slowly dying from dehydration.

After eight hours, his head began to pound, and his lips grew dry. He managed, for a few hours at least, to manufacture sufficient saliva by turning and rolling his tongue, and this helped keep his mouth moist. He even took small, but not insignificant pleasure in swallowing tiny sips of this self-produced saliva, his mind running through favorite beverages like some sort of desert island game—Dr. Pepper, how he'd discovered its sickly sweetness as a child while on holiday in Florida, or no, how about Canadian Dry Ginger Ale, truly "the champagne of gingers ales", or what about that rare Rusty Nail he allowed himself on special occasions, the rich marriage of single-malt scotch and a shot of honey-sweet Drambuie…

At the twelve-hour mark, even this self-generated hydration became nearly impossible, and Tim realized his best chances were in conservation. He tried to sleep with his chin on his chest, and when he could not sleep, he breathed through his nose rather than his mouth to reduce the drying effect.

At eighteen hours, his mind began to play tricks. His thinking process was muddled. He woke with a start several times, his world plunged to darkness, shivering and likely feverish, and he couldn't produce tears any more.

The dirt-throat thirst was nothing compared to the excruciating pain, then the numbness that spread from his bound arms to his shoulder blades. There was the indignity, too, in those first confused hours. Sitting there on the cold concrete floor, he had tried to hold it at first. The cramps had made it impossible. He sat there in the dampness of his own making, and he wondered what he had done in this or a previous life to deserve such a fate.

The things a man thought about in these long hours. The small worries that had occupied his life, the guilt or the hard feelings, the grudges held, the hours lost sitting waiting at red lights. It occurred to him he had never been to Las Vegas. He wasn't a gambler, but still. He had never been to New York City, either, for that matter. Wasn't there something inherently wrong with a man who approached his fortieth year without ever having been to a strip joint? He had never accepted that rolled joint at a house party, never really thrown caution to the wind for a night. Perhaps it was his parents, teachers both, and their moral and ethical guidelines, but he suspected it was something else. It was *him. It's me,* he thought. *I've been afraid my entire life. And not just since the death of my wife. No, it was long before that. Since I was a boy. Always content to take a back seat and watch the world roll by.*

Why, he wondered? What was there to be afraid of?

Especially now, Tim, now that you are tied and blindfolded. Now that you are going to die…

TWENTY-THREE

One down, one to go. This is what Kad was thinking as he walked along the street with the sunshine on his face. He wished the woman were alive to see the look in Bojan Kordic's eyes in that final moment. *Donia.* She had played her role, however, and it had helped extricate them from the mess of this school teacher and his meddling police officer friend. *Donia.* Yes, he tried now to recall her real name, her birth name, but it was gone. He stopped walking. He stood there on the sidewalk and tried to remember his own name. It was there, yes, but it did not come to mind immediately. It required a moment to pause and reach back.

He resumed walking. He had employed Turner's assistance in tracing the home number on the police officer's business card. It was right here, just up ahead. Unit number four. He moved a hand to the inside jacket and felt for the case with the syringe. At his back, tucked into his pants, was the handgun. And lastly, snug alongside his ankle and held in place with his sock and a Velcro strap, was the four-inch jackknife. He felt he was ready for anything.

He walked past the condo building and stopped a few doors down. He turned, and with his hands in his pockets, leaned against the bricks, looking back towards the building, just to get his eyes on it. It was no different from when he and the boys had cased a particular building in a nameless town, having on good authority that either Serb troops or paramilitaries were housed there. You wanted to mitigate the risk to the greatest extent possible. Note all possible exits, areas where a lookout or a scout might hide. To determine clear lines of fire that any sniper worth his salt would have previously mapped out. Operations were two thirds planning, one third action. The devil, as they said, was always in the details.

Satisfied and ready, he took a couple of deep breaths and walked back to the condo. He opened the front door and stepped inside the small foyer. It smelled fresh, the scent of flowers, as though they sprayed the place with potpourri fragrance. There was a bank of chrome-plated mailboxes to the left. The names were etched onto the front of the mailboxes, giving a sense of expected permanency. Kad scanned the names. The last one.

McKELVEY C—#4

The second inner door, he noted to his surprise and good fortune, was propped open with a stone. His old trick. The oldest trick of thieves in the night. He marvelled at the laziness. He smiled and opened the door, moving the stone aside with the toe of his shoe.

He climbed the stairs.

*   *   *

McKelvey was deep in thought as he made his way east on Front Street. He looked over his shoulder, half expecting to see Leyden skulking back there. What this thing *was,* he was unsure—it was too convoluted to make sense of just yet—but whether love triangle, sex traffic, organized crime, it hardly mattered. He had to get to Fielding before the cops found him and he was charged with murder. It seemed likely, given the scant facts and his professional experience with the human animal, that sex or drugs, or perhaps both, were at play here. It was quite possible, he surmised, that Fielding had simply fallen for the wrong woman.

217

Perhaps Hattie was right: Donia was a sex worker or a sex slave or otherwise "owned" by bad men with Eastern European accents. McKelvey knew half the strip joints around town were infused with a revolving bevy of women from Russia and Hungary and Croatia, these women working with so-called "entertainment visas". Fielding had unknowingly stumbled into this dark new world, and now the woman was dead and Fielding was either dead himself or being held.

Held *why*, though? There had been no ransom demand, no contact at all.

They're using Fielding as a red herring, he thought. Holding him somewhere long enough to give them time to wrap up their business and make a clean cut.

He stopped walking. It was possible. Every Metro cop was looking for Tim Fielding. It was a good plan. And, quite frankly, the only plan to which McKelvey could realistically prescribe. The alternative was not worth considering. In the alternative, Fielding was dead, had been dead two days now. In the alternative, McKelvey was responsible for his young friend's murder.

He continued on. As he approached the condo, he caught sight of the old Italian from the first floor unit. Giuseppe was hobbling up the street with a plastic bag that McKelvey was certain contained links of Italian sausage infused with garlic. Giuseppe had explained in one of their brief and rare conversations how he had survived the war on bread, cheese, and a little bit of sausage, so why tempt the fates by changing his diet now? The only new element Giuseppe had added to his regimen was a single daily prune taken to coax some consistency from his weathered bowels. The St. Lawrence Market was closed, so the old man had gone across to the twenty-four hour grocery. McKelvey waited, holding the door open.

"You should get delivery," McKelvey said.

Giuseppe squinted, and his face folded in against a sea of deep wrinkles. His hair was bone white and swept back, and his eyebrows were unruly, thick as jungle caterpillars.

"Those l'il buggers always holding their hand out for a *teepa*," he said, and because his accent was so thick, McKelvey didn't get the gist right away. "I give them a *teepa* for free. I say, cut your goddamned hair and smarten you up."

McKelvey held the door while Giuseppe grunted and lifted his ruined legs across the threshold. The old man went to pull the second door, and he grunted again when it did not give as expected.

"Ah, Jesus, the stone is gone," Giuseppe said.

"I've got my key," McKelvey said, and he moved in to unlock the door. "You know, Giuseppe, I'm not one to lecture, but…"

"Listen to me, young man," Giuseppe said, moving through the doorway, "someone wanna come in and kill or rob you, they gonna find a way, believe me. Locks, they for the honest people. And not many of those left, okay?"

* * *

Kad stood inside the apartment. It was still and quiet. He slipped the locksmith's tool back inside his wallet and looked around. It was spare, bordering on Spartan. Just the basics—something to sit on, somewhere to hang a coat. He thought perhaps he understood this man, the appreciation for simplicity, and he felt that they were really not so different. He wondered if this man, like himself, felt at odds within the context of these modern times. Kad often thought he should have been born in an earlier century. He took a few steps, and went into the kitchen, opened the fridge door and stared at the emptiness. Spare parts, leftovers, but nothing to make a meal. He closed the fridge and looked at the pictures that were stuck to the door with magnets from takeout pizza and Chinese food places. One photo featured a little girl with dark curly hair. There was another of a woman who appeared to be in her early twenties, olive-skinned, silky hair dark as coal. There was a page torn from a notebook posted on the door. It looked to be a grocery list which the occupant obviously had yet to fulfill. He looked in a few cupboards. They were stacked with plates and mugs, and there was an uncracked bottle of Jameson's Irish Whiskey next to a half empty bottle of red wine.

It did not matter to Kad that the occupant was apparently a police officer. It mattered not at all. He was tainted by the work of the police back home, where bribery and family connections turned the wheels. There was the heavy influence of the Russian mob. No institution, no senior official, was to be trusted without risk. Most of the cops were former soldiers. These men no longer believed in the myth of law, justice, truth and consequences. After all they had seen and done, they were beyond the notion of working within a righteous cause. It was every man for himself.

He checked all the rooms and came back to the kitchen. On top of the microwave he found a notebook from which a page had been torn in order to make the grocery list. He thought this was the best way to do it. This would prove to the policeman both the seriousness of the requirement for discretion, and also the ability for Kadro to come and go from his life as he pleased. There was the element of violation here, slipping in and slipping out.

He found a pen and sat down to write.

*   *   *

McKelvey took a few steps towards the staircase, but Giuseppe stuck his head out his door and said, "Come in, justa one minute. I show you something…"

McKelvey went to say that he didn't have the time, but he looked at the man's weathered face, those eyebrows shrugging above rheumy eyes, and for an instant he saw a vision of himself at that age. Alone. He stepped inside Giuseppe's apartment and was immediately assailed by the strange perfume of sausage, garlic and something else entirely—a strong scent of sharp fruit and yeast. He sniffed again and knew what it was. Fermenting grapes. The old bugger was making homemade wine.

"You smell that?" Giuseppe said, and finally he smiled. McKelvey saw what the man must have looked like when he was younger. Handsome and steely-eyed back in the war.

"Why am I not surprised," McKelvey said.

"I have bottle just for you," Giuseppe said, and he hobbled over to the kitchen. He bent down with some difficulty and opened the cupboards beside the dishwasher. "Old Giambi family recipe. We work the soil in them hills of Umbra, see, making the *Torgiano*." He set a plain brown bottle on the counter and pulled himself back up. "Till the fucking Tedeschi came, that is. And then we fight in them same hills, through the vineyards, the same boys who picked grapes with their grandfathers."

Giuseppe got a faraway look in his eyes, and McKelvey wondered what images played across the back of his eyelids at night. If he himself startled awake at times, shivering through the memory of some violent encounter from his patrol car days, visions of suicides and stabbing victims, he couldn't imagine the variety of scenes that were scorched into the veteran's brain screen for continual replay.

"You take," Giuseppe said and held out the bottle. "You're a good boy."

221

McKelvey accepted the bottle. "I'll save it for a special occasion," he said.

"Today is special occasion," Giuseppe said. He straightened his back with a long, deep breath. "You above ground, ain't you?"

McKelvey laughed and patted the old man on the shoulder. He had turned to the door and had his hand on the doorknob when Giuseppe said, "I have a *teepa* for you, my friend. If you don't mind."

McKelvey turned back. He said, "Shoot."

"That woman, the redhead. She's too young for you. You gotta marry her, or, you know, set her free like a little bird. One day soon you be old like me... "

McKelvey was taken aback, not just by the honesty of the remark, but the fact that the old man who hardly ever left his apartment was aware of the particulars of his personal life. The old Italian was just full of surprises.

"Thanks for the wine," McKelvey said.

* * *

McKelvey was three steps from the second floor landing when he looked up and saw a man coming down. McKelvey stopped there on the stairs. Their eyes met and locked. McKelvey's mind clicked. It came back to him in a flood of images.

The face, the shaved head, the build, the jacket...

Kad stopped, too, but just for an instant. He used the advantage of gravity and momentum. He rushed forward, using his shoulder like a ram as he came down the stairs. McKelvey was pushed to the side, but he didn't go down, and he turned and gave chase.

Kad jumped the last few stairs to the first floor landing,

222

grabbing the banister pole with a hand and, like a gymnast, using it to speed his turn on the pivot. He landed with heavy boots in the foyer, pushing the door with both hands.

McKelvey came around the landing and caught sight of the man's jeans and boots halfway through the inner door. He got to the middle of the stairs and, looking to avoid a race down Front Street—a race he certainly had no hope in hell of winning—he gripped the wine bottle like a football and cocked his arm. But the man was already out the doors, and McKelvey had no choice but to push his way through.

The city closed in on McKelvey, cars and trucks and taxis and pedestrians. Sounds shut out as he looked left and right, finally catching sight of the man running across Front towards the Market Square near the grocery store. A car honked and screeched to a stop as McKelvey dashed across the street, eyes on his target. He would not slip away this time, he would not leave McKelvey sprawled on his back in an empty apartment…

The man jumped into a parked car. *White.*

McKelvey squinted as he ran flat out, trying to get the make and model, the license plate. He was going to die out here, his heart and lungs and guts and everything else ready to burst open.

The car started and the driver backed up a few inches to make his escape from the curb. He jockeyed enough space between the other parked vehicles and was set to pull away as McKelvey came within six feet of the driver's side. He gripped the bottle again and launched it with all of his strength. The bottle exploded against the window, which shattered, broke apart and crumbled in a thousand pieces. The driver had a hand up to protect his face, but they made eye contact again as he hit the gas and tore away.

Next time, fucker, McKelvey thought. *Next time…*

He was left standing there on the street with this taste of acrid bile rising in his throat, then sure enough, he stumbled on a wave of dizziness and set his hand on a parked car to steady himself. Pins and needles, blurry vision. He bent and put his hands on his knees, sucking air, then he felt his stomach clench, and he turned and spat a mouthful of watery vomit beside the curb. He wiped his mouth, feeling suddenly better, and straightened up. People on both sides of the street had stopped to watch the scene unfold.

"Mommy, is that man drunk?" McKelvey heard a little boy's voice over his shoulder. The mother said something in a hushed tone and whisked the child away.

Not drunk, he thought. Just ancient. He exhaled, squared his shoulders and walked back across the street to his condo.

*   *   *

Maxime sat in his rental car yawning, trying to stay awake. He watched as the two men came rushing from the building, darting through traffic like a couple of shoplifters. The wine bottle had been unexpected. Who was this second man, and what was his connection to all of this? Rather than follow the target in the white Corolla—he would rely on the embedded GPS later— Maxime wrote the details of the activity in his notebook then got out of the rental and stretched and yawned. He looked both ways, waited for a hole in the traffic, and walked across the street towards the condo building.

TWENTY-FOUR

The torn page was posted to the centre of McKelvey's fridge door with a magnet from a Chinese take-out place. The note was printed in large block letters, the careful writing of a child:

> McKelvey;
> Your friend is safe.
> I will call you tonight to arrange for you to see him.
> Do not involve the authorities. If you do, you will not
> see your friend again.
> Stay by the phone.

McKelvey's mind swirled as he collapsed into a chair at the kitchen table. His hands were shaking from the run across the street—he hadn't hoofed it like that in years, not since working patrol. As a dick on the Hold-Up Squad, he had left the chasing up to the foot cops who were young and looking for any excuse to expend some energy. The note shivered between his fingers. What was this, an upping of the ante in this game? And it *was* a game, wasn't it? Him against them. McKelvey against the clock. He sat there for a long time just thinking. Holding the note, reading and re-reading the instructions. How had this man made the connection, found his address? He scoured his mind. And then, like tongues fitting a slotted groove, it was there: the superintendent at Donia's building. McKelvey had given the man his business card. Hadn't Leyden said the man had died of a heart attack the next day? Jarko's Automotive, too. Burned to the ground. He'd been traced through his visits to these places, and these contacts had been erased in his wake. So he was no longer chasing a ghost in his search for Tim Fielding—the tables had been turned. He was now the hunted. They wanted McKelvey and Fielding in a room together.

He went to the phone and dialed Hattie's number. She answered on the fourth ring. The line was immediately filled with background sounds, voices and music.

"Hattie?" he said.

"Sorry," she said in a loud voice, and he heard her walking away from the sounds, trying to find a quieter spot. "We stopped in at this pub. Place is packed. Everybody's sucking the last few drops out of the long weekend."

He wanted to ask her about the "we" she was referring to, but he had no right. He pictured Anderson sitting there with his platinum hair and some fruity drink with a goddamned umbrella.

"Davis Chapman works for the government," Hattie said, reading his thoughts. "That's all I know. There's a level three security block on his ID. Must be a heavyweight of some sort."

"Does Detective Kennedy know about Chapman?" McKelvey asked. He held the note from his fridge and tried to think of a way to let her in on this. He had kept one too many cards against his chest, and now he was backed into a corner.

"What's to tell? The guy might as well not even exist in any system. He could be RCMP, CSIS, JTF2, anything."

"Peter Dawson, the executive director of the resource centre, he'd have Chapman's address on file," McKelvey said. "It might not be the correct address, but he must have something. Christ, even a phone number."

"So give Peter Dawson a call," she said, and McKelvey understood by her tone that he had managed to reach the end of Hattie's patience, perhaps her goodwill, likely even her trust or belief in him.

"Listen, Charlie, Kennedy gave me something about a half hour ago. I think he expects me to pass it on to you. Maybe he's hoping it means something, I don't know. But this is definitely on the down-low. The media has been blocked out on details. Leyden and Kennedy are working this murder in the fashion district now, on top of the Donia Kruzik case."

"What are you talking about?"

"You haven't seen the breaking news?"

Jesus, McKelvey thought. *I haven't had time to take a piss or eat a sandwich, let alone watch the news.*

"Victim was found this afternoon in his office. Guess he was in there doing some catch-up work while the place was closed. The dead man, Bojan Kordic, was Donia's boss. He ran the garment factory, which was her last known place of employment. It's hazy, but there's obviously some sort of connection forming here. Kennedy and Leyden are swamped right now, but I'd expect their attention to swing right back to you in the next twenty-four hours. I won't be able to help you when that happens."

McKelvey felt something give way within his core and drop to the bottom of his gut. He needed a white board and a marker, to start drawing the lines and the players back to a nucleus. The way they used to do it on the force. Not rocket science, just throwing everything up on the wall and standing back to see the full spectrum.

"What was the piece of information Kennedy wanted me to hear?"

"They found a note pinned to the dead guy's shirt," Hattie

said. "It said something along the lines of: 'My name is Bojan Kordic. I am guilty'. And then his signature. Question is, guilty of what?"

"Did he say if the note was typed or printed or anything?"

"Hand-written. Block letters," she said. "Like a kid trying too hard to be neat, his words exactly."

McKelvey looked down at the note in his hand. "What a fucking fiasco," he muttered.

"Sorry," she said, "it's so loud. What'd you say?"

"Forget it," he said.

"Hey, listen," Hattie said. "I'm out of this now, okay? I mean really out. I have my interviews for Homicide this week, Charlie. Talk to Kennedy, for God's sake. He's a good cop. Leyden too."

"Have a good time," he said and hung up.

He stared at the phone, willing it to ring. The doorbell sounded instead. It broke McKelvey's concentration, and he started. He walked quietly to the door and leaned in, squinting through the spyglass. He did not recognize the man who stood there looking up and down the hall, then down at his shoes as he waited. Could be anybody, McKelvey thought. But what were the chances? This thing he'd stepped into. He looked around. He wished he had a gun he could slip in his pants under his shirt. But that had been part of the agreement after the shootout with Duguay. A clear case of self-defense—Duguay had broken into his home armed with a .45 Browning automatic, after all— had been made somewhat complicated by the fact McKelvey defended himself with an unregistered .25 pistol he'd kept locked in his garage for more than a decade while a friend sorted out the licensing during a tumultuous divorce. Rather than charge a recently retired officer for defending himself against certain death at the hands of a biker, the cops and the crown had agreed to seal the affair on McKelvey's word that he would not own or operate a firearm for a period of one year. It seemed reasonable at the time.

He had no pistol, no means to defend himself, and it was a terrible feeling. His eyes darted around the room quickly, then settled on the kitchen. He took a serrated steak knife from the drawer, slipped it carefully into the back pocket of his pants then went and opened the door a few inches.

"Yes?" he said.

"Excuse me," the man said. "I am looking for Mr. Giambi?"

The man spoke with an accent, pronouncing the name *Gee-am-bee*. French perhaps, and fancy.

"First floor," McKelvey said.

"Ah yes," the man said, and smiled. "Please, excuse me."

McKelvey closed the door. He returned the steak knife and went back to the living room. He sat on the sofa and stared at the phone, thinking of Hattie and how she would end up working in Homicide, and he thought about old Giuseppe's remarks from out of the blue. *That woman, she's too young for you.* Was it really so out of the blue? Perhaps McKelvey was guilty once again, as Caroline had often charged him, of living his life with blinders on. He was using Hattie, her youth and energy to fend off the inevitable slow shuffle to the nursing home. He was certainly using and abusing her position on the force. But he thought perhaps it was mutual, that they were using each other. McKelvey had not pressured her to live with him, though there were times when he certainly would have preferred it. As long as she was considered to be "with" McKelvey, Hattie didn't have to deal with her own version of his and Caroline's unfinished business. She had an ex-husband out on the east coast who still fished for lobster in the spring and early summer, who still, McKelvey knew, had hooks in her of one kind or another.

When he grew tired of the endless mental masturbation, he went to the phone and dialed 411 for directory assistance.

"English," he instructed the automated attendant.

"English!" he yelled again when it did not immediately click in. "Residential listing. Dawson, Peter. Toronto."

TWENTY-FIVE

Kad stood in front of the mirror in the tiny bathroom of the east-end safe house and stitched his scalp beneath the dim glow of a single forty watt bulb. It was not the first time he had stitched himself. Or someone else, for that matter. In the war, they were all medics. Basic first aid was learned in the field, under fire. If a man's limb was not entirely severed, then anyone on the line was expected to jump in and help. The thing was to stop the bleeding. Try to keep the wound as clean as possible, which was not an easy task under the circumstances. Mitigate the effects of shock on the human body.

The wine bottle had come as a surprise, a missile from the corner of his eye. Oddly enough, the bottle itself had not broken. It was intact, sitting on the spare kitchen table right now. The act made him like this policeman, this detective McKelvey, all the more—this absence of fear, this willingness to charge across a busy street in the name of vengeance. He could understand that variety of internal drive, the mechanism at play. Still, he would have to kill the man in order to close the circle entirely. He leaned into the mirror. The broken glass from the imploding window had stuck in a few places above his left ear. He pulled the jagged bits free with a pair of tweezers then washed the wounds with tap water. Only one of the gashes was large enough to require stitches, and even then it required only four quick loops with needle and thread to keep the flap of skin closed. It was a good thing he had little more than stubble on his scalp; it made this job all the easier.

He dabbed the wounds on the side of his head with some toilet tissue and turned off the light. He was bare-chested, and he pulled his shirt back on as he walked into the kitchen. He was hungry, but there was little other than canned soups and beans stocked in a cupboard, and he couldn't be bothered heating it up in a saucepan. He selected a can of tomato soup, opened it, and sat down at the table. He picked up a spoon and ate the concentrated mush straight from the can. For the first time since he'd landed in this country, he allowed his mind to move beyond the operation. *What happened after this?*

There was no "after this". Not in his original thinking. He supposed he had planned all along for his inevitable demise. Perhaps it was his heart's wishful thinking. To complete his task and to die over here, thousands of miles removed from his homeland, a body with no traceable identification. He would be John Doe. And why not? He *was* John Doe.

He ate the cold soup and thought of these last details to be put in place. The final phase of the plan depended on timing and the orchestration of set pieces. He would organize for McKelvey to meet him and Turner at a scheduled time the following afternoon. This would provide him with sufficient time to kill the second target, Mitovik, then gather all of the players together in one room. The school teacher and the policeman would necessarily be eliminated. As for Turner, well, he was to ensure Kadro's safe exit from the country. But Kad did not trust Turner. He expected Turner had similar plans in mind for him—this elimination of all loose ends.

He contemplated the car's broken window and the require-ment of a new vehicle. This would be the third. It wasn't worth the phone call to Turner, the admonishments, the wasted time. Besides, the weather was beautiful. It would be an easy thing to drive around for another day with the window rolled all the way down. Yes, it seemed there was little to do now but set the final plan in motion. He put the can of soup aside and belched. It echoed in the empty, lonely apartment. It was during moments such as this that Kadro truly wished he had died in the war like so many of his contemporaries. It was so much more complicated to be a survivor. The dead had already fulfilled their duty and their obligation. What was his duty now, to remember?

How could he forget?

He thought of Krupps and the day he had died. How Kad had insisted they check this one last house where he swore he had seen two enemy soldiers ducking in. Krupps wanted to move the group, to keep on going, but Kad had told him of this instinct he had, this gut feeling. Krupps had relented. And so he had followed Kad into the house through a back door, stepping quietly on the toes of their combat boots, and they found the two soldiers in the midst of raping a lone teenage girl. The girl's father and young brother were dead, their bodies sprawled in the hallway.

Kad and Krupps came into the living room as they had been trained, one aiming high, the other crouched low, and they each shot one of the soldiers, who both died with a look of surprise and guilt on their faces. Kad kicked their bodies off the girl. He looked down at her and told her to put her clothes on. The girl was wild-eyed, maniacal. Kad stepped out of the room to make sure their gunshots had not attracted reinforcements, while Krupps set about checking the dead soldiers for weapons and papers.

And then a gun fired.

Kad ran back, expecting to find that Krupps had killed the girl for some reason. But no. She sat there in her heap of clothes,

233

one of the soldier's handguns pointed at Krupps' body. Kad remembered these details: the girl's hands were shaking badly, and a tendril of smoke curled from the end of the gun. Krupps was on his side, and Kad could see the pool of blood spreading beneath him. Kad ordered the girl to put the gun down, but she was insane. He levelled his rifle at her. She held the pistol, her hands shaking, then slowly turned it on herself. She slumped backwards, and the gun hit the floor. Every sound was hollow. Kad remembered that scene as though it were a tableau made up of actors or statues—the two dead soldiers, his dead squad leader, and even the girl they had tried to save…

All dead.

"I turned my back on her," was all Krupps could say. In fact, these were his last words. "I turned my back on her…"

Here in the safe house, Kad could not say whether a minute or an hour had passed. He blinked and looked around the kitchen. He got up and began to rifle through the drawers. He supposed it was his wish all along, that he would complete his mission and die in the process. But first he had an obligation to clean up all loose ends to ensure that none of this came back to the Colonel, or perhaps more importantly, anyone from his village who was involved. Yes, he supposed all along this had been his desire, to die upon completion of the mission. There was no life beyond this, there was only the anguish of remembering, from time to time, who they had been, who they might have become.

He found a corkscrew. He set the wine bottle between his knees and removed the cork with a sharp popping sound. He poured a couple of inches of the dark burgundy wine into a coffee mug. It looked like blood. He raised the glass and smelled it, then he closed his eyes and drank to Krupps and the other dead from his unit, and he drank to himself, too, for he was among them.

TWENTY-SIX

Garrity's was busier than usual, due to the fact the liquor and beer stores were closed for the holiday. It was almost nine o'clock, and McKelvey was sitting at the bar with a pint of draft beer. His third. He didn't know where else to go or what else to do. He had walked a few blocks down towards the water then found himself drawn to the promise of relative companionship like a magnet pulled to its centre. He had no idea how he would make it across the span between today and tomorrow since the call had come. Sitting there for four hours staring at the phone. When the phone finally had rung, he'd snatched for it like a lonely teenager waiting for an invitation to the prom.

Leyden had called first. "Some new developments," he'd said. "We'll need some of your time tomorrow."

"You know where to find me," McKelvey had said.

"Don't be leaving town," Leyden said.

"Only the guilty skip town," McKelvey said.

Leyden said, "Right."

Then the call he had been waiting for. He held the receiver, spoke his name, and waited. There was silence. Then the faintest sound of breathing.

"McKelvey," a man said. He had a strong accent that McKelvey could not immediately place. Eastern European. He pronounced the name "*McKeelvy*".

"Yes," McKelvey said. And again he waited. It was torture. He couldn't wait for the opportunity to meet face to face with the caller. No sucker punches this time. This time he would finish the job.

"Tomorrow at ten a.m.," the man said, "I will call the middle pay phone against the far wall of the arrivals level at Union Station. You will answer. I will give you instructions on where to meet so you can see your friend Tim Fielding."

"I want to talk to him first," McKelvey said, and he suddenly felt like a character in some B-movie. He was at the end of his patience with this game.

"Not part of the plan," the man said.

"Listen to me," McKelvey said, and he felt the familiar ring of heat on the back of his neck, spreading across nerve endings like a spider's web. "I'm not bringing the cops into this. Like you instructed in your letter that you so neatly printed and left on my fucking fridge. I'm keeping my end of the bargain. I need to hear his voice."

There was a long pause, and McKelvey thought for a moment there was a chance he had blown the phone call. The one and only chance to make contact with Fielding.

"We are out of time," the man said. "No tracing of the calls. I will call the pay phone at ten a.m., and you can hear your friend's voice."

The caller had hung up.

Now McKelvey finished the last swallow of the third pint of beer, and he looked at himself in the mirror behind the bar. The lighting was dim, a soft amber, and it was normally quite complimentary. But tonight there was no amount of makeup or lighting or smoke and mirrors that could hide the fact that McKelvey looked like a piece of hammered shit. He wasn't sleeping, he wasn't eating properly, and the bruising on his face had turned that yellow-brown hue that bruises take on as they wane.

"You're in rare form tonight, Charlie," Huff said. He put his big hands on the bar and leaned in. McKelvey could almost count the scars, the nicks and cuts across the canvas of the man's face. "You celebrating or contemplating?"

"You ever get yourself into a jam that you weren't sure you could get out of?" McKelvey said, turning the pint glass in his hand.

"Every time I put on a pair of skates," Huff said, and he smiled. "Yeah, I got myself into a few corners over the years. I figure the only thing to do is fight your way out. Keep swinging, and eventually you'll land a good one."

McKelvey digested the advice. It was true. He had to keep swinging here, try to get one step ahead, gain some leverage. His call to Peter Dawson had perhaps provided a means to do so. In the process he had also likely shortened the window of time before Leyden and Kennedy and the whole fury of the Homicide Squad came crashing down on his head. Once they found out this unknown man was quite possibly somehow involved in the death of the building superintendent, christ, once they found out he was taking calls from this stranger, well, it wasn't a stretch to make a case for obstruction of justice. If a prosecutor was in a particularly bad mood, it could even look more like accessory after the fact. Either way, he had no choice now but to get to Fielding. And he had to get there first.

Dawson had not appreciated the call to his home number. "I think you'll agree this is a rather odd situation. If the police want to speak with me, they can contact me at the office," he had said. "I've already provided you with more information than I should have."

"I appreciate that," McKelvey said, "but let me help you out here, Peter. You didn't do anything wrong. Why should the centre come under the microscope, maybe even get shut down, just because of Davis? The sooner I can sit down with Davis and clear some things up, the better off you'll be."

McKelvey had asked the man two questions. Two questions and the promise that he would provide the full back story before any officers approached Dawson for an interview.

"Does the name Bojan Kordic mean anything to you?" McKelvey asked.

"I don't think so," Dawson said. "Doesn't ring any bells."

"Do you have a home address or phone number for Davis?"

"That's part of the problem, I can't reach him," Dawson said. "He always used a cellphone, and his number was constantly changing. I mean, like every couple of months. The last number I had is disconnected. Like I said, he travelled a lot for work. In the last year I probably only saw him three or four times at the centre. I think his interest had waned."

"What about an address?" McKelvey said. "He must have had to provide some basic information when he applied to volunteer."

"He sure did," Dawson said. And here the man laughed a little, a mixture of nerves and stress and frustration. "One Bathurst Quay."

McKelvey tried to picture the address. Bathurst Street. At the Quay. There were high-rise condos sprouting up along the waterfront like wild flowers.

"One of those new condo buildings?" McKelvey said.

"How about Lake Ontario," Dawson said. "Davis was fucking with me. You don't really think much of these details when you have bodies willing to roll up their sleeves and volunteer. I suppose I thought it was strange, I mean you don't often see 'one' in a street address, but it didn't concern me. Davis volunteered off and on

238

for almost three and a half years. He was getting us funding. I never had reason to go over to his house. We weren't buddies."

Now McKelvey sat on the stool at the bar, trying to line up the bits and pieces. It was now obvious that Davis Chapman—or whatever his real name was—had used the immigrant resource centre to get Donia Kruzik set up. Davis Chapman worked in some capacity for the "government". Donia had been found murdered in Tim Fielding's apartment. Donia's boss, Bojan Kordic, had been murdered. Tim Fielding had stepped into the middle of something that was beyond the experience of McKelvey's time on the force. What was the objective here, the motive?

As McKelvey sat thinking, his eyes glanced to a man sitting at a small table beneath a black and white portrait of James Joyce. This was the same bearded rounder he'd seen in the bar a couple of times over the past week. The man was not doing a very good job of hiding the fact that he was looking at McKelvey.

TWENTY-SEVEN

Maxime had fallen asleep on his bed at the Royal York after making contact with his office in Lyon. The time difference, about five hours, meant that his support staff had to be available at all hours of the day and night. Such was the life of a young officer looking to make the grade. Maxime had certainly paid enough dues to earn his tenure. When he lifted his head from the floral bedspread, the digital clock read quarter past nine. At first he wasn't sure if it was morning or night. The curtains were sufficiently multi-layered to block out all natural light. He blinked and reached for his wristwatch on the night table. As he slipped it on his wrist, he was happy to note that it was still evening.

He had dozed off in his jeans and his dress shirt. He paused in the bathroom long enough to wet his hair and splash some water on his face. He smiled as he recalled the brief conversation he'd had with someone at the Toronto airport upon his arrival. He had been looking for the toilet. The young woman had smiled and said, "The washrooms?" Yes, he supposed he would need to wash as well, but what he was really interested in was a toilet. *La toilette*. It was all just a matter of nuance, he thought. Much like police work or being in love. Or, he hoped, being a father.

He put his coat on and headed down the hallway to the bank of brass-fronted elevators.

*   *   *

McKelvey sat there at Garrity's for a long time thinking, looking but not looking at the bearded man sitting alone. He had a last swallow of his fourth beer and got up. He was halfway to being full-fledged intoxicated. Everything on him, pressing down, these traps of his own setting. On his way past the bar, he leaned in and asked Huff if he still kept that umbrella under the bar.

"Sure," Huff said, and smiled. "Are you expecting rain on the long trip home?"

McKelvey took the umbrella and tucked it along the inside of his left arm. He gave Huff a wink and headed out of the bar. On the street, he walked briskly past his building then ducked down the alleyway between the condo and the sushi restaurant beside it. He waited a beat. Then he heard it, as he'd somehow expected, his cop's instinct still firing on a few cylinders. The door to Garrity's opening, letting the soft Irish music bleed into the street. Footsteps. He waited, the umbrella in his hand like a night stick. He hugged the side of the building and listened. It sounded as though someone had paused at the door to his condo. Then they continued on, closer now, steps from the mouth of the alley. McKelvey let the dark figure pass by just a few steps before he turned to look around the corner, and he was there, right there, the same rounder from Garrity's with his shaggy black goatee and his oilskin crop coat.

"Looking for me?" McKelvey said, and he stepped from the bricks of the building, the umbrella still hugging his forearm.

"Your name McKelvey?" the big man said.

McKelvey didn't hesitate—not when someone on a dark street was asking your name. He stepped in, swinging the umbrella out and upwards the way they'd been trained to do with their police batons, a tool he'd used on the streets and in

241

the housing projects, an extension of his will. The curved wood handle caught the stranger hard on the side of his jaw, and he went down, sloping sideways like a buffalo felled by an arrow. As he hit the sidewalk and teetered there, McKelvey became aware of the man's sheer bulk, the heavy upper body and thick shoulders, and it summoned images of prison weight pits. McKelvey understood he had no chance against the man if he allowed him to get to his feet again, so he came in quickly from behind and put the umbrella under the man's neck, then pulled back hard with a knee to the back for leverage, choking him.

"You looking for me?" McKelvey said. "What, did I arrest you ten years ago and you want to square things away, is that it? Who the fuck are you anyway?"

The man was on his knees, and he used one hand to fight the pressure of the umbrella at his neck, and with the other he reached back and fought for purchase against McKelvey's leg. The man's grip was strong. McKelvey felt his foe's energy surging with the adrenalin, knew he would pull up from the sidewalk within seconds. And then, toe to toe, it would be McKelvey who would find himself on the losing end of the equation. He pulled back with all of his weight, and the man's arms flailed, then he was pulling up, this great wildebeest rising from the concrete.

McKelvey was shucked off like a kid wrestling with his father, and he fell backwards, the umbrella gone from his grasp. He looked up at the city sky, dark and glowing with halos of street lamps. It was happening so fast, this action, and it occurred to him briefly that he was about to die here on the street in front of his building. From the corner of his eye he saw a third figure coming in, running across Front to the alley. The man was of small stature, but he bent low at the waist and came in with his hands held by his jawline as though he'd had some boxing lessons. He walked into the rounder's heavy swings like a log being pushed into a wood chipper, and the punches from the bigger man either failed to land or had no effect. The new stranger came in with his chin tucked into his neck, and he delivered two or three hard jabs, pistons of bone, and the rounder was dropped for the second time, flat on his ass on the sidewalk.

The smaller man went to jump in with his foot, but McKelvey called him off. The man stepped to the side, and his face, for the first time, was washed with the yellow light of the lamps. McKelvey's mind clicked. He'd seen this man before. Yes. That was it. It was the man who had knocked on his door looking for Giuseppe just that afternoon. He was sure of it.

He turned his attention to the rounder. "Who are you?" McKelvey asked.

The big man sat up, rubbed his jaw, and turned and spat a little blood on the sidewalk. He brought fingers to his mouth, fiddled inside, and pulled out a tooth.

"I used to run with the Blades," the man said, catching his breath. "Pierre Duguay sent me on a mission...he wants you to know... "

"Wants me to know what?" McKelvey said. He had picked up the umbrella and was tapping it against his palm like a nightstick. Old habits.

"He's not gunning for you. He won't be sending anyone. He considers your business closed. I guess it was important to him that you know there won't be anybody coming for you."

Pierre Duguay, the former head of the fledgling Toronto chapter of the Blades, who was right now awaiting trial. The ex-con was easily looking at a ten- or fifteen-year sentence for violating the conditions of his previous parole when he'd broken into McKelvey's home, drawn a handgun and fired.

"I had to be sure I had the right guy," the rounder said, and he pulled himself up. "And after what you did to Duguay, fuck, I didn't want to get shot or anything. You're a piece of work, man."

"You can tell Duguay the feeling is mutual," McKelvey said. "And listen, I'm sorry about your tooth."

"Fuck it," the rounder said. "But just so we're square, you do know that you'd be fucken dead right now if it wasn't for Duguay."

"Agreed," McKelvey said.

McKelvey watched the big man swagger down the sidewalk as though this sort of thing was simply a part of day to day business. And it was, at least in the world of bikers and underground crime. As for McKelvey, he'd had more than enough excitement for one day. His heart was just starting to find its natural rhythm again. He was suddenly sober, acutely aware of the cool evening air and the smells of the city, the world around him.

"I'm seriously too old for this shit," McKelvey said.

"You handled yourself—how do you say—*adroitly*," the man said. He put his hand out and said, "Maxime Auteuil. Interpol."

McKelvey put a hand against the bricks of the wall and drew air through his nostrils. *Interpol*. Jesus, what next? He fought off a wave of nausea, unwilling to vomit in the street more than once in any given day.

"You knocked on my door earlier today," McKelvey said.

Maxime smiled. "Ah yes," he said. "One of the first tricks I was taught while working the beat in Marseille. In these housing projects where nobody has eyes or ears. It is effective only if you have visual identification of the suspect. In your case, I knew you lived in the building, but I did not know your name. And so I knocked on every door and asked for a different occupant. Until I knocked on your door and saw your face. It is a pleasure to meet you, Mr. McKelvey."

"What do you want with me?" McKelvey said.

"I believe we can help each other," Maxime said. "Concerning a certain woman whose alias is Donia Kruzik."

He had McKelvey's attention now.

"Can I buy you a drink, Mr. McKelvey?" Maxime said.

"I should buy *you* a drink," McKelvey said. "Your timing was impeccable."

*   *   *

They went back to Garrity's. McKelvey laid the umbrella on the bar.

"I won't even ask," Huff said.

"A Jameson's on ice for me," McKelvey said, "and—"

"A red wine, please," Maxime said. "Pinot noir, if you have it."

They moved to a back table. McKelvey took a drink of the whiskey and saw that his hand was shaking. He exhaled a long sigh. His heart was still palpitating, and he was a little dizzy. He felt as though he had reached, and more than likely exceeded, the limits of his physical capabilities. An old man in a young man's game. Maxime took a drink of his red wine, rolled it in his mouth, swallowed and shrugged.

"So," McKelvey said. "First off, my thanks for jumping in. Looks like you know how to handle yourself. You move fast."

"I am glad I was walking by at the right time," Maxime said. "Growing up we learned how to fight in the streets a little bit, you know, and then when you're a cop in Marseille, well, you are ready for anything. My father followed the fights a little bit, professional boxing. He was always telling me I reminded him of this little champ named Willie Pep, small but fast. I saw you earlier today with the wine bottle. That was fantastic. You have had quite a busy day, yes?"

"So you were staking me out. What does Interpol want with a retired Toronto cop?"

"I had my friends at the Intelligence Command Centre back in Lyon do a little legwork, as you say over here," Maxime said. "They need all the work they can get, these computer cops with their soft hands. Yes, we have a new generation of coppers, Mr. McKelvey, happy to play their video games."

"You checked up on me," McKelvey said. "Interpol can do that sort of thing? I always thought you guys were like the British Bobbies, unarmed and with no real authority."

"With the proper co-operation, anything is possible. I found some areas where I believe we share a common philosophy in our approach to police work, Mr. McKelvey."

McKelvey swallowed a mouthful of the amber Irish whiskey. "Call me Charlie," he said. "And let me see your ID. If you don't mind."

Now he felt like Peter Dawson asking to see McKelvey's business card. Maxime reached into his jacket pocket and produced his wallet. It contained a couple of credit cards, then he flipped a section and revealed his identification beneath a plastic window. It looked authentic enough, though McKelvey had to admit he had no idea what he was looking for. In his own career he had worked with the RCMP, a few state police departments on cases that crossed jurisdictions, but he had never worked with Interpol.

Maxime slipped his wallet back into his pocket and said, "You are not afraid of getting your hands dirty in the pursuit of a righteous cause. I am very sorry about your son, but I can appreciate the lengths you went to in order to, how would you say—shine a light on the darkness. I think you, of all people, will appreciate the delicate dynamics of what is at play here."

Maxime paused for a sip of the red wine. He made a face when he swallowed it, as though it were just barely palatable. McKelvey used the pause to break in.

"I'll be straight with you, mostly because I don't have the time to fuck around. My friend is caught up in this thing, whatever this thing is. The only mistake he made was falling for this woman, this Donia Kruzik, and now he's been framed for her murder, and I believe he's been kidnapped. I've done my best to dog this thing down, but there's a connection I just can't make with these people."

"And there is no shame in that, Charlie, because it would take a hundred policeman a hundred years to make that connection. As I said, there are delicate dynamics at play. We are talking about the ripple effect of war. There is a righteous cause, to be certain, and there is a thirst for international justice. This spans many continents, dozens of characters. You and I may agree with the pursuit of a righteous cause, but our—"

"What are you talking about?" McKelvey interrupted. A headache was coming on like a tight band being twisted around his skull, and he was squinting through the pain. "I've been straight with you. I told you, I don't have the luxury of time. What is this whole thing about?"

Maxime moved his wine glass aside and leaned in, his head tilted a little to the left, and he said, in a low voice, "What I am talking about is a killing squad."

McKelvey took the last swallow of his drink to buy a moment and process the information. But the whiskey seemed to have no power or taste to it. "A killing squad," he repeated. "Here, in Toronto."

"We believe they number around one dozen around the world. The core group, that is. We have tracked this for two years now.

We know they are operating in Canada, the U.S., Britain. They were formed with the consent and support of a rogue element within the security and intelligence branch of the independent government of Bosnia-Herzegovina in the dying days of the war. They have one goal: to locate and eliminate those members of the Serb paramilitary unit they hold responsible for the mass execution of men and boys at Srebrenica and the surrounding villages in the summer of 1995. There are two caveats for membership in the league. First, you must be a direct blood relative of a victim. Second, you agree to end your identity when you sign up."

"Who's in charge of this league?"

"An individual known as 'The Colonel'. He funded the establishment of a paramilitary unit during the war. The unit's job was to disrupt enemy activity to the greatest extent possible. They were highly effective."

McKelvey felt weak. He saw where things were headed, understood he had enrolled himself in a new school. Suddenly the connections began to click into place.

"Our security guys must be aware. CSIS, the Mounties," McKelvey said.

Maxime sat back. He took the wine glass and turned it by the stem. "That's where things get very delicate, Charlie. You see, one of the lead operatives we have been tracking happens to work for your government."

"Davis Chapman," McKelvey said.

"Very good. Yes. He goes by various names. Turner is the current name he is employing for this stage of the operation."

"And what about Donia Kruzik? What's her role in all of this?"

"She is—or was—a member of the league. It's not her real name, of course, we are still digging where that is concerned.

But we believe she was assigned, along with her colleague—the man you threw the wine bottle at—she was assigned the names of two former soldiers who are living here in Toronto. I suspect her role was to seek these targets out, to shadow them and record their routines in preparation for their assassination."

McKelvey nodded, letting the information sink in. So Tim and Donia had simply made the oldest mistake in the book—they had fallen for one another under less than ideal circumstances. Love during a time of war was a dangerous undertaking. And then McKelvey had stirred the hornet's nest by poking around her apartment, by tracking the man from her apartment to Jarko's Automotive then the immigrant support centre. If he had minded his own business, if he had taken Fielding out to cry in his beer instead of acting like some private detective, they would all be none the wiser. Fielding would be at home asleep, and McKelvey would be wrapped in the covers with Hattie.

"I was too late today," Maxime said. "Bojan Kordic was assassinated."

"Who's the other target?"

"A man named Goran Mitovik. Former platoon leader. A very nasty man. Both he and Bojan are wanted for war crimes by the international courts. I have a red notice for both men, as authorized by the Secretary-General of Interpol."

"Your interest here is in arresting Kordic and Mitovik?"

Maxime finished the last of his wine and pushed the glass aside. "My interest is in bringing those men back to face justice by the international court, and also to close down this vigilante operation. How do you say, two birds with a single stone? As you know, Charlie, one death only begets another death. These people are still fighting a war that ended almost six years ago. What was done is done, Charlie. There can be no justice in murder."

"I assume you're working with the local authorities on this? Or the RCMP?"

Maxime shook his head. "The RCMP is aware of my presence here, but this is where I believe you can appreciate my approach. Like you, Charlie, *je suis un loup seul*—a lone wolf. I have been working on this case for two years now. I want to close the file, put the bad guys away, and put an end to the Colonel's work. And then I will retire and leave this job to the young people. *C'est tout.*"

"What about the second target, this Mitovik," McKelvey said. "He's obviously in danger."

"He will wake up to my smiling face tomorrow," Maxime said, "and that is when your local police will get a chance to put their thumbprint on this case, to pose for the photographers after the heavy lifting is done."

This was beyond McKelvey's professional experience. Organized gangs, punks, thugs, hammerheads and crackheads, pathological liars, sure, even the heavyweight cons who walked into banks with sawed-off shotguns; that was the world he understood. But this, this was geopolitics, talk of a war he had not understood in the slightest when it was actually happening, let alone now, years after the fact when they were stepping into a new war. He remembered the newspapers, the TV footage of the siege of Sarajevo, daily artillery salvos, snipers taking out old ladies waiting in line for bread, the horrific news of entire villages being rounded up, the men shot or exiled to prison camps, the women and girls raped and tortured. But he was never able to decipher the starting point in the whole mess; who were the good guys, who were the bad guys, and how could one tell the difference? As though one minute there had been a unified country and the next the whole thing was shattered into a hundred little pieces.

"This man, the one I threw the wine bottle at. He's holding my friend, Tim Fielding. I guess we're both what you'd call loose ends in this," McKelvey said. "We stumbled into the middle of their operation and fucked things up for them."

"That man is the only operator we have yet to positively identify," Maxime said. "I believe his operational name is Kadro. He served in the Colonel's unit with some distinction. He is a dangerous man, believe me."

"What do you think the chances are he'll let Tim Fielding go?"

Maxime looked at him and shook his head. "We must help each other, Charlie," he said. "You get your friend, and I close my case."

McKelvey sat back and relayed the details of the phone call from the stranger, the letter on his fridge, the whole series of events of the past few days. Maxime listened, nodded and offered explanations where he could.

"Closing time, boys," Huff said, and he flicked the lights off and on.

When McKelvey looked up, he saw that the bar was empty. It was one o'clock. He was utterly exhausted. Now that the adrenalin had ebbed, his body was spent. The two men shook hands and agreed to meet in the morning to put their plan in place.

"I'm on my way," Maxime said, following McKelvey out the door.

"Where are you staying?"

"The Royal York," Maxime said. He pronounced it "royale yolk".

McKelvey stopped at the door to his building and fished in his pocket for his keys. He said, "Interpol isn't hiring, by any chance?"

"You would not like the paperwork, Charlie," Maxime said over his shoulder. "*Bonne nuit.*"

*   *   *

McKelvey opened the door to his condo and flicked on the lights. He stood there at the threshold for a full minute listening, half expecting someone to jump from the shadows in this strange new game he was playing. The apartment was still and quiet. He went to the bedroom and dug through the sock drawer, twisting and turning and spilling pairs on the floor. His fingers finally found what they sought: a tiny cylindrical tablet. One of the old ones from the original prescription for his leg wound. Tiny submarine of original bliss. He'd stretched out on the sofa for nearly a month after his release from hospital, getting reacquainted with daytime television, popping the pain tabs and drinking herbal teas as suggested. He'd floated, and he hadn't thought of anything at all. He liked Ellen, she was funny, and he liked some of the game shows, too, but he couldn't help but notice how fat most of the contestants were. How fat everybody on television was. What had happened to their civilization, he had wondered in those days of recovery and recuperation. Now he swallowed the tablet and stretched out on the bed. He didn't bother removing his clothes or his shoes. The mattress ate him alive.

TWENTY-EIGHT

Maxime was up early and parked down the street from Goran Mitovik's semi-detached home on Evelyn Avenue in the neighborhood of High Park North. Goran had not done as well as Bojan in his new life in this country, but then again Bojan had come from better family money, and he had been an officer in the war. Goran had served as a non-commissioned officer leading a platoon, and these days he managed a Pickle Barrel restaurant in the north end. Maxime watched the house, but there were no signs of activity, and no sign of the white Corolla either.

He glanced at the GPS receiver. The vehicle had not moved since the previous afternoon. Not since shortly after McKelvey had broken the window with the wine bottle. It was possible the car had been stowed to keep it from public view—which would seriously thwart his ability to trace the target. He had followed the signal first thing in the morning to an east-end neighborhood of strip malls, car washes, fast food restaurants, but there were too many laneways and parking lots to check feasibly. He glanced at his watch. It was twenty to nine. He had promised to pick McKelvey up at nine. He started the rental and pulled away from the curb.

"*Ce n'était pas encore votre temps,* Monsieur Mitovik," he said.

McKelvey was standing on the sidewalk when Maxime pulled up.

"Did you rest well, Charlie?" Maxime said as McKelvey hopped in the small car.

"I think I died last night," McKelvey said.

He was still wearing the same clothes, which were badly rumpled, and his face was wrinkled on one side from sleep. He had tried to eat something, but his stomach would not take it. There wasn't much selection, either, beyond some cereal, a dried heel of cheddar and some celery that was well into the process of decomposition.

Maxime pulled away from the curb in front of McKelvey's building, and they joined the stop-and-go flow of morning traffic. The core of the financial district undulated with human activity, these ant-like columns of commuters pouring out of Union Station towards the glass and mirrored banking towers.

Something in the glove compartment made an electronic beep.

"Aha, good timing," Maxime said. He reached over and opened the compartment and took out the GPS receiver. "Our friend is on the move."

Maxime drove and glanced down at the small LED screen.

"You've got him tracked," McKelvey said. "How did you manage that?"

"Long story. See, he is heading southwest," Maxime said. "Yes, he is coming down south and headed our way."

"This Davis Chapman," McKelvey said. "I still don't get the connection. If it's not CSIS or the Mounties, what branch of the government would be involved in this sort of thing? I mean, it's safe to say he's a spy or an operative of some sort."

"A spook, a spy, we don't call them that any more, Charlie. That was the Cold War. They are *les agents provocateurs*. When it comes to these affairs, your country may not be as loud as your neighbours to the south with their paranoid CIA and their FBI and their Homeland Security, but believe me, you are playing the same games. Davis Chapman is simply a—what do you say—a puppeteer."

They drove west and south then came back eastward along the Lakeshore Boulevard. Maxime glanced at the GPS receiver.

"The vehicle has stopped for a few minutes," Maxime said. "Perhaps he is getting gas or visiting the toilet."

The washroom, McKelvey was going to say, but he glanced at his watch and saw they were fifteen minutes from the scheduled phone call.

"We need to head over to Union Station now," McKelvey said. "He's calling on the hour."

Maxime drove, and McKelvey felt his chest tightening. It was unbearable.

"Our friend is heading due south," Maxime said, "towards the lake."

*   *   *

Maxime could not park the car in front of Union Station, so he dropped McKelvey off at the main doors and pulled a U-turn to park across the street at the Royal York. McKelvey glanced at his watch as he ran down the ramp to the arrivals level. Two minutes to ten. He came through the doors and headed straight for the bank of pay phones against the wall by the stairs that led to the departures level for the trains. One minute to ten. There was an old man standing in front of the phones, fiddling in his pockets

255

for change, suitcase at his feet. McKelvey came up and stepped in to block the middle phone. He was out of breath.

It rang. He snatched the receiver. "McKelvey," he said.

"Charlie—"

It was Fielding's voice. Hoarse and weak, but it was his voice. He was alive, and it was all that mattered in this moment. The phone was pulled away, and the other man was on the line again.

"Eleven," the man said quickly. McKelvey heard something in the background, the drone of an engine, and it grew louder. "The parking lot of Exhibition Place. I will drive you to the location from there."

The line went dead. McKelvey hung up. The old man with the suitcase was staring at him. McKelvey looked over at the newsstand in the centre of the station, watching the people flowing in and out. He knew the sound he'd heard on the phone was an airplane engine. And not just any engine, it was the roar of a smaller prop plane. Christ, he had it. He dropped a couple of quarters into the phone and dialed directory assistance. He had to plug his free ear and yell into the receiver before the automated attendant understood his command. Goddamned fucking automation of everything. The line rang a few times before a cheery voice answered.

"Toronto Island Airport," a woman said.

"When is the next flight arriving?" McKelvey said.

"From which destination, sir?"

"Anywhere," he said, "just the next arrival."

"A flight just landed from Montreal," she said.

"Like right now?"

"It just touched down, sir. Ten a.m. arrival," she said. "Can I help you with flight details or…"

McKelvey hung up. He ran up the ramp, pushing through

256

travelers and students on his way to the car across the street at the hotel. Maxime was waiting at the wheel with the engine running. McKelvey slammed the door and took a deep haul of air.

"How close can we get with that thing?" he said, indicating the GPS receiver.

"It depends on the signal strength, interference," Maxime said, "but usually within a block. Why?"

"I know where they're keeping Fielding," McKelvey said. "Or at least the general area. And with this thing, we can narrow it down. Come on, drive. Head west on Front."

Maxime popped the car into gear and rolled them through the always-clustered gaggle of cars parked by the western entrance to the hotel.

"How are you so positive, Charlie?"

Dawson's words came back to him. *He was fucking with me.* Chapman's address. One Bathurst Quay…Lake Ontario.

"Near the Toronto Island Airport," McKelvey said. "There are a few warehouses, condos under construction. Chapman must know the area somehow, it must mean something to him. The address he listed on his application for the immigrant support centre is the end of the street. Nothing there but water."

TWENTY-NINE

The GPS confirmed McKelvey's hunch. Maxime brought them across Front Street then south on Spadina Avenue to Lakeshore Boulevard. At Bathurst Street they turned left and headed south to the Toronto Island Airport. Maxime kept one eye on the road, the other on the GPS receiver.

"We are close," he said.

"Keep going towards the water," McKelvey said.

The airport ferry terminal to the right, the old Canada Malting Company silos and plant to the left. This is it, McKelvey thought. This area would be One Bathurst Quay.

"Pull up over there," McKelvey said. His heart was beginning to hammer in his chest. "Let's check this out."

They got out of the car. Maxime went around to the hatch and opened his small black gun case. He looked around and discreetly clipped the sidearm to his belt in its holster. He picked up a slim flashlight and tested it against his palm.

"After you, Charlie," he said.

McKelvey led them over to the fences that encircled the old plant that had at one time stored and processed malt hops. The facility had been built in the 1940s and operated until its closure in the 1980s. It loomed over the waterfront as an emblem of the city's industrial past. There were "No Trespassing" signs posted every six feet. McKelvey found a section of fence that had been cut at one time, likely by youths looking to tag their graffiti on the pock-marked cement and brick of the landmark silos.

They stepped through the fence and were among the overgrown weeds and wildflowers of the yard. Old beer bottles and cigarette packages. McKelvey looked up. Most of the windows had been smashed years earlier. They reached a steel side door, which was locked with a new piece of chain and a padlock. On the ground McKelvey spotted a rusted length of chain and what must have been the original padlock.

"They replaced the lock," McKelvey said. "He's in here…"

"There must be another entrance at the back, Charlie, for them to come and go. They could not lock themselves in like this," Maxime said.

"I don't have time to find their secret fucking passage. This is the quickest way in."

"Try this," Maxime said, and he reached down and picked up a red brick.

McKelvey used the brick as a hammer. Sparks shot as he struck the padlock. Any hope they had for the element of surprise was surely lost. The sound bounced and echoed from the side of the massive structure. The lock blew apart. McKelvey pulled the chain and tossed it to the weeds. He gave the door a tug, and it opened with a groan.

They stepped inside the near-darkness. Their nostrils were immediately assailed by the deep funk of must and mould mixed with the lingering pong of rich malt hops. Water dripped from overhead pipes. Maxime led with his flashlight and his weapon drawn.

"This way," he said, aiming the band of light at a set of iron stairs.

McKelvey picked up a length of rusted pipe from the ground and followed.

* * *

Kadro had been preparing to leave the abandoned factory and meet McKelvey at Exhibition Place. He had a length of rope and a band of cloth which he planned to use to tie McKelvey's hands and blindfold him for the drive back to the plant. He had asked Turner to meet them at the factory at eleven, providing Kad with enough time to eliminate both the school teacher and the police officer. Kad had even contemplated ambushing Turner and perhaps staging it so the one-eyed Canadian could take the blame for the killings. He had left the rest of the afternoon completely open for the assassination of Goran Mitovik, who generally worked late afternoons and evenings. He wouldn't be coming to work this evening, however. Since the previous day's epiphany, Kadro now believed it was his obligation as a survivor to endure. It was his job now to live and to remember. He would return home after all of this.

Kad had put the cellphone in front of the school teacher's mouth so the policeman would know that he was alive. He realized, as he took the phone back, that the incoming flight could give away his location, at least to some degree. So they were near the airport. He doubted McKelvey had the ability or the equipment to triangulate a precise location based on the sound of an engine. Still, it had been an error in judgement, and he had admonished himself for the lapse. Now Kad was finished re-tying the knots on the school teacher and gathering his tools when he heard the banging on the door.

He was on his haunches. He stopped. Listened.

"He's coming," the school teacher croaked.

Kad moved to him. He ripped a small length of the cloth and shoved it in Fielding's mouth. He turned and pulled the handgun from his belt. He cocked the weapon, sliding a bullet into the chamber. Each office on the top floor was connected to an office on either side by a single door, so that it was conceivable an employee could walk from one end of the hall to the other by passing through each office. Kad walked on the balls of his feet over to the door on the right side, he slid the lock latch, turned the knob and stepped into the darkness. He would come out at the far end of the hall and surprise McKelvey.

*   *   *

Maxime and McKelvey reached the top of the stairs. There was a long hallway with offices along the left-hand side. It was open on the right-hand side, with a railing overlooking the plant floor, presumably so supervisors and foremen could stand and watch the workers' progress below. There was stronger light on this level, coming through the shattered windows, falling in broken bars across the dirty floor. Maxime nodded for McKelvey to head left to the end of the hallway.

McKelvey crept along the hall with the rusty pipe cold and rough in his hand. He noticed he was shaking, and he couldn't catch his breath. He paused at the first door, put his hand on the knob and turned. The broken light illuminated Fielding on the floor, his hands tied behind his back and around a foundation pole.

Jesus, McKelvey thought, *he's alive…*

He pushed the door wide to make sure there was nobody behind it, then he went to Fielding. He pulled the cloth from the man's mouth. Fielding gulped for air.

"Tim," he whispered, "where are they? How many?"

"One," the teacher managed, and he nodded towards the door leading to the adjoining office.

261

McKelvey worked furiously to untie Fielding's hands. When he had pulled the ropes off, Fielding did not move his arms. McKelvey went to help him bend them slowly, but Fielding cried out in pain.

"It's okay," McKelvey said. "I'll be back."

* * *

Kad could hear the soft footsteps, then he heard the cry from the school teacher. He was inside the last office now. He paused at the door, then turned the knob slowly. He opened the door a crack and listened. The hunted rarely had the advantage, so he crouched low and peered into the hallway. Put them on the defensive, Krupps had always said.

Kad felt the presence of the man an instant before he felt the barrel of the gun touch his scalp. He held his breath, motionless.

"Put it down," Maxime said. He was flush against the wall, hiding in the shadows. "Come this way, Charlie," he yelled without turning his head away.

Kad was reluctant to lay his gun down. But he had other tricks, and he could wait for the right moment. He set the gun on the floor and put his hands in the air. McKelvey closed in on them. He was gripping the piece of pipe.

"Put it down, Charlie. Please. No disrespect," Maxime said.

McKelvey stared at him. He didn't move. Maxime took the gun off Kad and kicked it into the hallway.

"Just put it on the ground, Charlie," he said.

McKelvey bent at the waist and put the pipe down. "You mind telling me what the fuck is going on?" he said.

"There will be time for that," Maxime said. "Right now I need your help. We will need to tie our friend to a chair."

"And then what?" McKelvey said.

"And then," Maxime said, "we get him to tell us everything he knows about the Colonel. He looks very stubborn, so I expect it to be a messy job. You have a strong stomach, Charlie?"

Maxime kept the gun trained on Kadro while McKelvey was to tie the man's hands behind his back. Out of habit, he first checked the man's pant pockets, as he had done a thousand times before throwing a suspect in the back of his cruiser. He found a few papers and stuffed them in his shirt pocket without looking at them. He was about to sweep the rest of the man's body when a knock on the door to the adjoining office startled the three of them.

"Put your weapons on the floor," came a voice from behind the door. "I've got the school teacher here."

Maxime motioned for McKelvey to open the door. The man with the eye patch was standing there with a gun to Fielding's head. Fielding was barely conscious, held up on his feet by the collar.

"Davis Chapman," McKelvey said.

"Or Chapman Davis. Today you can call me Turner," he said. "Looks like we have a decision to make. Drop the gun, Frenchie."

McKelvey glanced between Turner and Maxime. He shook his head. "You guys know each other?"

"Interpol here has been doggedly following us with interest for some time now, I do believe. I must admit, I had no idea you were this close," Turner said. "I have little faith in the general level of talent at Interpol these days. Now why don't you tell your friend here what you're really doing over here."

"I am here under the authority of the Secretary-General of Interpol with a Red Notice for the arrests of Bojan Kordic and Goran Mitovik."

"And to collect your bounty from the Serb mob at the same time," Turner said. "Don't forget to tell that part."

"What's he talking about?" McKelvey said.

"That's right," Turner said. "Mr. Interpol here wins a medal for bringing the lot of us to justice then pockets a couple hundred grand for making sure we don't ever make it to trial. But it sounds like he double-crossed the mob, too. You let us kill Kordic, and we will get Mitovik, too. You played both sides. Just like the French during the Second World War."

"Shut up," Maxime said. "You have no idea what you are talking about." He still held the gun to Kadro's head where he was crouching on the floor. "We are the same, you and me, Charlie," he said. "It is the same with your son, no? Why can't we have both justice and revenge in the same meal? These men Bojan Kordic and Goran Mitovik, they are not worth the cost of a trial."

"It's true?" McKelvey said. "You're here to kill these two? You used me and Tim to draw them in?"

McKelvey felt weak at the knees. He looked over at Fielding held up by the shirt, the gun at his head. He should have taken Fielding out of the plant when he'd first untied him. He would have gotten him to the safety of the car. Now Turner pushed the gun to the teacher's temple and stared at Maxime.

"Okay," Maxime said. "I'm putting it down."

He was lowering himself at the knees, the handgun still in his grasp, when a man stepped into the doorway facing the stairs. The light was at his back, and his features were indiscernible. When he took another step forward, the light fell across half of his face and McKelvey saw that it was Leyden. He had the department issue shotgun from the trunk of his unmarked cruiser. He racked the action. Turner pushed Fielding forward so that the school teacher stumbled headlong into McKelvey and Maxime, then used the moment of confusion to slip away into the darkness.

Kad did not hesitate within this window of opportunity. He was up on his feet throwing himself at Maxime, hands thrusting, grabbing for the weapon. McKelvey jumped in, got his arm around Kad's neck and pulled back hard, getting the man off balance. Kad was too strong, and he rolled his shoulders and wrestled free. McKelvey didn't see the pocket knife Kad had pulled from the strap on his calf, a flash of silver. Leyden set Fielding on the floor and was taking his pulse, using one hand as the other levelled the shotgun out in front. Maxime disappeared after Turner.

"Krupps!" Kad said, breathing hard. His eyes were wild.

McKelvey saw the glint of the knife, then knew he had no choice, and he took two fast steps with a hand out in defense to catch the blade, and he brought his head down against Kad's forehead. It was a concussive blast, bone on bone, and the adrenalin surge allowed McKelvey to maintain the momentum, to use his weight to drive Kad backwards. He put a foot behind the man's legs to trip him, then they were both going down in a heap of dead weight, McKelvey on top. It was a full second before he realized that in the commotion, in their falling together, the blade had punctured him. Somewhere in the middle of his stomach, below the solar plexus. There was no pain, just the warm rush of blood.

"Put it down!" Leyden yelled, but Kad was up now, blood running in a thick line from the cut McKelvey had opened across the centre of his forehead.

Leyden swung the shotgun and fired. The blast rang like a bomb going off in the cavernous factory, and the load caught Kad in the centre of his torso, knocking him off his feet. The knife flew from his grip and skidded across the floor. Leyden stepped in and used a foot to nudge the body. There was no response. McKelvey was on his back, and his breath was coming in short bursts. He was shaking again.

"Is it bad?" Leyden said.

He was standing over McKelvey now, the shotgun raised at his shoulder, index finger prone alongside the trigger guard. McKelvey sat up and felt his stomach, his hand sticky with blood. He pulled his shirt from his pants and raised it to have a quick look. It was a puncture wound, but he was sure the blade had not made it past the layers of fat and muscle.

"Not too deep," he said. "Jesus, Leyden, you were following me again."

"Thank your girlfriend. She told me not to let you out of my sight."

"Go," McKelvey said. "Get that crazy son of a bitch."

Leyden nodded, levelled the shotgun, swung out into the hallway and disappeared. McKelvey held a hand to his stomach then went and picked up Kad's handgun from the hallway where Maxime had kicked it. Tim was sitting with his back to the wall. A band of light fell across the upper half his body, and he looked ghastly. He was white-faced, lips and cracked and bleeding from the days of dehydration.

Shouts echoed throughout the plant, disembodied voices across the distance. Then two shots rang out. It wasn't the shotgun, McKelvey knew. A handgun. Pop-pop. He stepped into the hallway. The sounds were coming from the far end. Voices, taunts, metal against metal. He came to the corner and hugged the wall, staying low and coming around with the handgun gripped in both hands. The hall opened up to a catwalk that spanned the entire work floor. It was too dark to see what was

266

going on at the far end.

McKelvey came upon a dark figure sprawled in the middle of the catwalk. Leyden. The tall man's legs were splayed at an odd angle. The shotgun was just out of his grasp. McKelvey knelt and checked for a pulse. There was nothing. He rolled the detective from his side to his back, and he saw immediately that he had been shot twice in the chest, the rounds grouped close together. The shirt was soaked with blood. No protective vest. McKelvey wondered what sort of marksman could make these shots in the dark, at this range. He tucked the handgun in his belt and grabbed the shotgun, hoping to even out his odds. He crouched and racked the action, delivering a fresh shell to the chamber.

He made his way along the catwalk.

Two more shots tore the silence, bounced and echoed.

Then a return shot from a handgun, smaller caliber.

A man yelled out then moaned. A wounded animal.

McKelvey walked on.

THIRTY

Maxime clutched at his belly, legs pulled up to his chest. He went to speak, but he choked, and a roll of blood came out of the side of his mouth. Dark red, thick as pudding. He began to shake, and he looked for a moment like a kid play-acting in drama class. Arching his back, knees twisted, bucking back against the pain. It was as though the shot had splintered him at his very core.

McKelvey put fingers to Maxime's throat, checking the heart rate.

"Ch-Charlie...listen...*je ne suis pas un criminel*...I want you to know. I was a good cop. Like you. The money, it was for my chocolate shop..." here Maxime laughed a little and coughed again, and there was more blood. "My chocolate shop...I thought why can't something good come from all this war. One stone and two birds, as you say...let these bad men die and still collect some bounty... "

"Is he up ahead?" McKelvey said. His only focus.

"He was lying d-d-down on the catwalk in the dark. He surprised me."

McKelvey snuggled the butt of the shotgun against his shoulder and did his best to slow his breathing. He ran through an image in his mind of what he would do so that when the moment came, he would not hesitate. He knew that he would kill Turner if it came to it. Or Davis Chapman, or whoever or whatever he was.

Maxime Auteuil held his belly and rocked himself. His face was slick with sweat, and it had chilled against his skin. He thought of his wife and his unborn child. Gabriel. Yes. But maybe it wasn't a boy after all. A girl? The protection it would require in this wicked world. What wonders and joys and mysteries would that bring into his life? Dresses and hair ribbons and a whole new language of the heart. He clenched his eyes, and he held onto an image of the three of them, just the three of them—him with his wife and his daughter in the back of their chocolate shop, the place filled with the rich scent of cocoa bubbling on the stove like dark sweetness…

His mind flipped then to a technical thought: how he had always heard that a gunshot wound to the stomach was the worst way to die. He guessed, as he lay there with his hands pressed to his belly, with the warmth of his life spilling from him with each beat of his heart, sirens coming from somewhere in the distance, he guessed that he was about to find out firsthand.

*　*　*

McKelvey made his way along the catwalk, stepping through sheets of light and tunnels of darkness. He squinted and made out a rectangle of light at the far end. A window. He caught the edge of movement down there, a blur of activity. The light coming in this way would put him at a distinct disadvantage. He would have a spotlight on him long before he could make out the figure in front of him.

He stopped, crouched and listened to the darkness. There was a voice. A lone voice. He made progress an inch at a time, swivelling his old hips in this low duck walk, the gun growing heavier by the minute.

He got close enough so that he could make out the trace of a human figure in silhouette against the broken window. He squinted. This lie he had been telling for years now, that he didn't need eyeglasses, well, what good had it done him? Curse your vanity, Charlie McKelvey. Eyeglasses and an oxygen tank were definitely in order.

He kept moving. Suddenly, without realizing it, he was washed in a band of dirty light pouring through the shattered panes. He froze.

"This is my fort," Turner said.

McKelvey edged himself just out of the light so that he could make out Turner standing at the ledge of the window. The window was twelve feet high, and half its panes were missing entirely or cracked. McKelvey could smell the fresh air out there, the stink of the harbour, sounds of gulls.

"You can see everything from here. The whole city. All the boats out there like toys. I used to come here when I was a kid. My dad worked at this plant. Until he died in an industrial accident. That's what they call it, you know, an accident. But there are no accidents in life."

Turner moved his feet so that he was half facing McKelvey now. And McKelvey saw the handgun hanging from the man's left hand.

"Easy," McKelvey said. He could hear the laboured sound of his own breathing.

The wail of sirens drew closer. McKelvey knew the Emergency Task Force would surround the place within minutes after receiving a call about multiple gunshots in the populated downtown core. McKelvey needed to keep Turner talking, to buy some time.

"I've made a living at engineering accidents," Turner said. "Falls down stairs, from buildings, hotwired light switches, exploding toasters. Coups and victory parades. My only mistake was in not getting rid of Peter Dawson. I was soft. He could have had a peaceful passing, no pain whatsoever. See what you get for being Mr. Nice Guy?"

"Why the eye patch for someone looking to go unnoticed?"

"I lost my eye in Bosnia in the first days of the war," Turner said. "It pissed me off, what can I say. I don't want to ease anybody's discomfort. I don't want anybody to forget. Sacrifices are being made each day, and not just by soldiers. Look at 9-11. There are heros among us. This," he said, and he tapped the patch with his index finger, "is my badge of honour."

The two men stared at one another. A dead draw. Their guns at their hips. McKelvey had firepower on his side, and at this range he'd have to be blind not to hit at least some part of Turner's core. But he'd seen the shots Turner had made, in the dark against moving targets.

"Even dumb beat cops like you make sacrifices for things you don't really understand," Turner went on. "You just do what you're told. It's how the chain of command works."

"Who do you work for?" McKelvey said.

Turner laughed. "For you, of course. For queen and country."

"And the Colonel," McKelvey said. "You work for him, too?"

Turner shifted his weight just slightly, and his face for the first time was fully illuminated by a band of daylight. "I *am* the Colonel," he said.

McKelvey saw the first indication in Turner's left shoulder as he raised the handgun. Turner got it to hip level before the load from the shotgun struck him square in the chest. The blast was seismic, concussive, as though Turner was yanked by a rope

271

backwards through the window, a stuntman doing tricks on a movie set. Shards of glass rained down.

McKelvey set the shotgun on the grating, a tendril of smoke curling from its long barrel. His ears rang. He pulled up on his aching knees and went to the end of the catwalk. He put his hands on either side of the window frame and he looked down. Turner's body was floating, back side up, in the green-blue waters of the Toronto harbour.

*　*　*

Maxime was still breathing, but he was slipping in and out of consciousness. His hair was drenched, matted to his forehead. There was nothing McKelvey could do. He felt lightheaded himself. The sirens wailed from just outside the building now. The screech and squawk of a megaphone, a sergeant ordering his men into position. McKelvey set a knee on the grating of the catwalk, and tried to catch his breath. His chest was tight, and he could feel his heart pressing against his ribcage. Each beat sent a rivulet of pain to his chest wound.

"I'll get help," McKelvey said.

He went to pull up. The catwalk tilted on an axis and the floor came up to meet him. It was the last thing he remembered. A smell of damp concrete, mildew and must.

THIRTY-ONE

Three Dead in Harbour Gunfight

(Staff)—Three men are dead following an exchange of gunfire late yesterday afternoon in the vacant Canada Malting Company factory located at the end of Bathurst Street along the Harbourfront. Unconfirmed reports indicate one of the dead is a Toronto Police detective and another victim may be a foreign police officer.

Patrol officers from 51 Division, along with members of the Emergency Task Force (ETF) responded to multiple reports of gunfire at about 10:50 a.m. Officers found two dead and two wounded on the second floor of the former malting plant; a third victim was found floating in the waters of the lake on the east side of the building.

Homicide and Forensic Identification officers cordoned off the entire yard area of the facility located adjacent to the ferry depot for the Toronto Island Airport. Responding officers were joined by members of the provincial Special Investigations Unit. The dead have not yet been identified pending notification of next of kin.

A source within the police department said late last night that the detective believed to have been killed in the shootout was a twenty-four-year veteran. A former member of the Metro force is also believed to be among the wounded. The source indicated the former cop is ex-Hold-Up Squad detective Charles McKelvey, who was involved in a shootout with reputed biker, Pierre Duguay, just over a year ago after the police officer allegedly conducted an unauthorized investigation into his son's murder.

A senior investigator with the SIU said it would be a number of days before they pieced together what happened in the factory.

THIRTY-TWO

The doctor said it was part of his routine, that every time he took blood from a man of a certain age, he would run a series of standard tests that might not otherwise find their way into a regimen of infrequent medical visits. Cholesterol. Liver enzymes. PSA. And the thing is, he said, you require some follow-up tests. McKelvey was tongue-thick and groggy from a restless sleep on the gurney in the emergency department, the hall lights and the equipment and voices running all night as he fulfilled the mandatory observation period. He woke to yellow curtains, the sounds of institutional function.

"With this sort of elevation in the numbers," the doctor said, "although I can't be certain until there are further tests, of course, and the oncologist can provide…"

The doctor was a young man in his early thirties, and his words trailed off as McKelvey wondered when this had happened—when exactly he had crossed the threshold and become old. Not just "middle-aged" any more, but old. It was official. The future held for him a whole new vocabulary, a foreign landscape over which to stumble—scanning the daily obits for names of friends and former colleagues, storing a cornucopia of multi-coloured pills in a seven-day container, pouring over nursing home pamphlets, these places with bullshit names like "Emerald Meadows" and "Serendipity Manor". *Fuck, right. Shoot me now.*

"How many stages are there?" McKelvey asked the doctor.

"Well, four," the doctor said, "but again, as I said, we need to…"

McKelvey tried to picture a glass half full. Or perhaps it was already three quarters empty. A pie with one piece left. The doctor had some brochures and a list of contacts for suggested follow-up appointments and tests, and he left McKelvey to sit there on the gurney. His mind lately had been meandering back home, even before this, the news that most likely explained the stopping and the starting, the trickle and the flow. Just thinking about home. Up there, Ste. Bernadette. It was the river that saved their lives. The green river that was never any good for fishing, too slow and too reedy. When the mercury disappeared and it was so cold that the tip of your nose went numb within a few minutes, still they laced their skates on rough benches made of two-by-fours, and they went together down to carve up that translucent blackness. The white puffs of their breath peppered against the gun metal grey of the winter day, that sound of their skates cutting and slicing. They picked teams and they fought, and someone always got hurt, but it was like a religion. In a small town that offered but one industry, a killer goal or a shutout or a really good fight came with enough glory to make a boy a hero for a weekend.

They went down there to the tall grass along the shoreline in late October, around Halloween, and they brought beers stolen from their fathers' cases, and they saw who could walk out the farthest on those first sheets of late autumn ice. They watched and waited as the river's edge turned grey then a crystalline blue-black. And then one day in late November, the river was frozen shore to shore. From that day on, and everyday until the farthest lip of spring, it was their home and their church and their escape. On a moonlit night they played the greatest game

276

on earth, their young voices loud and carrying across the river. It was everything. And sometimes it was enough …

*   *   *

He had rested on the gurney in the emergency department through the long night and into the early morning. It was as though once he stopped moving, his body shut down completely. He stared up at the rows of buzzing fluorescent lights, thinking of Leyden and Fielding, thinking of Maxime, and he closed his eyes each time one of the investigators from the SIU or Metro stepped inside the curtain with a notepad at the ready.

"He's resting right now," the young nurse would tell them.

McKelvey especially didn't want to see Detective Kennedy. He couldn't face the man, not just yet. He had drifted into the deepest of sleeps after they first brought him in. He had woken with a start, some imagined threat, and he lifted his head and saw Hattie. He blinked to clear his vision. Her red hair was untied and hung to her shoulder, licks of flame. They didn't speak for the longest time. They searched each other with their eyes.

"God, you lied to me, Charlie. Or at least you didn't tell me everything that was going on, everything that you were doing," she said. "It's one and the same. I thought you trusted me. But I don't think you can trust anyone, not fully. You really scared me this time."

"Hattie," he said. And that was it. What else was there to say?

She leaned in and kissed him on the cheek. It was the innocent kiss of a friend to a friend, a daughter to a father. He deserved even less.

"Get well," she said. And he saw that her eyes were red.

He lay there on the gurney and watched her walk away.

*   *   *

The young nurse came through the curtain with a plastic bag filled with his personal items. His watch, his wallet, some papers from his pockets.

"Don't tell anyone I was snooping," she said, and she smiled. "I'm a bit of a lottery fanatic. Congratulations."

"What are you talking about?" he said. His head was still muddled.

"The scratch ticket from your shirt pocket," she said. "You won five grand on the Game of Life. Congratulations. You look like you could use some good news. You know, you're lucky you didn't get the wrong paramedics. We hear stories all the time about personal stuff going missing, and then who gets blamed? We do. I think it's mostly an urban legend."

The papers he'd taken from Kadro. He wanted to laugh, but it wouldn't come. She set the bag on the tray table and slipped out through the curtain.

*   *   *

McKelvey's wound had been sutured, and he was given a prescription for strong antibiotics to ward off infection from the blade, and a little something for the pain. He had a series of business cards from both SIU and Metro Toronto investigators, the RCMP. Everybody wanted to talk to him. There were interviews scheduled the following morning. He understood that it would be a grueling process, the questions, the answers, getting things lined up. One of the more sympathetic investigators told him that Goran Mitovik had been picked up at the restaurant he managed and was being questioned by authorities. Interpol had agents on their way from an office in New York.

He pulled his jacket on carefully, clenching his teeth through the pain. It wasn't bad, though, nothing compared to the gunshot wound from Duguay's .45, so close to his balls. The thought still made him shiver. At the nursing station, he asked for Tim Fielding's room number. Then he went downstairs to the gift shop. The front pages of both the city papers that morning featured block letter headlines about the shootout and aerial photos of the malting plant. He didn't want to read anything about it. Not today, not ever.

He fingered through a bunch of trashy magazines, paperback mysteries and thrillers. He hadn't read a book himself in what seemed like years. He stood there and nodded at himself, at this notion that he might like to do that now, find a good book and see what he had been missing. He wasn't sure he could get through one of these mysteries, though, if they were anything like the cop shows on TV. These writers who thought they could get it right, sitting there at a typewriter in the safety of their cardigan and slippers. He picked out two books and the latest issue of *The Economist*, which seemed sufficiently cerebral for the school teacher.

Fielding was asleep when McKelvey came into the room. He had lost perhaps fifteen pounds, and it was significant on a man who had no weight to spare. His lips were severely swollen, cracked and bloody. His flesh was pallid as candle wax. His eyes fluttered and he blinked.

"Hey," Tim said. His voice was hoarse.

"Looks like it might be a long winter for you," McKelvey said.

"Give me time to think about things," Tim said.

They were quiet for a long time. McKelvey opened the

plastic bag and set the books and magazine on the sliding tray at the bedside. The breakfast was still there, untouched. The first attempt at solids, this grey, moldy-looking oatmeal now congealed to a plastic sheen.

"I should have asked for help a lot earlier," McKelvey said.

Sorry, that's what he was saying, or trying to say. Sorry for almost getting you killed. *My stubbornness and pride, those dual afflictions,* McKelvey thought. Caroline had been right about him all along. And now Hattie had reached the point of exhaustion as well. He supposed a person could only take so much.

"I was the one who dragged you into this," Tim said. "Anyway, it doesn't matter. I did a lot of thinking. Funny how being tied up gives a man a lot of time to think about his life. What he's done or failed to do. The space that he occupies in this life… "

Tim got that distant look in his eyes that sometimes made McKelvey uncomfortable when they had a few beers together. It was a crapshoot whether that look would lead to a few tears over the death of Fielding's wife, or a philosophical statement on a level that McKelvey could hardly decipher.

"And what's the verdict?" McKelvey said.

"I think," the school teacher said, "I have bad luck with women. Generally speaking."

McKelvey smiled and said, "Makes two of us."

"My face has been everywhere. I mean, even though I'll be cleared, that will always be out there hanging over me. Hey, isn't that the night school teacher who murdered his student?"

"You're thinking of starting over somewhere else?" McKelvey said. He pictured Fielding squatting in the middle of a circle of school children in some quaint African village.

"I need to leave everything that I know," Tim said. "Start somewhere with nothing, just to see if I can do it on my own."

McKelvey liked the sound of that coming from the younger man. It was the only thing to do. There was nothing left here for either one of them.

"I don't want to have any regrets," Tim said. And then, after a long moment, he said, "What's yours, Charlie? What's your biggest regret?"

McKelvey didn't have to reach. It was there, right there. "I let Caroline slip away," he said.

The younger man looked at McKelvey then seemed to get lost again. He cleared his throat and said, "So, what about you?"

"Me?"

"Any plans?"

McKelvey thought about it for a minute. Plans. Yes. He had plans. For the first time in what seemed like a hundred years, he knew what he wanted to do, where he wanted to be. Propelled, that was the word.

"I guess I'm going home for a little while," McKelvey said.

"Home home?" Tim said.

"Yeah, home home," McKelvey said. "Ste. Bernadette."

"You're heading in the wrong direction," Tim said. "Should be going south in the winter. You're supposed to be retired, remember?"

"Maybe I'll wait for the spring thaw and the blackflies," McKelvey said.

He reached out, and the men shook hands. He held the younger man's hand and, for just a moment in there, he felt like he was holding the hand of his boy, Gavin. They were all together in that hospital room right then, his boy and Fielding's wife, all these ghosts with which they had made some sort of quiet peace.

"I'll check on you tomorrow," McKelvey said.

"Smuggle me in a beer, will you? It's all I thought about while I was dying of thirst. That sound of a nice cold can opening, pfffft." Fielding closed his eyes and drifted.

McKelvey said, "You got it."

He went out and walked down the hallway to the bank of elevators. He hit the button and waited. The door chimed and opened, and he stepped aside to let out a few visitors. People with bouquets of flowers, greeting cards, tired looks on their faces. He thought of what the doctor had told him, what lay ahead in the coming months, and cringed at the thought of people showing up to see him lying there dressed in a hospital gown, his old white arse flapping in the breeze.

When the visitors had cleared, he stepped inside the elevator and pushed the button for the ground level. He lifted his head and looked across the floor to the nursing station. There was an attractive woman dressed in baby-blue scrubs standing there to gathering a few files. She looked up. He smiled at her. She smiled back just as the doors closed on him.

THIRTY-THREE

Hassan drove McKelvey home from the hospital. It was warm in the taxi, and he opened the back window as far as it would go. The smell of the city came to him like the familiar scent of a lover. Only rather than flowers and vanilla, this was muffler exhaust and a hint of chromium and coal ash.

"Traffic seems heavy," McKelvey said.

"Rush hour. Summer is over now, my friend, everyone has been back to school and back to work for two days now," Hassan said. "It is like the world has woken up from a slumber. Do you know this city has more than three hundred and fifty school buses? Some days I feel like they are all lined up in front of me."

McKelvey had lost track of the days. Of course it was back to school. After Labour Day. He wondered how much Jerry Lewis had raised this year for muscular dystrophy. He had always watched the telethon with his boy, Gavin. He remembered how Gavin used to mimic the comedian, unbuttoning his pajamas and mopping his brow with a hankie. The memory made McKelvey smile. It was a small smile, but it was foreign, and it felt good the way anything new feels.

"Did you happen to catch any of the Jerry Lewis telethon?" McKelvey asked.

"I'm afraid not," Hassan said. "We do not have the cable television."

They inched their way the last few blocks to Front Street.

McKelvey slid out and handed the driver two twenties for the twenty-five dollar fare, along with a piece of silver paper stock.

"Keep the change," McKelvey said.

Hassan had his hands in the leather fanny pack which contained his float, but McKelvey was already limping up the street. Hassan watched him for a minute, but he had to squint against the strong September sun, then he lost sight of his fare altogether.

He held the piece of silver paper up and saw that it was a lottery scratch ticket.

*   *   *

The apartment was still and quiet, and he stood there just inside the door for a moment. He thought it looked more like a hotel room than a home. It was true, Hattie had tried in her way to push him in that direction, to really start his life over again, to fill his space with new things. Build something, unpack the suitcase of grief. Perhaps she was still too young to realize that changing your address or changing your hairstyle didn't really change anything about who you were or where you'd been. Or perhaps he was simply unwilling to fully let go of the past.

He crossed the floor to the telephone by the window. He picked up the receiver and dialed from memory. She answered on the third ring.

"Hello?" she said.

"Hello," he said.

There was a beat, a moment of silence wherein he lived and died.

"Charlie," Caroline said. "How are you?"

He stood there at the little desk by the window. He looked

outside. It was a beautiful day in early September. A good question posed by the person who knew him better than anyone, better than himself—how are you?

"I'm okay," he said.

There was no sense burdening her with information about which he himself was unclear. The truth was, he was scared. Of how close he had come to losing his friend, the days of questions that were to come, of what lay ahead for him with the news from the doctor. More tests required. He reached into his coat pocket and found the small white paper bag with the prescriptions. He cradled the phone between his ear and shoulder, set the antibiotics aside and opened the pain medication. He shook two tablets into his palm.

"It's good to hear your voice," Caroline said. "It's been a while. I was getting worried about you."

"You've got better things to do than worry about me," he said.

"Jessie called the other day," she said. "She's worried about you, too, Charlie. She said you looked like you had gone a few rounds with somebody. You have a black eye?"

McKelvey laughed it off. "Just getting clumsy," he said. He popped the tabs in his mouth, snapped his head back and swallowed them dry. "Otherwise, I'm right as rain."

"Speaking of rain," Carline said, "we're on day six out here. I don't miss the snow, but the rain can get a little monotonous. I've been thinking of coming out for a visit. See Jessie and Emily. And you, of course, if you want. I always liked the fall in Ontario. We used to go on those long drives up through Georgian Bay just to see the colours. Do you remember?"

He felt what was perhaps the first faint glow of the pills, or it was his mind wishing for it. He looked out the window at the day. Everything was moving. Nothing went unchanged. The world existed in your memories. Things as they were.

He closed his eyes. "I remember everything," he said.

Acknowledgements

With very special thanks to Sylvia, Allister and Emma at Napoleon.

I would like to thank the following for their support of my writing today and over the years: Tracy Forrest; Graham and Susan Forrest; the New Brunswick Forrests; Ariane Sabourin; John Churchill; Stephanie Smith; Ulrike Kucera; Katherine Hobbs; Brenda Chapman; Sue Pike; Pauline Braithwaite and Greg Poulin; Mary Jane Maffini; Barbara Fradkin; RJ Harlick; Rick Blechta; Lou Allen; JD Carpenter for his correspondence and Bushmills wisdom; Allan Neal and CBC's *All in a Day*; Steve and Andrea Clifford; Bob and Leslie Grace; Patty Brundritt and the Marsh clan (don't forget little Dougie); Capital Crime Writers and Canadian Crime Writers; and lastly, those reviewers and their publications who still believe that Canadian writing is worth talking about.

This is entirely a work of fiction; as such, the author has taken liberties with historical timelines and the facts in general. Several sources of information provided inspiration during the writing of this book, including: *Seasons in Hell: Understanding Bosnia's War* by Ed Vulliamy; *My War Gone By, I Miss It So* by Anothony William Vivian Loyd; *Love Thy Neighbor: A Story of War* by Peter Maas; *Slobodan Milosevic and the Destruction of Yugoslavia* by Louis Sell; and *Ghosts of the Medak Pocket* by Caroline Orr.

photo by Stephanie Smith

C. B. Forrest's first literary crime novel, *The Weight of Stones*, was shortlisted for the Arthur Ellis Award for Best First Novel. He has also published short stories and poetry in Canadian and U.S. publications. A member of the Crime Writers of Canada and the Capital Crime Writers, he is currently at work on a third McKelvey novel. He can be visited online at www.cbforrest.com